HYPERSPACE OUTLAWS
©2022 LUKE T. BARNETT

Book 1: Hyperspace Outlaws
Book 2: Artificial Malevolence
Book 3: The Dark Weight of Justice

THE GALACTIC RANGER OATH_

On my honor, I will never
betray my badge, my integrity,
my character, or the public trust.
I will defend the helpless, uphold the weak,
and bring to justice those that would
threaten the well-being of others.
I will always have the courage to hold
myself and others accountable for our actions.
I will always uphold the
Code of the Rangers.

THE RANGER'S CODE_

Defend the helpless.
Uphold the weak.
Bring lawbreakers to justice.
Never shoot a sentient in the back.
Never shoot an unarmed sentient.
Lethal force is a last resort.
Never take a bribe.
Always seek justice.
Never seek power.
Never seek revenge.

PROLOGUE_

Johns McCormick glanced over his shoulder for the tenth time since leaving the market district. Normally he'd just order through the holo-net, but he wanted to get out and find a gift for his new niece. Something truly unique you could only find at the local markets.

Sweat rolled down his cheek.

Stop it, Johns! He chided himself. *You're being paranoid!*

He'd gone out plenty of times before without anyone spotting him. No one ever called him out or shouted for law enforcement. No one knew him here. Why would they? This was a large city on a core world. The type of place someone like him could disappear into. Someplace he could forget his past, start a new life…

And never be found.

Unlike those other times, today the distinct feeling he was being followed and watched lingered. He stopped at the threshold to his apartment complex and scrutinized the street and sky. No weary eyes found him. Zip crafts, speeders, and personal flyers flew past overhead. Except one. It was just across the way, ten stories up. Johns's cybernetic eyes zoomed in. A man in a black visor sat in the driver's seat, staring down at his area of the street, looking every bit the suspicious figure.

No. He was staring down at *him*.

Johns's hand drifted to the blaster concealed beneath his jacket. It was more instinct than anything. No way he could hit the guy at this distance.

Johns was about to make a break for it when the window the speeder was hovering in front of slid open. A woman jumped out and tackled the man. They laughed and kissed. The woman slid into the passenger's seat and buckled in. The man didn't even give Johns a second glance, pulling away from the building and out of sight.

Johns let out a breath, his hand falling from his blaster.

See? Nothing to worry about.

He entered the building, chiding himself for jumping at ghosts. The long ride up the elevator, Johns tried to calm his nerves, focusing on the channels he needed to send the gift through. His trail would remain clean while ensuring the package arrived safely. The panel chimed, indicating he was on the three-hundred and twelfth floor.

Johns reached his apartment, giving his voice identifier. Once inside, he initiated the security seal on the door. In the living room was a massive window making up one wall of the apartment. The view of the twin suns of Jandalore Prime sinking behind the massive city was spectacular.

"Quite a view, ain't it?"

The voice hit Johns's nerves like a hammer. He turned his head. A man in a wide-brimmed hat and large duster overcoat lounged on his couch, his booted feet propped up on the transparasteel table. The man had a gleaming badge on his shirt and a blaster in his hand, the barrel leveled at Johns.

A Ranger? How'd he find me?

"How about you put the package down and turn around nice and slow," the man said in a New Texan drawl.

Johns gripped the parcel, his muscles tense. In a swift move he threw it at the Ranger and drew his weapon, firing off several bolts. The pulsing light met the Ranger's own stun blasts, canceling each other out. The Ranger slid behind a wall and Johns continued to fire, burning scorching holes in the particle steel barrier.

Johns ducked behind the kitchenette counter, eyes and gun trained on where the Ranger disappeared. He holstered the blaster pistol, opening a drawer where he kept his spread blaster and pumped the spread, priming it. He crept toward the corner, his aim steady.

He'd made it out. He'd left that life of killing behind. Galaxy's edge if he was going back. Finger on the trigger, he rounded the corner.

No one.

A trickle of sweat ran down the side of his face.

Where the space did he go?

He crept toward the door at the other end of the room, still glancing around, trying to watch everywhere at once. Johns hit the open button. The door slid up with a *WHOOSH* and he realized he hadn't heard it open before. He dove inside. The edges of a stun blast brushed past him, sending a tingle down his arm. He shook it out and pressed himself against the wall. If not for his other enhancements, that brush would have been enough to paralyze him.

"Come on out!" the Ranger called. He was smart enough not to follow Johns. "There's no way out of there. Come along peaceful-like and no harm'll come to you. I won't even use the stun blast."

He smiled. This Ranger didn't know what he'd gotten himself into. Johns could withstand a full-on stun blast, maybe two. But he only needed to bare one to take the Ranger out. Gripping his spread blaster, he spun around the corner, the Ranger in sight with his blaster ready. *You're mine, Ranger.* The impact of the stun blast tingled through Johns's every nerve, forcing him to grit his teeth against the pain.

Johns leveled the barrel of his spread blaster and pulled the trigger.

CLICK.

Johns's eyes went wide. He dropped the blaster and charged. Another stun blast hit him. His limbs went dead and he crumpled to the floor.

"Hope you don't mind," the Ranger said, holstering his gun. "I helped myself to your weapon."

He moved over Johns, his face shadowed by his hat, and pulled out a pair of stun cuffs.

Except the Ranger didn't account for how quickly Johns's strength was returning. It wasn't one-hundred percent, but it was enough. The Ranger reached down. Johns grabbed his arm and slammed him to the ground, getting on top of him. He threw a fist toward the Ranger's head. Even pinned, the Ranger dodged. Johns's fist connected with the floor, leaving a dent in the impervisteel beneath.

He wrapped his hands around the Ranger's throat. One squeeze and it would all be over. He'd figure out what to do about the body later. He recognized a pressure at his side too late. A horrible surge of electricity shot through him. He toppled off the Ranger, dazed. Burnt flesh and ozone assaulted his senses.

What was that?

He got to his hands and knees. His coughs sounded electronic. Was his synthesizer damaged?

He risked a glance at the mirror across the room. The clothes and skin on the left half of his body had been burned away, revealing the cybernetic exoskeleton beneath.

He needed to get out. Get away.

But the Ranger...

His enhanced ears picked up on the Ranger getting to his feet. Behind him. In front of the window.

In a last-ditch effort, Johns leapt to his feet and charged, his mass sending them crashing through the glass. He grappled for the ledge, hoping the Ranger enjoyed his three-hundred floor drop.

Irregular wind screamed in his damaged ears as he dangled like a wind chime. Shards of glass scraped his exoskeleton, digging into his skin. He winced. It was an intermittent, distorted grasp of his senses. He could hardly tell what was even still working. Whatever the Ranger hit him with, it was messing with his circuitry.

Despite the fritzing, he managed to drag his upper body into the apartment but his leg didn't want to budge. Why was it so heavy?

Lifting his leg revealed the Ranger's hand gripping his ankle. Johns tried to shake him off, but the stubborn Ranger swung his other hand up and caught the window ledge.

Why wouldn't this Ranger die?

Johns struggled to his feet, yanking his ankle out of the Ranger's grip. Falling was too good for him. Johns hauled him up with his thick fingers wrapped around his throat. He squeezed, knowing his cybernetic exoskeleton was on full display. His smile widened, willing his red eye to pierce the Ranger's soul.

Johns wanted his enemy to look him in the eye as he died. To wallow in his failure before Johns let him drop to the permacrete three-hundred and twelve stories below.

A sudden surge of pain shot through Johns. He screamed a fluctuating, electronic scream, his body spasming before collapsing onto the floor of the apartment. The pain left him, his exterior nerves burned away. His damaged nodes could barely process the burnt smell into thoughts in his still very human, but very scrambled brain.

"I want to thank you for pulling me off that ledge," came the Ranger's casual voice. "That gave me the free hand to pull out the nullizer."

A smoking, half-melted device dropped to the floor in front of Johns's vision.

"The thing most people don't realize about Rangers," the Ranger continued, "is that we always come prepared. Course, I wasn't expecting to have to disable the limiter on that thing in order to take you down, but I guess some folks are tougher than others."

Johns tried to force out an expletive, but all that came out was a warped, drooling mumble.

"Tell me again when your circuits reboot," the Ranger said, cuffing him. "Or don't. All the same to me. Oh, forgive my manners. Doug Lancer, Galactic Ranger. Let's make this official, shall we? Johns McCormick, for the murder of countless sentients in five systems, including your own wife and son, you're under arrest."

CHAPTER ONE_

Doug twirled the stun cuffs on one finger, catching them with each rotation. He stared after Johns being hauled away in electric binders. The former mobster glared back.

"Please confirm your identity," came an electronic voice beside him.

Doug held his gaze on Johns until he was escorted out of sight, then turned to the bot standing behind the counter.

"Douglas Lancer," he replied. "Galactic Ranger."

The bot worked its console. "May I scan your badge?"

Doug pulled back his duster, unpinned the badge from his shirt, and held it up. The identifier chip inside was unique to him, coded specifically to identify him as a Ranger. With it, he was granted access to areas and information most beings didn't have. And because the Rangers didn't share their tech, it couldn't be faked. At least not well enough to fool anyone.

"Confirmed," the bot said as Doug replaced his badge. "You are a Galactic Ranger. Yet I cannot find you in their official roster."

"That's cause I'm not on it. Is that a problem?"

"Since you are not a Bounty Hunter sanctioned by the Empire, nor on the Galactic Ranger roster, I am only authorized to offer unsanctioned pay for the bounty."

Doug sighed. He expected as much, but hoped he was wrong. He'd have to take what he could get. He just hoped Tlirik wouldn't be too upset.

"I'll take it."

The bot handed him a data chip which he pocketed. He tipped his hat at the bot and walked out into the corridor of the space station. Tlirik would be in the food court.

The lift doors opened. Doug paused, taking in the tan-skinned female occupying the lift, sipping on what looked like a marko-bian foam drink. She wore navy-blue, skin-tight, polymer under-armor, the kind that covered the torso and pelvis, designed to deflect light blaster fire. A black, leather flight jacket, pants, and boots were overlaid on top. The blaster holstered on her tactical belt and the helmet cradled in her free arm didn't escape him either.

Imperial fighter pilot.

Her crystal-blue eyes were sharp, staring into his as she sipped her drink. Her hair was light brown with highlights in gold, a curly, golden lock hanging in her face. After a moment, he stepped aside, tipping his hat toward her.

"Ma'am."

She eyed him as she passed, a slight smile forming on her lips, the sound of her sipping punctuating the air around them. He noted her determined step and caught the quick glance back in his direction.

Doug smirked and stepped onto the lift.

He found Tlirik in the crowded food court easily. The alien was a hulking figure of gray stone wolfing down a half-dead squid creature as big as Doug's head.

"You get the bounty?" Tlirik asked, minding his meal.

Doug handed him the credit chip. Tlirik inserted it into the datapad resting on the table. He paused in his chewing as he viewed the information. His head swiveled slowly to stare up at Doug, purple smatterings on his stone chin, anger burning in his eyes.

"Three-hundred?"

"That's all they'd give me."

"You're giving all of this to me."

Doug shook his head.

"Deal was fifty-fifty for every bounty."

Tlirik stood, towering over Doug.

"I didn't sign on with you to get such petty pay. A hundred and fifty credits won't even pay for this meal."

"Maybe you should get something less expensive."

Tlirik glanced at the squid-thing in his hand, then tossed it behind him.

"Get sanctioned," he ordered.

"No."

Tlirik's frown twisted into a scowl. He swiped up his data pad, tapped a few buttons and tossed the data chip at Doug who caught it with a quick hand.

"You're walking a fine line with me, Ranger," Tlirik said. "I'm going to get the ship warmed up. If you're not on it by the time it's refueled, I'm taking it as payment and stranding you on this rock."

He stalked away, leaving Doug next to a table splattered in purple goo. Injustice roiled within Doug. An ancient verse popped in his head.

He could save others but he couldn't save himself.

"Yeah, sounds familiar," he mumbled.

After checking the Bounty Net for new bounties on a public console, he headed for his ship. Tlirik was in the cockpit, his bulk rather comical in the human-sized pilot chair.

"Where do you want to go?" the alien asked in a sour tone.

"Idis nine," Doug replied. "New bounty just came on the net. Worth a lot. Should make up for what we lost on this one."

"Idis nine is on the other side of the Galactic Ring. And I'm not taking this ship through the Mid Dark."

"Well, if we hurry, we may be able to catch this one before anyone else does."

Tlirik harrumphed and busied himself with the controls. Not wanting to be around the surly rock man, Doug excused himself and headed for his bunk. The ship rumbled and vibrated, telling him they were lifting off. He steadied himself against a wall until they escaped the gravity well of the moon.

Each lift-off was nerve-racking, driving him to wonder if this would be the time the old rust bucket finally gave up and flew apart.

It was no question he needed money. But being sanctioned by the Empire meant joining those Rangers gone turncoat. That wasn't something he was prepared to do.

The vibrations ended and he made his way to his quarters. Once inside, he locked the door, then hung his hat and duster on a hook. Another shudder, likely the ship going to hyperspace. Fatigue washed over him. He removed his gun belt and hung it next to his coat. Pinching the bridge of his nose, he heaved a heavy sigh.

He viewed his bed, longing to lie down and sleep away his cares. Instead, he sat down on it and pressed a button on the ancient console sitting on a side table. After warming up, the screen displayed words in Terran.

/2 Messages/He hit the button to retrieve them, skipping the first. The second was a message in simple Basic text.

/Still awaiting your decision./

Doug grimaced, not needing to look up the sender to know who it was. He deleted it. The other one was an old video message from nearly two years ago. It was rendered in holo, but his display didn't have that capability. The effect made a double image on the screen. It almost gave him a headache.

A beautiful red-skinned Hassa smiled back at Doug and he played the message.

"Hey, Doug, it's Arta," she said, speaking in Basic. She gave a nervous laugh. "Of course it's me. Anyway, I know you said to use this line if I have an emergency, but I was just wondering how you were doing. It's been so long since I've seen you. I'd like to again. Give me a call."

Doug paused the video and stared at Arta's endearing smile. It was nice to be appreciated. Perhaps that was why he kept the video. He shut down the console and lay back on his bed. A flitting thought of getting a cat entered his mind before he drifted off to sleep.

———

A violent shudder woke him. He checked the time. They were still three hours out from the Idis system. He keyed the com for the cockpit.

"Everything all right up there?"

No reply came.

"Tlirik?"

Nothing.

Doug hurriedly strapped on his gun belt on his way to the cockpit.

The door was closed.

Doug drew his blaster and hit the open button. The door clunked, revealing an empty cockpit. The instrument panel was intact with no sign of a struggle. The view outside was empty space. The ship came out of hyperspace in the ring, but not at their intended destination. At least that explained the shudder that woke him.

One of the status lights—labeled hanger bay—started rapidly blinking. Doug watched out the viewport as Tlirik's personal ship came into view.

He keyed the com, somehow knowing what the answer would be.

"Tlirik? Were we boarded? Are you under duress?"

"Don't play dumb, Ranger. I've made my choice. You can find yourself a new pilot, if you can figure out how to fly that junk pile. So long."

Tlirik's ship leapt into hyperspace and was gone.

Doug plopped down into the co-pilot's seat and glanced over the instrument panel. He knew basic ship operation for sublight engines, but had never properly learned how to operate the hyperdrive. He scratched the stubble on his chin, shrugged and reached for a toggle labeled "hy-drive." The ship vibrated horribly, flashing warning lights at him. He flipped it back with lightning speed. The rumbling and alarms stopped.

He sat back, wondering if he had the food stores to make it to a place where he could resupply, or enough credits for a tow. Only… he didn't know where exactly he was or how to find out.

He propped his feet up on the controls and sat back, his hat placed low over his face. He dimmed the lights and prepared himself to wait. Something would come up.

It always did.

CHAPTER TWO_

Loni Taraska pulled hard on the yoke. Her SJ Interceptor barrel rolled, avoiding the hailstorm of red blaster fire streaking past. Her fingers danced on the controls, getting the computer started on a jump vector. Her ship bucked and an alarm blared. She toggled a switch and read the status message on her visor.

Hyperdrive damaged.

"Galaxy's edge," she swore. A few more switches and she re-routed power to the sublight engines.

"SJ Interceptor Zero-Zero-Six," came a voice over the com. "You are acting in defiance of direct orders and are operating stolen Imperial Property. Cut your engines and surrender your vessel."

"Fat chance of that," she muttered, muting the com. She pushed her throttle all the way forward and her ship shot away from the pursuing carrier.

Her sensors alerted her the carrier's engines fired. They were in pursuit. No way they would catch her…

Until her fuel ran out and they went full burn. She ran through her options.

No hyperdrive, so light-speed was out, as well as reaching

anywhere significant. She scanned the system. There was nothing nearby, not even a planet to set down on. She was in the middle of nowhere. Once the carrier caught up, even if she was able to take out all their laser batteries and the other interceptors, they'd just tractor her in or wait for another capitol ship. She was so slagged.

A beep drew her attention to her long-range sensors.

A ship.

Daring to hope, she set coordinates to intercept. At her speed, it was a short time before the craft came into com range. And the carrier wasn't far behind. In fact, they were closer than they should be.

Space heads probably micro-jumped to keep up. I hope their engines lock up for that.

She opened a com channel. "Unidentified craft, this is Loni Taraska aboard the fighter *Barracuda*. I am being pursued by an Imperial carrier. My hyperdrive is damaged and I'm almost out of fuel. Please render assistance."

"This is Unidentified Craft," replied a casual male voice. "Galactic Ranger Doug Lancer speaking. Why exactly are you being pursued by the Empire, Ms. Taraska?"

A Galactic Ranger. She had a chance.

"Ranger, I lawfully defected from the Galactic Federation under Galactic Federation amendment law fourteen, sub-section Twelve. I was fired upon by my carrier vessel and told I was defying orders and piloting stolen property."

"Are you?"

The voice remained nonchalant, but nonetheless ground her nerves. And the beeping from her sensors didn't help either. The carrier just jumped again. They would be on her in moments.

"No, Ranger, I'm not. I announced my defection to my commanding officer as per protocol. Then I boarded my ship, which is significantly modified by my own funds as to claim ownership. My commanding officer objected, but as I was operating according to Galactic Federation protocol, he had no grounds for refusal."

"Don't know if anyone told you, Ms. Taraska, but the Galactic Federation ain't around no more. They've gone Imperial."

"Yes, Ranger, I'm aware of that. Please, render assis—"

The carrier appeared above her and a squadron of interceptors flooded out of its hanger bays.

"Edge!" she shouted and pulled on her yoke, angling her ship to fly out from under the carrier and away from the squadron.

Interceptors fired off their batteries, assisted by the carrier. Loni rolled and swerved, avoiding the blasts. Her low fuel alarm screamed in her ears. A blast caught her wing assembly, sending her into a spin. She flipped switches, initiating emergency stabilizers. She was able to right herself and gain some distance before her fuel gave out. She was running on inertia and the Ranger hadn't answered. She sat back and closed her eyes, waiting for the inevitable.

"Unidentified Imperial Carrier," came the Ranger's voice over the com, "This is the Galactic Ranger ship *Horseshoe*. You are in pursuit of a craft under the official protection of the Galactic Rangers. Break off your attack and cease pursuit."

Loni grimaced at the name. *Horseshoe?*

"Galactic Ranger," came the carrier's response, "This is the Imperial Carrier *Dominator*. The craft is stolen Imperial property and the pilot is an AWOL officer. This is an Imperial matter. Stay out of it."

"Now that's no way to talk to a Ranger," he said.

A text burst came across her visor.

Port Thrusters. Coming along starboard.

One of the ugliest ships Loni had ever seen eased its way toward her. It was a U-shaped, half-cobbled together mess. Even the hanger bay underneath looked like someone just slapped it on and called it a day.

"This so-called criminal you're chasing claims to be innocent," the Ranger continued. "I'm taking her into Ranger custody per Galactic Law until we can get this mess sorted out. Call off your attack or you'll be in violation of Galactic Law yourself."

The *Horseshoe* positioned itself between Loni and her pursuers, its opening hanger baya welcome relief. Using her stored oxygen supply, Loni fired her maneuvering thrusters. It might be a rusty hunk of junk, but it was better than her dying flyer.

She lowered her landing gear and initiated the shutdown sequence.

"Ms. Taraska," the Ranger said over com, "with this change from Federation over to the Imperials, they may or may not abide by Galactic Law. I find it's hit or miss with them. You better get up here to the cockpit. Take the first lift to the top and head left. I'll keep the doors open."

"Acknowledged."

Loni removed her helmet and hopped out of her cockpit onto the auto-stair that unfolded from the side of the ship. She took a moment to take in the group of interceptors hovering just outside the force field of the hanger bay. She could see a few of the pilots, men and women alongside whom she fought in multiple engagements. Good people. Good friends. And all their faces showed contempt and betrayal. They really would blast her into vapor at the first opportunity. Where had it all gone wrong?

———

Loni ran down the corridor into a cramped cockpit. Four chairs total—a half-crushed pilot's chair next to the co-pilot, and two seats behind.

"Welcome aboard, your highness." The man had a casual way about him. He extended a hand. "Doug Lancer."

Loni instinctively moved to the pilot's chair but froze before she sat down. The man, wearing a simple button-up shirt, pants, heavy boots, and a distinctive wide-brimmed hat occupying the co-pilot's spot, was the Ranger from the space station elevator, and he'd just identified her as royalty.

"Loni Taraska," Doug continued, withdrawing his hand. "Second daughter to the royal family on Tarsek Prime, lawful rulers of the Tarsek system. Enrolled in the Galactic Federation at eighteen, but retained your rights to the throne. Became one of the best fighter pilots in the Federation until now."

Loni was unsure what to make of this man and how he knew so much about her already.

"What do you think took me so long to hail the carrier?" he said, as if reading her thoughts. "Now if you don't mind, my pilot jumped ship about six hours ago and I haven't the foggiest of how to operate the hyperdrive."

He pointed to the pilot's chair. Loni plopped into it and immediately began flipping switches and cycling through systems checks, getting the ship ready to jump.

"You operate that thing like you grew up in that seat," Doug commented.

The recognition forced a smile from Loni, despite the situation.

"Never met a bird I can't operate. Controls are generally the same on most Terran design ships anyway. Okay. Calculations are underway. Should be ready in two minutes."

"Good. Soon as they're ready, go ahead and punch it."

"Won't that look bad?"

"Here's what I didn't tell you: The Rangers, officially as an organization, have folded into the Empire. Though a few of us haven't assented. If your carrier does its homework they'll find the Rangers are under Imperial control. It'd be in our best interest to high-tail it out of here."

"So you just saved me to get a pilot."

"Your accusations are not appreciated. Like I said, not all us Rangers assented. Those that haven't are still Rangers and are still independent from the Empire. We're dedicated to protecting the innocent, helping people in need, and seeking justice.

"You were completely within your rights to do what you did. The royal family, as a sovereign system, has the right to resign their commission from any force at any time. Your ship is mostly of your investment, so it's officially yours. Imperial totalitarianism hasn't yet caught up with Galactic Federation Law, so you're in the clear.

"I was fully prepared to leave myself drifting if your story didn't check out. But it did, so I'm obliged to help, regardless of whether it benefitted me or not."

Loni gaped, her mind reeling from the honor this man showed.

"Never met a Galactic Ranger, have you?" Doug asked.

The com chirped to life.

"*Horseshoe*, this is *Dominator*."

The console beeped.

"Calculations are ready," Loni said.

Doug pointed to the hyperdrive lever as the *Dominator* continued, "The Rangers are officially under the auspices of the Empire. You will power down your ship and—"

Loni pushed the lever forward, cutting the voice off. The stars streaked into hyperspace.

CHAPTER THREE_

Commodore Evelyn Ferris stood at the forward viewport, gloved fists clasped tightly behind her back. The ship was gone; flashed into hyperspace to who-knows-where. They could be in the Mid Dark, the vast area of starless space around which the galactic ring swirled. They could have gone to some core world or a backwater, low-star system. There was no way to track them, not for an Imperial warship.

"Com officer!" Ferris barked, turning to the appropriate station.

A young man with junior lieutenant bars on his shoulder swiveled in his chair to face her. "Yes, Ma'am!"

"Contact the Bounty Hunter's Guild."

"Right away, Commodore."

Captain Staltz walked up and spoke quietly to the commodore, "Ma'am, bounty hunters? For an AWOL officer?"

"She's not just AWOL, Captain. She's guilty of treason of the highest order."

"Treason? All due respect, Ma'am, Lieutenant Colonel Taraska—"

The commodore held up a hand, her face softening. "I understand your feelings, Captain. She was a fine officer. I don't deny that. But she's betrayed the Empire. This may be hard to hear, but I've learned that she has vital intel she is taking to the rebellion."

"Lieutenant Taraska? I can't believe that."

"Believe it, Captain. She was planning on defecting her entire squadron. Fortunately, or unfortunately, on their last mission they all contracted White Scars. We were able to neutralize them in their bunks. Except Lieutenant Taraska. She's a threat to the Empire and every living creature she encounters."

Commodore Ferris sighed and pinched the bridge of her nose.

"This isn't any easier for me to accept than yourself. But accept it, we must. Loni Taraska is now an enemy of the Federation and thus the Empire. And she must be hunted down and executed before she can do any more damage."

The captain gave a solemn nod.

Staltz was a far cry from his ancestor, the famed captain who led the expedition into this galaxy. This man before her had no spine, no command in his posture or voice. How he made captain escaped her and boiled her blood. She, in contrast, clawed her way to the top with hard work and determination, making commodore at only thirty years old.

Some called her ruthless. But over the course of her career, her actions saved many lives and quelled rebellions that could have turned ugly given enough time.

Since the time of the Alien Wars, the galaxy remained peaceful but not in Ferris's mind. She'd always been at war. Perhaps her ruthlessness and warring mindset is what grabbed the attention of Admiral Traik, moving him to bring her into the circle of trust. What she learned solidified her convictions.

Terrible times were coming.

They didn't need captains who fraternized with their crews. They needed warriors. They needed her.

———

Nearly an hour later, the commodore examined five figures assembled on her bridge.

Aoo, a gray-ish blue blob.

Initinni, a short, hooded figure whose true form was obscured by loose robes.

Iptol and Lotpi, from the race of Glipts where every being was a twin.

And Lo Jinal, from the Creedo, a warrior society that preferred death over failure.

Ferris stopped in front of Lo. His body armor most likely surpassed that of the Armored Corps, which meant it was illegal or incredibly expensive. Ferris chose to ignore this. Infractions of Galactic Law were the Rangers' territory. There were far greater threats to thwart.

"Your target is former Lieutenant Colonel Loni Taraska, former Imperial pilot and traitor to the Empire." She gestured and a full-body, holo image of a tan-skinned female with wavy hair, dressed in the flight suit of an Imperial fighter pilot appeared. "She will be flying an SJ interceptor, but was last seen docking her stolen ship in the hanger bay of a Terran Wars era UTF Frigate." The image shifted to a rotating view of the *Horseshoe*. "You have all been provided with their last known trajectory. Based on the capabilities of that ship, we have also provided likely distances and destinations. The rest is up to you. Find them and eliminate all parties involved. The bounty will be sent out on the Bounty Net in four standard hours, so I advise you to be quick. If you work together, you stand a better chance of success and will split the reward equally."

They had no intention of working together, she knew that. She was counting on their competition to make them move faster to claim the entire bounty. Why else hire four bounty hunters instead of just one?

"Questions?" Ferris asked.

Initinni raise a small, gloved claw.

"Yes?" The Commodore asked.

A jabbering sound emitted from the hood. Ferris turned to the sleek, black translator bot standing behind her.

The bot responded in a feminine voice with an accent the origin of which was lost to time.

"I understand there was a Galactic Ranger involved."

"The Rangers are officially under the auspices of the Empire. If there is a Ranger involved, he is also to be eliminated. You will be duly paid if that is the case."

Initinni gestured wildly, its robe flapping about as it jabbered away.

"No," the bot translated. "I am not going up against a Galactic Ranger."

"I assure you, you will be well compensated."

Initinni continued his behavior.

"No amount of money can convince me," the bot continued. "You are insane. Keep your money. I will not do it."

The short alien ceased its rant, its body undulating with breath. Ferris sighed and signaled for a security officer.

In a smooth motion, Ferris snatched the officer's blaster pistol and fired a single bolt into Initinni's hood. The hooded figure crumpled to the floor while the other bounty hunters stared on impassively.

"Anyone else refusing the commission?" Ferris asked.

None responded.

"Good."

She handed the blaster back to the stunned officer and dismissed him.

"You all have your assignment. Get to it."

The bounty hunters headed to the hanger bay as a security officer removed the body. Ferris noticed some of the bridge crew staring.

"Anyone who sides with our enemies is an enemy of the Empire," she announced. "Anyone who refuses to hunt our enemies when so commissioned is an enemy himself. Only being united in purpose will allow us to withstand the days ahead. Let this be a lesson to us all. You all have your orders. See to them."

Ferris returned her attention to the forward viewport. The crew couldn't know the enormity of the task they faced. Even she didn't know the totality of it. But she'd be spaced if she was going to allow any semblance of dissention to distract those under her command.

The consequences if she did, frightened her to no end.

CHAPTER FOUR

Loni pulled open an access panel to her fighter and noted the fried wiring inside. She slammed the panel, causing a loud *BANG* to reverberate through the hanger bay. The panel hit wrong and swung back down, its damaged state mocking her anger.

"She's pretty shot up," Doug observed.

"Oh, ya think?" Loni snapped. "Took me six months to get this bird in prime shape. Now look at her."

She kicked the landing gear.

"You always this temperamental? She's just a ship."

"She's not just a ship, Ranger! She's my baby. I spent most of my earned credits making her the fastest, most agile bird in my unit. No one could out-fly me in speed or maneuverability. Now she's shot to pieces. By my own comrades no less!"

Loni plopped on the deck and rested her arms on her knees, her head hanging. She sat there for several minutes, mourning her ship and wondering where she would ever get the funds to rebuild it.

Yeah. Nevermind the pilots under your command. You know, the ones that are all dead now? Don't worry about them.

Guilt stung her and she almost burst into tears. She'd barely escaped with her life, but her pilots hadn't even heard the shot that killed them.

Doug's voice cut through her sadness.

"I'm assuming you don't want to rely on your family's wealth to repair it."

Loni didn't raise her head.

"My family doesn't use our money on personal pursuits. But no, I wouldn't want to do that anyway. I built her myself. I want to keep it that way, so no one can say I had to lean on my family."

"You opposed to having help outside your family?"

Loni raised her head, her brow furrowed.

The Ranger squatted next to her. His face was young, Caucasian, and handsome. Coal black hair smoothed back, five-o'clock shadow, and dark, piercing eyes. It was quite a contrast to her tan skin, curly hair and eyes of blue.

"Look, I know something about being shot at by people you once trusted with your life. So, except for your ship, I know where you're at right now. I'd be happy to help if you're willing to let me."

"What did you have in mind?" Loni asked, realizing how croaked her voice sounded.

"You got any credits?"

"Some."

"I know a Ticksar, sells ship parts. Always gives me a discount cause he's afraid I'm going to turn him in for some of the shady stuff he does. But his products are legit and he can pretty much dig up anything you'd need. If you built it, you can repair it. So that'll save you on labor. I have some credits too. Maybe we can come up with enough to get her ship shape again."

Loni raised an eyebrow. "What's the catch?"

"I'm a Ranger. Ain't no catch. I'm happy to help. But if you're looking for what to do with your life next... Well, I'm pretty much reduced to unsanctioned bounty hunting to survive out here and I could use a pilot. You fly my ship and on occasion help me catch bounties, I'll split the reward money with you. Fifty-fifty."

Loni hadn't even had time to think about what she'd do next. She didn't want to go running back to her family. A job as a pilot and part time bounty-hunter didn't sound like an entirely bad move.

"Alright, Ranger," Loni said, offering a hand.

Doug gave it a firm shake.

"Doug."

"Doug. On one condition, though," Loni said, their hands still locked.

"What's that?"

"You let me upgrade this tub *and* teach you how to pilot it."

"Can't turn that down. You got yourself a deal."

———

"Are you sure you're alright, Jumba?"

Loni smiled at the holo-image of her parents, their images and voices reassuring after a day of betrayal.

"Yes, mother, I'm fine. My ship is just a little damaged and the Ranger is helping me get it repaired."

"Be sure to thank him for us," her father said. "You sure this is the path you want? Bounty-hunting can be dangerous, and with a fugitive Ranger."

"He's not a fugitive, Father. The Empire doesn't care about him, just the other Rangers. And they only want to convince him to join in their defection. I figure he could use an ally and so could we."

BOOM!

The sound rumbled through the hull and the lights momentarily dimmed.

The com squawked to life.

"Loni, get up here."

"I have to go," she said, killing the transmission. She sprinted for the cockpit.

She arrived just as the ship rocked again, throwing her into a control panel. She stumbled over and plopped into the pilot's seat, strapping herself in. She paused at the looseness of the straps.

One more thing I'll have to upgrade.

"Are we being fired at?" she asked, bringing the engines online.

"Looks that way," Doug replied, craning his neck to see out the main viewport.

"You'll have better luck with the sensor display. Do you know how to operate *anything* on this ship besides the com?"

"A few things, yeah," Doug mumbled.

Loni reached over and tapped a button. A screen inlaid into the console lit up, displaying two dots moving from the outer edge toward the center.

Loni pushed on the yoke.

"A screen display, are you kidding me? Doesn't this ship have a holo-display?"

"Ship's kindof old. Belonged to my grandfather. Held up pretty well over the years. I think they're closing in."

High intensity blaster bolts struck the hull, rocking the ship. Two fighters zipped past the viewport.

"Those look like modified snub fighters," she said.

"Bounty hunters."

"Bounty hunters? You have bounty hunters after you? I thought the Rangers didn't use bounty hunters."

"We don't. They're not after me. They're after you. I just checked the bounty net. There's a one-million credit bounty out for your death."

"What? Why?"

"You tell me, Princess. Empire wouldn't put out such a high bounty, much less any bounty at all on a member of the royal family, for a simple AWOL and theft charge."

Loni gritted her teeth. She knew she should tell him what she found out, but now wasn't the time. "Weapons?"

"Defensive lasers only."

"Shields? Tell me we have shields."

"We have shields. I think."

Loni gave him a flat stare.

"They're moving in again," Doug said.

Loni cycled through her options. Defensive lasers wouldn't make a dent in the shielding those fighters carried. The shielding had probably been upgraded anyway. No missiles. Maybe no shields of their own. A single impact would probably…

"How old is this bird?" Loni asked.

"She was built around the time of the Terran Wars and modified to be a mobile carrier. Took a beating in the Alien Wars and was refitted afterwards."

Loni made some calculations in her head. It just might work. If it didn't, they were dead either way. May as well go out with a bang.

She fiddled with different switches on the panel, testing their use. The ship jostled as thrusters fired in different directions. Inertial dampeners were probably slag like everything else on the ship.

"Okay, got it," she said. "Which direction are they coming in from?"

"Uhmmm…" Doug said, scratching his head. "Either below us or behind us."

Loni let go of the yoke and undid the useless straps long enough to lean over the display. "Below us."

She resumed her seat and pulled back on the yoke, angling the ship so they were flying directly away from the fighters on the same vector.

"Tell me when they're within two-hundred meters," she said.

"Uhmmm…"

Loni was about to open her mouth in exasperation when Doug blurted out, "Oh, I got it. Okay. All set."

Loni hovered her hand over the thruster controls.

"Now!"

She hit reverse thrusters, throwing them forward in their harnesses, then hit the underside thrusters immediately after, sending the nose of the craft spinning upward along the Y axis from their previous vector. Two loud impacts followed one after the other, rocking the ship and jostling her around her loose harness. Loni winced, dreading the bruising she'd have. The noise of the impact was so loud, she expected hull breach lights to flash on her console. But there was nothing beyond a single flashing light, partially labeled, "Imp—ct."

"Did you just cause them to crash directly into my ship?" Doug asked.

Loni breathed out a relieved sigh.

"Yup. Terran War stuff is as tough as they come. Modern blaster bolts might cut through these old hulls like butter, but when standing up to matter impacts, the beating these ships can take is unmatched. They don't make them like this anymore. Guess this old tub is actually good for something besides scaring the children of ship builders."

Doug was pale as a ghost.

"You just crashed two star fighters into the hull of my grandfather's ship."

"You want to survive in this tub, Cowboy, you'd better learn to trust me. I can pilot your ship, but there's only so much I can do. There was no out-running them. By the time the hyperdrive spooled up, we'd have been so full of holes we'd make space look full. I doubt this thing has a jump drive and I didn't see any other option of getting us out of that mess. Did you?"

Doug leaned back in his chair, wiping his face. "Just…tell me before you do something like that again."

"If I think of it."

"You're not a very compliant pilot, are you?"

"You don't need compliance. You need someone that can keep you alive."

"Speaking of which," Doug said, regaining his composure. "What is it you have that the Empire wants you dead?"

"After we've jumped to some place more remote," Loni said, and started entering coordinates.

CHAPTER FIVE_

Loni glanced over the hyperdrive engine and scribbled notes on a datapad.

"So?" Doug asked.

"So, your ship is a piece of junk," Loni said, moving to examine the energy coils. "Sure, it's Terran War stuff which is both tough and designed to last, but it's light years behind everything else out there. Your hyperdrive is a class C. Class C! They don't even use Terran letters for hyperdrive classes anymore!"

"Not about tha—"

"On top of that, your shield array is practically non-existent when going up against weapons of today."

"Loni."

"Your sub-light engines are sub-standard, power relays are worn, there's no A.I. driving this thing."

"Loni."

"Oxygen recycle is barely working. Space, it's a wonder we can even breathe in here."

"Loni, will you shut up for a minute! I'm not talking about the ship."

Loni gave him a blank stare. What else could be so important?

"I'm talking about what you have the Empire doesn't want you to know."

"Oh, that," Loni said as if it were a minor thing, returning to her examination of the engine compartment. "They're planning on wiping out the core."

Doug waited for her to continue, but she just muttered something about replacing the entire compartment and made more notes on her pad. Doug cleared his throat. That confused expression crossed her face again.

"Can we focus on the Empire and their plans to wipe out the core? How'd you even find this out?" Doug asked.

Loni's hands started to shake. "I-I need to finish my work here."

She ducked her head down, focusing on her datapad before moving to examine a set of power couplers.

Doug moved around to stand next to her. She wasn't shaking anymore, clearly trying to distract herself.

"Hey," Doug said in a gentle voice, drawing her attention. "I'm here to help. If something happened, you can trust me with it. Ranger's honor. Talk to me."

Then he saw it. That look in her eyes he'd seen plenty of times before. The woman had encountered something truly traumatic. Her head went on a swivel, her breaths quickening.

"You want to go to your ship?" Doug said, thinking it might help calm her.

She bolted for the ladder that led out of the engine compartment onto the main deck. Doug followed and hadn't even stepped off the ladder before she said with a wide-eyed stare, "Kitchens?"

Doug pointed and Loni rushed off, Doug on her heels. The door to the kitchens slid open to a room just as outdated as the rest of the ship. She turned to Doug.

"There's some ready-soup in the cabinet and some water in the chiller," Doug said.

Loni pulled out a bowl of ready-soup and ripped off the lid. The contents immediately hydrated, drawing moisture from the air, and heated to a boil. The smell of cooked chicken wafted around them. After wiping down a bench and grimacing at the dust on her glove, Loni sat down.

Doug handed her a spoon, sitting across from her with his own soup, and pushed a bottle of water toward her. Loni grabbed it, chugging its contents, then dove into her soup. After consuming half the cup, her panic quelled and she sat back.

"Yesterday, my squad and I were briefed on an attack run planned on a Space Pirate base in the Diltan sector of the outer asteroid belt. My squad was picked because we were the only ones skilled enough to fly in without getting obliterated. During the mission, we encountered some resistance. Mostly older, short range fighters from a decade ago, modified transports, medical carriers, it was a hodgepodge. There was nothing that looked anything like Pirate tech.

"My pilots noticed the same thing. I ordered a temporary cease-fire while I contacted one of the fighters. Their weapons couldn't do much against us anyway, so I figured what's the harm?

"The man identified himself and their colony as a peaceful human settlement having nothing to do with the Pirates, which confirmed what we'd seen so far. I commed back to the *Dominator* to confirm our coordinates and intel. To my surprise, the commodore commanding the *Dominator* came on the com.

"'Interceptor squad, you are being misled by ghost talk. This is a rebellion outpost housing Pirates and rebel leaders. Follow orders and destroy the base.'

"We were monitoring their coms and the moment the order came back, the fighters went to full engagement again. We had no choice but to wipe them out and take out the base. I got another static filled transmission, probably coming from the base, pleading with us to break off, saying they were a peaceful non-Federation colony. I followed my orders and ignored the transmission, blasting the rock to slag. Before the transmission cut off completely, I thought I heard children's voices. I couldn't be sure. Might have just been my own doubts. But it bothered me enough to wonder…

"The carrier ordered the complete obliteration of the enemy fighters and any debris we found floating. That wasn't uncommon for virus containment, but this was supposed to be a Space Pirate base, then it became a Rebel base. I had a gut feeling if I questioned our orders I would be told it contained some deadly outbreak of White Scars.

"It was zero-one-hundred this morning when we were sent out. When we got back, the rest of my squadron went to sleep. I started digging as discretely as I could, trying to find information on the op. Everything was blocked with a high rank lock-out. I contacted a slicer friend of mine, genius kid. Told him what I was trying to find out. He got back to me at zero-three-hundred with temporary access to all top-level info. Said it would only last for twenty minutes before the security protocols went back up. It took me the entire time to secure a terminal that wasn't being monitored and wouldn't be unusual for me to be using."

She paused, her hands gripping the ready-soup bowl, her head bowed and her eyes closed. When she continued, her voice was quiet.

"I located the file. It was marked with official orders from an Admiral Trai mentioning there was a mole hiding out on the base who was in possession of confidential plans the Empire had to 'wipe out the core.' That was all I saw. The security protocols went up, setting off an internal alarm. I got my tail out of there and headed for my squadron. I had to tell them. When I got there…they were massacred. All of them were lying about the bunk, their eyes were just staring…not moving. Little white streaks on their skin."

She grew quiet, her brow knitted. After a moment, Doug reached out and touched her shoulder. Loni gasped and bolted upright.

Doug held up his hands.

"It's okay. You're all right."

Loni brought a shaking hand to her face, wiping away a tear. She took some steadying breaths and continued.

"There was a stealth bot there. It was injecting something into one of my pilots. It turned and came at me. The thing was so fast. I drew my side arm and fired. It dodged. I don't know if you're familiar with stealth bots, but they're designed for evasion. It shot an arm toward me, a needle on the end. I caught it with my free hand. It clamped its other hand onto my throat. The thing had a grip like a repulsor press. I pressed the barrel to its torso and fired over and over again, until the thing fell limp. Then, I just ran. I don't even remember getting into my ship. Just the duty officer yelling something at me, and a squad of Armored Corps Troopers coming in and firing at me. I probably incinerated a few of them as I did a full burn shooting out of the hanger bay. The rest you know."

Doug remained silent, taking in the whole of the story as she attacked her soup with more vigor than before. She drank the last bits, dropping bowl and spoon to the table with a satisfied burp.

"I'm sorry about your squadron," Doug said.

Loni nodded, mostly back to normal.

"They were good people."

"I take it you *didn't* report your defection to your commanding officer?"

Loni shrugged, the look on her face showing how little she cared.

"I may have made a rude gesture at him through the canopy. That's notice enough for me."

Doug couldn't help but grin.

"I'll tell you one thing," Loni said, pointing at Doug, "whoever gave that order better hope I never find out."

"Best revenge you can get is by stopping their plans."

Loni rolled her eyes and glanced around.

"If you need the incinerator, it's on the far wall," Doug directed her.

"This whole ship needs an incinerator." She left her bowl where it was and walked out of the kitchens.

"She ain't wrong," Doug mumbled and went back to his soup.

CHAPTER SIX_

Loni maneuvered her straw to suck up the last of the pink foam. She tilted her head back, a euphoric smile on her face.

"Fix my ship and treat me to a markobian foam drink," she said to Doug. "A girl could get used to this. You sure you don't have some hidden agenda?"

Doug smiled and took a sip of his own mug of a dark, frothy liquid. At Loni's suggestion, they headed for Eisen Ro, a space-port orbiting the scrap planet of Graigt. It wasn't where Doug's contact resided, but it was just as good and Loni knew how to get deals there.

"Not that I'm aware of," Doug replied. "Just figured after the day you had you could use a treat."

Loni regarded him with searching eyes.

"What's your story, Cowboy? What made you join the Rangers and why haven't you turned with the rest of them?"

"You like calling me that, don't you?"

"That's what you are, aren't you? A Ranger turned bounty hunter? I thought that's how you Rangers referred to men like yourself."

"We do, but I just don't see it that way. As far as I'm concerned,

I'm still a Ranger. I'm still upholding the law and bringing criminals to justice. Only difference is the Rangers ain't paying my salary, so I have to make money by bringing in bounties."

"Splitting hairs if you ask me, but whatever you like."

Loni thought she detected a hint of sadness flash across his face.

"As to your other questions," Doug said, "the Rangers have always been independent. We answer to each other. If we're all abiding by the code, ain't no way anyone's getting away with being dirty. There's no need to come under the auspices of the Empire. Something's fishy. And if what you found out about the Empire is true, I've got a haunting suspicion the same thing may have happened to my fellow Rangers."

Loni thought on Doug's claims, swiveling her barstool to face the interior of the cantina. It was a long strip of area on the space station in between the docks and the main arcade. The air was a bit stuffy though, and the place was crowded.

She didn't mind. This was an underground establishment, frequented by people who wanted to stay clear of Imperial eyes, but needed to stay near this particular core system. A few aliens milled among the crowd, but most were human enough. Her eye caught a man with a red beard and a birthmark over one eye staring at them. He averted his eyes just as she saw him. Loni casually swiveled back to the bar.

"Doug," she said, quietly, "there's a man at a table who's been staring at us."

"Yeah, I spotted him when we came in. He's a Ranger. Don't know if he's turned or not, though."

"How do you know he's a Ranger?"

"I just know. No, don't reach for your weapon. He may have spotted you as an Imperial. Might be wondering the same about me as we are about him."

The doors slid open and a group of four men walked in, scanning the crowd. Their long duster coats and badges clearly identified them as Rangers.

Uh, oh, Loni thought.

———

Doug saw the Rangers enter and minded his drink. He was thankful he wasn't wearing his badge or duster. Unless one looked real close at him and his demeanor, he wore nothing else to identify him as a Ranger.

"Which direction are they headed?" Doug asked.

"For that Ranger, the one that was staring at us. They don't seem to have noticed you."

Doug chanced a look. The four Rangers were surrounding the table.

"We better leave while they're distracted," Loni said.

Doug held up a hand, halting her. He needed to know what they were up to, but was only able to catch snippets of their conversation.

"…time to make a decision…"

Two chatty aliens, a Druul and a Corsican, passed by, creating a pause in the exchange.

"…don't be stupid…making it worse…"

Doug slid off his barstool. That was enough for him.

Loni grabbed his arm.

"What are you doing? This is our chance to get out of here."

"Go and get the ship ready."

"Don't be stupid, Cowboy, this isn't—"

"I ain't leaving a Ranger behind," Doug said, his eyes intense. Loni reluctantly removed her hand. "Now go and get the ship ready. I'll be right behind you."

Doug walked up behind the group just as one's hand drifted to his blaster.

"Keep that hand off your weapon, Ranger," Doug said.

The group whirled on him, all four going for their holsters. Doug remained still, hands casually hanging near his blasters.

"This is Ranger business, Texan," the lead guy said. "Be best if you stayed out of it."

"From what I recall, Rangers don't gang up on a fellow Ranger and try to bully him into making a decision. Now why don't three of you clear out and one of you sit down and talk to the man like an equal. And don't be so hasty with your weapons. Someone's likely to get hurt."

Another of the men spoke up, "You shut your mouth, Mister. Don't tell a Ranger how to do his job."

"Your job? Thought that was upholding the law, not turning on your own."

The man stepped forward. The leader held up his hand, stopping him.

"What's your name, Texan?"

"Doug."

"Doug what?"

"Doug your own grave if you don't back off."

"You threatening a Ranger?"

Doug shook his head. "No. Just know the pattern. Folks who make trouble tend to fall into it themselves. You keep on this path, you're asking to get a blaster bolt through your skull. Don't matter who carries it, you'll have done it to yourself."

The leader waivered under Doug's steady gaze. Out of the corner of his eye, Doug noticed the seated Ranger with the birthmark over his eye making slow, deliberate movements. The other four didn't seem to notice.

"Nice blasters you have there," the leader said, gaining back some of his confidence. "Let's see if you know how to use them." He backed away, hand hovering over his blaster.

Some of the locals quietly shuffled back and exited the building. "I don't want to kill you, Ranger, and definitely not here with all these innocents around," Doug said.

"I don't think you have a choice, Texan." The leader stopped a good distance away.

A large, red-skinned alien roared, tackling the leader from behind a side-wall. Two more aliens lit up with twisted smiles and joined the fray, dog-piling the Ranger. Quick as lightning, Doug drew his blaster and fired off a stun blast, catching one of the aliens and knocking him out.

The cold barrel of a blaster pressed against Doug's head. "Drop it, Texan."

"Hey!" came a shout from the booth.

The three Rangers turned and two were hit with a stun blast. The third dodged and fired a red blaster bolt through the booth man's shoulder. Doug slugged that one across the jaw and the man crumpled to the floor. A burley human lunged at Doug, his meaty fist already mid swing. Doug barely had time to doge and fire off another stun blast.

Next thing he knew, the entire cantina erupted into one big bar fight. He hurried over and helped the bearded man out of the booth.

"C'mon, we gotta clear out," Doug said.

"Much obliged," the bearded man huffed.

Loni appeared, blaster in hand, and the three of them worked their way through the chaos and out into the hall that led to the docking bays.

"Thought I told you to get the ship ready," Doug said.

"You looked like you could use a hand, Cowboy."

"You mean to tell me you started that fight?"

"I might have told the Druul and a few others the Rangers

were here to collect their women. The Corsicans were just happy there was a fight. You know how they are. It just kind of ran out of control from there."

"You didn't have to do that. I had it handled."

"Sure you did," Loni said.

"I hate to interrupt," said the bearded man, "but you mind telling me who you are?"

Doug stopped and held out a hand.

"Ranger Doug Lancer."

The man shook it with a firm grip.

"Deputy Pen Olster."

"Where's your Ranger, Deputy?"

"Back in the cantina. He offered me a promotion to full Ranger, with a few strings attached. Told him I needed time to think about it. After today, I'm pretty sure my answer is no for the Empire. Not sure what to do though. May just have to resign."

"We're really sad for you," Loni said, grabbing Doug's hand. "But we have to go."

Doug stood his ground. "It ain't a hard decision, just a hard path. You believe in the Rangers?"

"Doug!" Loni urged.

"The true Rangers? Yeah, I believe in them, if there's any point in believing in them anymore."

"I guarantee you there is. You ever betray your badge, your integrity, or the public trust?"

The fire in Pen's eyes was unmistakable.

"I've lived my entire adult life by the code. When I swore that oath, I meant it. I'll still live it. Even if I never become a Ranger."

"We ain't got time for ceremony—"

"We don't have time for *any* of this!" Loni interrupted. "We have to go, Doug!"

Shouting alongside heavy boots sounded from down the hall.

"—and I don't have a badge to give you," Doug

continued unabated. "Here's what I can give you: Deputy Pen Olster, by my witness of your actions of holding to the code and by your word to hold to said code, I promote you to the status of full Galactic Ranger with all the rights, privileges, and responsibilities that office holds. Swear to stand true to the code of the Rangers until the cold sleep takes you."

Pen beamed.

"I so swear."

Doug held out his hand, the shouting closing in, and they shook again.

"Congratulations, Ranger," Doug said. "Stay safe out there."

"You as well."

They parted ways. Doug and Loni ran down the corridor away from the approaching danger following them. Doug started off one direction at an intersection but Loni grabbed his arm and hauled him the other way.

"But we're docked—"

"Nevermind, just come on." She activated her com. "This is Loni Taraska. Is everything ready? Good. We're heading your way now. Have the ship prepped for lift-off. Yes, I'll pay, just put it on the ledger."

They had maybe half a minute before the people attached to those boots caught up.

Doug and Loni reached a docking bay door and she entered a code. The door slid up into the ceiling, revealing a shiny blue, crescent-shaped ship, the two points aimed at the exit doors. The cockpit sat between the points in the center, with a hanger bay underneath running half the length of the ship. Heavy gun emplacements were mounted above and below along the hull, and a heavy, repeating blaster cannon was mounted on the belly in the center below the cockpit just in front of the hanger. A crew hustled around the ship disconnecting cables and fuel lines. A portly man waved from the cockpit and Loni led Doug up the ramp.

"Loni, what is going on?" Doug asked as they ran down the ship's corridor to the cockpit.

The man greeted them with a smile and a data pad.

"Welcome to your—"

"Thank you," Loni replied, snatching the data pad. She skimmed through the data, made a sloppy signature, then shoved it into Doug's hands.

"Thumbprint that," she said, sliding into the pilot's seat, activating holo-controls and bringing systems online.

"Loni, tell me what is going on," Doug insisted. "Where is my ship?"

"This *is* your ship," Loni said, still cycling through checks. "I sold your old one."

"You what?" Doug shouted.

"That's a fine piece of history," the portly man said. "Don't see many of those around anymore."

"Loni, how could you—"

Loni reached back and clamped her hand down on Doug's, pressing his thumb to the identifier. The data pad chirped and Loni handed it back to the man.

"You better get clear, Tes," she said. "Trouble's coming for us and you don't want to be with us when it does."

"Nice doing business with you," Tes said, hastily making his way out of the cockpit.

Despite his chagrin, Doug slid into the co-pilot's seat and strapped in.

"Loni, you've got a lot of explaining to do."

"Later, Cowboy."

Confirming Tes was huffing away from the ship, Loni raised the ramp. Two Rangers burst into the docking bay, and started firing. A green shimmer appeared and faded before the cockpit as the shields absorbed the blasts. Loni flicked a final switch and grabbed the yoke. The Rangers dove back through the doorway away from the backsplash of the thrusters blowing through the docking bay. The ship lifted and shot through the still opening bay doors, throwing them into their seats.

"Wooo!" Loni whooped, her smile wide. "He wasn't kidding. This thing really moves!"

The inertial dampeners caught up with their momentum and the pressure eased.

"What about your personal ship?" Doug asked once they were out in open space.

"The *Barracuda?* I had it loaded onto this one along with all your personal affects. Figured you'd want a ship like your old one."

"My old one was just fine. And where do you get off selling someone else's property?"

"We had a deal, Cowboy. You said I could upgrade your old tub, so I did."

"Upgrading does not mean replacing."

"It does if the components are worthless."

Doug opened his mouth to reply, but Loni cut him off.

"Doug, the ship was a relic. It couldn't outrun a tow barge. You needed something fast and powerful. This is it. It would have cost more to upgrade everything on your old tub than to buy a whole new ship. And I got the credits to repair my ship and plenty left over."

"And did it ever occur to you to ask me first?"

"You'd have said yes."

"That ain't the point! You don't just go and sell someone's ship without asking them first. You of all people should know that."

"How about you risking our lives so you can spout off some ceremonial garbage to someone you just met?" Loni said.

"Don't change the subject. You sold my ship without clearing it with me first. I don't take kindly to that."

Loni crossed her arms. "Fine. Douglas Lancer, would it be alright if I traded your old, junk pile of a ship for something that would actually allow us to catch the criminals we're chasing, get away from the Rangers chasing us, and have all the amenities of your old ship, plus a brig and a firing range?"

"That ain't fun—There's a firing range?"

Loni smiled and nodded. Doug paused, then shook away the thought.

"That don't make up for it," he said.

"You hired me to fly your ship. You want me to do that, I need something that will keep the both of us alive. It's a deadly galaxy out there, Cowboy. And with the Empire after me and the Rangers after you, that relic was a death trap."

She closed her eyes, her shoulders relaxing slightly.

"I admit I should have asked you first. And I planned to. But you had to stop and do your little ceremony and we lost the time to do it."

Doug's temper cooled.

"That ceremony was important. The galaxy's gone topsy-turvy. People doing the right thing and holding to their standards should be commended. People tend to just give up otherwise and let things fall to the wayside."

Loni didn't answer, didn't even bother to look his way.

Doug ran his hand through his hair. He wasn't happy about her decision, but what was done was done. No sense crying about it. It *was* a good decision. He couldn't fault her for that.

"Look, I understand your reasoning, not saying you're wrong there. But you need to communicate to me these kinds of decisions. Besides that, it was my grandfather's ship. Lotta history there. Sorry I got loud."

"Don't be sorry," Loni said. "I'd be mad to. But I'll be spaced if you think I'm going to apologize for a decision that will save both our lives in the long run, bad communication or not."

"Well, that'll just have to be between you and your conscience."

Loni scrunched her brow, trying to understand what he meant by that. Doug sighed and swiveled to the controls. The panel was new and shiny, switches clearly labeled. No broken components or spots of oxidation. The walls were immaculate. Even the seat felt stable, comfortable, and didn't squeak when he turned. He had to admit, it was nice being in something new.

"Controls look pretty much the same from the *Horseshoe*," he said.

Loni grimaced.

"Speaking of which, you might want to think of a name for this vessel. And please don't say *Horseshoe Two*."

"You got something against horseshoes?"

"No, but a ship should have a name that instills something. It should capture its essence and spirit."

Doug knitted his brow.

"Ships don't have spirits."

Loni put her head in her hand.

"Just pick something that sounds interesting. Like it fits. Think of what you want the name to convey."

Doug opened his mouth.

"And don't say crescent," Loni said.

Doug closed his mouth and pursed his lips. Loni waited patiently, but he just sat there, his face screwed up in concentration.

"You're really torn up about this," Loni said.

"Well, you ain't making it easy."

Doug sighed and scratched his head, knocking his hat askew. Loni tried not to laugh.

"*Blue Moon*," he said.

"*Blue Moon*? Had to go with the cowboy theme, didn't you?"

"It's all I can think of," Doug said, waving a dismissive hand. His voice was edged and his normal laxness gone. "I ain't got experience in this sort of thing. I ain't a pilot."

Loni felt a sting of regret for annoying him.

"I can live with it. It's not bad."

Doug threw her a look like he didn't believe her. She decided to change the subject.

"The reason the controls look the same as your old tub is because this is a newer model of your grandpa's ship. Like I said, I tried to find something at least similar to your old one. Frankly, this ship design is still ugly as sin, but at least the tech is up-to-date. It has a point-zero-six hyperdrive, and I was able to get some heavy weaponry mounted. Shields are nearly top of the line too."

"You did all that in the space of two hours?"

Loni shrugged.

"I started when we were en route. Once I knew where we were going, I researched what was available for sale. It was fortunate there just happened to be this exact model there. Everything else was pretty easy to find and have installed. By the time we arrived, all that was left was to transfer the *Barracuda* and your personal affects."

"You talk like you have experience in this."

"Like I said, I upgraded my own ship. I've learned where to find things on what planets and how to negotiate a deal."

Doug nodded appreciatively. An alarm blared and Loni checked her console.

"We're being fired upon," she said, grabbing the yoke.

"Really?" Doug asked, eyeing his sensor display. He added in a mumble, "Didn't feel nothing."

Loni had to smile at that.

"Yeah, I see them," Doug said. "Terran design. Probably the Rangers. Guess they ain't interested in Pen."

"Calculating hyperspace course. Any destination in particular?"

"Mid Dark, to give us time to repair your ship and me time to get to know this one."

"You got it."

A couple more blips on the display and Doug turned to Loni.

"Was that them firing on us again?"

"Yup. Scored two direct hits. Shields at ninety-eight percent. Jump calc is ready."

Doug raised his eyebrows. That was fast.

"Fire it up."

Loni pushed the hyperspace lever forward and the stars streaked into the brilliant colors of hyperspace.

"I set us a spot near the center of the Dark before we hit the interference clouds. Should be there in a few hours."

"Nice work."

Loni *mmhmmed* as she started running through systems checks.

"I mean on choosing the ship," Doug said. "Long as she doesn't break down every cycle, seems like you were real smart about it."

"Why thank you, Ranger. You sure know how to make a girl feel appreciated. Sometimes."

Doug cleared his throat and unstrapped from his seat.

Loni swiveled towards him. "Hey, you mind if we make a side trip afterwards?"

"Where to?"

"Not sure. I need to pick up a special item, but I don't really know where to find it. Maybe you can help me out with that."

"Okay, sure. We can talk about it while we work on your ship."

Loni raised her eyebrows.

"You're going to help me?"

"Yeah, why not?"

"Have you ever repaired a starship before?"

"No, but it can't be that hard."

"Uh-huh."

Doug didn't like the grin plastered on her face.

"Okay, well, I'll be in my bunk."

He exited the cockpit, then poked his head back in.

"Where *is* my bunk?"

CHAPTER SEVEN_

The market bustled with activity, thick with innumerable beings from a multitude of species buying and selling. Doug led Loni down a crowded, narrow walkway. Ancient-looking shops and well-maintained tents lined one side, and an old, rusted, steel railing guarded a sheer drop on the other.

Most of the beings they passed wore clothing denoting a working-class society, not a wealthy one. Children with dirty faces and rags for clothes milled through the crowd. There were beggars sitting in front of shops with enough frequency to cause wariness to override Loni's sympathy.

Scents of old metal and wood, body odor, savory meat, sweet perfumes, and others Loni didn't recognize blew past her in great wafts. Her head on a swivel, she held the straps of her metal pack tightly, determined not to let some pickpocket swipe it from her. Not that they'd have an easy time of it.

"You sure we're in the right place?" she asked.

"You wanted a shop that sells rare weaponry," Doug replied over his shoulder, his tone as casual as ever. "This is the best place I know of."

Tapolas was a moon, and although densely populated, not wealthy.

Doug led the way to a small shop built out of old, stained wood of some indigenous tree. Dirty glass windows obscured the inside. It was typical of the shops in this sector of the city.

They crossed the threshold into a small, dimly lit interior, a brass, analog bell attached to a steel cord announcing their entrance. Numerous weapons lined the walls, each illuminated by a spotlight. Blaster pistols, gauss rifles, disintegrators, vibro-swords, even slug launchers so large they were once tagged as "hand-cannons."

At the far end was a counter stretching from wall to wall. In its center was a glass case containing even more firearms. Atop the counter sat a black, sleek-furred feline, slightly larger than most cats Loni had seen. Its tail lazily whipped the air while it pawed at a data pad. It raised its head when they approached, its paw frozen mid-swipe, golden eyes sizing-up the princess.

"Who's the broad, Doug?" the cat said in accented basic. "You know I don't like women in my shop."

Loni scowled. It wasn't a cat, but an Ikati, a sentient cat-like race without a homeworld. She might have been sympathetic toward the creature had it not just insulted her.

"Loni Taraska," Doug introduced, "Whiskers."

"Whiskers?" the Ikati scoffed. It stood on its hind legs, paws on its hips. That's when Loni noticed the tactical vest covering its chest. "You pea-shooting, gun-toting, bi-pedal, hairless renegade. You come into my shop towing a female of your species who looks like she spent a week too close to a solar, and have the audacity to call me Whiskers? You're walking a thin line with me, Ranger."

"What are you going to do, pint-size? Morph into a giant Razorhulk and throw me over the railing outside?"

"Oh, you wanna go down that road? I'd be something far

worse than a Razorhulk. But let's be more practical. Maybe I should just call the *real* Rangers and let them know you're here. I hear they're looking for you and ain't too happy with you right now. What do you think of that, smart-mouth?"

That was enough for Loni, she reached for the feline, but stopped short at the blaster pistol aimed at her head. The gun whined, powering up. Loni barely saw him draw it, and she had no idea where from.

"Don't try it, toots!"

Doug was attempting to hold in his laughter.

"It's all right, Loni. That was just playful banter between me and him. Ar-Chitak ain't calling the Rangers. He'd be out of business in a week."

"It'd be worth it to wipe that smug smile off your face," Ar-Chitak said.

"We're here to make a purchase, Arch."

"You sure this broad isn't going to try anything stupid?" He jutted the barrel toward her for emphasis, his paws apparently possessing opposable thumbs that blended in to look like a normal cat's paw.

"Actually, she's the reason we're here. Said she needed some shells. Rarest of rare I believe is how she put it."

"Oh," Arch said, lowering the blaster. "Well, that's different then." He slapped the side of the blaster, collapsing it into a small square he attached to a belt hanging just below the vest. "What can I interest you in? I got some nice old-world slug-launchers, even older than that tub this Ranger calls a ship."

"Loni," Doug prompted.

"Unlock," Loni said and the latch on her straps clicked open.

Loni wriggled her arms out and set the case on the counter. Arch was immediately transfixed, rubbing a paw over the case.

"Solid duranium," he mumbled.

"What's duranium?" Doug asked.

"Y'know, for a Ranger, you don't know much," Arch shot at him. "Duranium is a rare metal used in the mixture to make impervisteel. It's expensive and hard to find, but they only need a small amount to increase the integrity of steel a hundred-fold. Oh, and it's also just the backing for the entire Federation Credit system. This case alone is worth a fortune."

Loni smirked and removed her glove.

"Wait till you see what's inside." She placed her palm on the top right corner of the case. "Open."

A beam scanned her hand and the case clicked open. Inside was a gun whose four-centimeter muzzle made hand cannons look like pea shooters. The sightless barrel was a straight cylinder, crimped in places where three, dark, narrow stripes spiraled up the length, ending in dots just before the tip. The entire weapon seemed composed of one solid piece, its brilliant silver sheen reflecting off the ceiling.

The Ikati's golden eyes widened.

"A singularity gun?"

He reached a paw toward it, but stopped, seeking Loni for permission. She nodded and he caressed the finish. His feline eyes closed and a soft purr bubbled up from deep inside him.

"This...this is the real deal," he said, opening his eyes. "I've waited my whole life to see one of these."

"Am I still some female that got too close to a solar?"

Arch withdrew his paw, rubbing it on his fur.

"Ah-heh. I'll, uh, have to verify its authenticity, if you don't mind."

Loni glanced at Doug.

"You can trust him," Doug said, eyeing some guns in the case.

Arch reached behind the counter and the far section of it slid inward, allowing for a path behind it.

"If you'll bring it over here," Arch said, jumping down and then hopping up onto the counter on the back wall. He pulled a sheet off a device and indicated for Loni to place the gun into its clamps. The thing clicked around the singularity gun. Arch tapped some buttons on a console, but stopped to address her.

"Uh, this will just take a minute. Feel free to browse. I'll give you ten percent off."

He waved her away and resumed his tapping. Loni wandered over to Doug who was staring at a long-barreled rifle on the wall.

"NK-47," she said. "Its rounds fire miniature versions of what used to be called nuclear weapons. Has a range of almost sixteen-hundred meters. The immediate area of destruction is twice that with more coming from nuclear fallout, depending on which way the wind blows. That thing is as old as your old ship. Don't make them like that anymore."

"Probably cause nobody can find radioactive material. You seem to know a lot about it."

"I know a lot about a lot of firearms." She pointed to an alien-looking blaster."Eei-klack high-impact blaster. Made of some metal from the Eei-klack homeworld they won't share. Four rounds per minute with a shorter range than your Nordon blasters. But the blasts are compacted energy. One hit from that will not only knock you across the room, but will blow a hole in you the size of a Gorman fist and stun anyone standing in close proximity."

"How close?"

"One-point-six meters."

"How about that one?" Doug pointed to a hand-held slug-launcher in the case.

"Polymer-framed, short recoil-operated, lock-breech semi-automatic pistol. Called a Glock after the makers somewhere back in history. No safety. Fires a forty-five-caliber slug. There were models that fired other calibers. Capable of eleven-hundred to twelve-hundred rounds per minute at three-hundred seventy-five meters per second at a range of forty-five-point-four-seven meters. These were sturdy pieces of hardware."

"Pilot, mechanic, and weapons expert. You sure are multi-talented," Doug said.

"I study starcraft design because I like efficiency in my star-crafts. If things aren't operating at peak efficiency, it could spell disaster. In order to keep things that way, I need to know my ship and its components inside and out."

"And the weapons?"

Her smile widened. "I like things that go *boom*."

"So, miss expert, tell me about that pretty piece of hardware you're buying shells for. I've seen my share of firearms and that's a new one for me."

Loni eyed the Ikati. He was watching the readouts of his testing device as the dark stripes on the gun pulsed with a blue light, his paws rubbing in anticipation.

"There are only four singularity guns in existence. My father, mother, and I each have one, and there's one sealed away in our home. My family invented it and we're the only ones who know how to operate it. The shells can do a number of things depending on the shell. From self-collapsing black-holes, to high-yield energy barriers, to molecular scattering."

Doug's eyebrows went up into his hat.

"You see why we don't like to hand these out to anyone," Loni said.

"Then how come we can buy the shells here?"

"The shells themselves are difficult to manufacture, but not impossible, thus their costly nature and rarity. But they're useless without a singularity gun to initiate the dormant astrophysics inherent in the shell. That doesn't stop some black market dealers from manufacturing and selling them. Some people try to create an approximation of a singularity gun or activate the shells in other ways. The results are either lackluster or incredibly destructive. That's why they're outlawed. Only with one of those properly calibrated can the reactions be controlled to the point of making an effective and precise weapon."

"I get the feeling it's not just the gun and the knowledge on how to use it that keeps it inside your family. Anything can be reverse engineered given enough time."

"I guess that'll just be my family secret then."

"I'm all done here," Arch called, disengaging the device. "It's the real deal all right. Perfectly calibrated too. And I heard you talking before. You know your weapons. I'm, uh, sorry for insulting you, your highness. I don't get a lot of women in here. Those that do don't know a barrel from straw. I gotta say, you're a credit to your species and gender. It's an honor to have tested your gun."

He gave an elaborate bow, one furry arm swung out to the side, the other over his chest. Loni inclined her head in return.

"Now I believe you were looking to purchase some shells," Arch said.

He hopped down from the counter and padded over to the forward counter. Placing his paw on a metal portion, he said, "Authorization: Shut your pie hole."

Loni nearly burst into laughter.

"You'd be surprised how hard that is to crack," Arch said, opening the door and pulling out a simple wooden case, handing it to Loni. She was surprised at the weight of it.

Arch hopped back up onto the forward counter.

"As you can imagine, I haven't had a lot of requests for these. Those that do, I turn away as no one can show proof that their gun is genuine."

He opened the case with a key he pulled from inside his vest. Fifty large-caliber shells lay in foam housings inside the case, each with different color markings.

"How's the quality?" Loni asked.

Arch raised a furry finger.

"Aha. Your highness knows what questions to ask. My seller assures me his process is quite thorough. But I always test my merchandise, and doubly so with these. I do have a special chamber in the back for testing if you want to give it a go. I'll give you a freebie test. If it's successful, you agree to purchase ten."

Doug opened his mouth to say something, but was cut-off by Arch holding up a paw. His ears twitched and his eyes widened.

"Get down!"

He jumped from the counter just as a hail of blaster fire tore through the shop. Loni and Doug were only a second behind him. They huddled beneath the small section of impervisteel while the shop disintegrated around them.

"What kind of trouble did you bring to my shop, Doug?" Arch shouted over the cacophony.

As if in answer, the blaster fire ceased and an amplified voice echoed into the shop.

"Loni Taraska, by Imperial order, you are under arrest. Come out with your hands on your head and your blaster on the ground."

Loni took advantage of the cease fire to grab the two cases off the counter.

"If you do not comply in ten seconds," the voice continued as Loni threw the duranium case back on, "we will firebomb the building with you in it."

"Firebomb?" Arch yelled. "Wait a second! They can't fire-bomb my shop for a fugitive! And why are you a fugitive from the Federation?"

"Empire," Loni corrected. "New rules."

"Oh," Arch said, "Well, in that case…"

He hopped back up onto the counter, pulled his blaster and

slapped its side. The weapon telescoped and unfolded to a shoulder-mounted, high-yield, fully automatic rifle.

"Here's her answer, meatheads!"

Bright cyan blaster bolts erupted from the weapon at a rate faster than Loni would have thought possible, shredding the front of Arch's shop. A feline scream screeched from his throat, and the fur on his back stood on end. He was barely able to hold the weapon steady against the recoil. Loni picked a blue shell from Arch's case and hit a button on the side of her gun. Two plates on top slid apart, exposing the breach. She slid the shell inside and the breach closed automatically around it.

Arch's blaster dry fired.

Loni and Doug peaked up as Arch gave a triumphant, "Haha! What do you say to that, you lousy Imperialists?"

The front of his shop collapsed into a pile of debris. Standing just beyond it was a squad of twenty Armored Corps Troopers, weapons ready, behind a glowing, blue energy shield.

"Aww, criminy," Arch said, just before he was yanked backwards by Doug.

In the same moment, Loni popped up, aimed, and pulled the trigger. Blue lights ran up the dark stripes. A bright blue beam shot from the gun, lighting up the energy shield. The shield fritzed out and the beam enveloped the troopers, spreading like electricity across a pool of water. Once the gun fully discharged, Loni ducked back down.

"Test successful," she said. The breach opened and the shell popped out of its own accord. Loni caught it in a gloved hand. "Halve your normal asking price and I'll take them all."

"Three-quarters," Arch countered.

"That directed EMP won't hold them for long. You get us out of here and we have deal."

"Doug, there's a big button underneath the counter there. Slap it," Arch said.

Doug found the button, hit it, and a door slid open on the back wall.

"This way." Arch led them through, sealing the doorway behind them and ran down the narrow hall on all fours. "I assume you have a ship on the way?"

Loni and Doug glanced at each other.

"Yeah, I should have figured as much. Alright, we'll have to cram into my ship. It'll be a tight fit, but I think we can do it. Just gotta grab one thing."

He stopped at a wall panel just before the end of the hall. Putting his paw to it, he said, "Toast." The panel slid open, revealing a metal case. The entire section of the wall next to it slid open to a narrow chamber. The three piled in and immediately felt their stomachs drop at the vertical acceleration. A moment later, they slid to a stop inside a cramped, one person flyer. It was more of a pod than an actual ship. Arch wormed his way into the pilot's seat and strapped in, leaving Doug and Loni crammed to get in positions that weren't too uncomfortable or compromising.

"I'd tell you to strap in, but uh…" Arch said as he activated switches. No sooner were they airborne, a shockwave impacted the flyer. "Whoa! Guess I didn't have the timing quite right."

The craft hurtled uncontrolled through the air, making Loni sick. Shortly, Arch got the craft stabilized.

"What was that?" Doug asked, Loni's elbow in his face.

"Have a look-see," Arch replied, maneuvering the craft. Far below was a smoking crater where Arch's shop used to be.

"Yeah, that's what I'm talking about!" Arch yelled, pumping a paw. "No one roasts my shop but me! Uh-oh."

Red blaster bolts shot up from the ground, narrowly missing. Arch rotated the craft and shot away toward the spaceport.

"You blew up your own shop?" Doug asked.

"You have any idea how bad it would be if anyone got their hands on half the stuff in my shop? It was an emergency ditch plan I'd hoped I'd never have to use. I like being prepared. We're free and clear for now. Tell me what dock your ship is at. Looks like we'll be bunk mates for a while."

"Dock thirteen," Doug said.

"Oh, perfect! All the bad luck we need. And here I forgot my lucky fur. So, where we going in that piece of scrap metal you call a ship?"

"The Diltan sector."

"Ain't that just a big asteroid field?"

"Yeah, but there's—"

"No, y'know what? Don't tell me. I'm already in it enough with helping you two out."

Guilt stung at Loni.

"I'm sorry, Arch," she said. "If there's anything I can do to make up for your loss…"

Arch waved a dismissive paw.

"Ah, don't worry about it. Place was a dump. Was probably holding me back. Besides, in case you haven't noticed, I ain't too friendly with the Empire. One thing you can do though is explain to me why a squad of Armored Corps Troopers is after a princess of the Tarsek System."

CHAPTER EIGHT_

Rocks.

They tumbled aimlessly through space, occasionally crashing into one another. They floated around in an endless circle from their creation, until now. Only a handful of settlements managed to navigate them and settle down amidst their slow, chaotic realm. Even fewer colonies survived long enough to become a thriving society or decent outpost.

This was not one of them.

Just outside the field of stone, a blue, curved ship appeared fresh out of hyperspace. Two of the occupants had never been here. The other hadn't wanted to come back.

"How do you plan to navigate through all that?" Doug asked as Loni sent systems into standby. "I know you're good, but this ship's awful big to maneuver through there."

"You're right on both counts," Loni replied, unstrapping. "That's why we're taking my interceptor, not your frigate. And just for the record, I could fly this ship in there and not make a scratch. I just prefer not to bust my brain trying to do it unless I have to."

"Never doubted you could. You coming, Arch?"

The Ikati sat on the control board, staring out into the asteroid field.

"Out there? No thanks. I ain't made for space-walking. Besides, I don't have a suit."

"You don't have an emergency suit in your ship?" Doug asked.

"Never got around to it. Never thought I'd need it." He shrugged. "Hey, I'm prepared, not perfect. Besides, I got some work to do here."

Despite his declaration, he remained on the console, fixated on space, his tail lazily whipping back and forth. They left him to his contemplations.

———

Loni expertly navigated the asteroid field and successfully made Doug sick.

"It's all in your head," Loni said. "Just don't look at the rocks."

Doug focused on his boots. That *did* seem to help.

She brought them down on a scorched and pitted landing pad. Doug donned his helmet which sealed with a hiss of air, and waited for the integrity indicators to register one-hundred percent. Upon sealing, it automatically shrunk to fit Doug's form like a glove. Loni's under-armor extended to cover her limbs, connecting and sealing with her gloves, boots, and pilot's helm. Loni vented the atmosphere and popped the canopy and they climbed out on the auto-stair.

"Grav unit must still be running, as well as the deflection field." Loni said over com, noting how the surrounding asteroids avoided impacts with this one. "Guess we didn't do as thorough a job as I thought."

"Let's hope so," Doug said, flipping on the ultrabeam on the side of his helmet, flooding the dark space with light. He drew his blaster and took the lead. "Keep your eyes sharp and your blaster up."

"You really think anyone survived?"

"Maybe. But who knows who found out about this place and came snooping since you vaped it. Scavengers, Pirates. No telling what we'll run into in here."

Loni scrambled back into her cockpit, reemerging with her singularity gun in hand. She loaded a red shell as she reached the bottom of the stair.

"You always keep that on your ship?"

"Why do you think I had it when I fled the *Dominator*? It's all I have left of my personal affects."

"We'll have to fix that."

Loni smiled, surprised and warmed by the gesture.

They proceeded cautiously toward the large blast doors, the outer-coating melted to slag. The doors were stuck halfway open and they easily made it inside. The entryway was filled with debris. Fallen and half-melted rock littered the floor and covered the few transports still in the bay when the attack happened.

"This was a space colony, so they're likely to have some records of their residents in a central location," Doug said. He pointed to a windowed door across the way. "That looks likely."

They crawled over debris and came up to the door, scanning the label. *Central.* Doug tried the panel. The door opened, albeit slowly, and they squeezed through. A corpse lay on the floor, covered in ice crystals.

Loni froze. It was one of her squadmates. When she blinked, the ice crystals disappeared, replaced by small, white scars covering the skin. Wide eyes stared up at the ceiling, mouth hanging open. Loni's chest grew tight. Her eyes swept the room, finding bunks stacked with bodies whose faces she recognized, all in the same condition.

Voices sounded around her, pleading for her to call off the attack.

She started to back away. Metallic hands grabbed her shoulders and she batted at them, lurching back. Loni slammed into an impervasteel wall. She was trapped. Trapped!

"Loni!"

The voice was urgent with a New Texan accent. She didn't know anyone like that. No, she knew one being.

Doug.

"Loni!"

Loni raised her head. Doug's concern shone through his visor. She glanced around, realizing how shallow her breathing became. She was in the control room of the asteroid colony, not the shared room with her squadmates.

Her eyes found the body. It wasn't anyone she knew, but she immediately turned away, swallowing and trying to shove the images out of her mind.

"Loni, come back to me," Doug said.

"I'm all right," she managed. "I'm all right. I just need a minute."

She leaned against the wall, slowing her breathing, eyes closed. A hand touched her arm and she started.

"It's all right. Let's get you out of here," Doug said.

Loni allowed herself to be led out of the room, but when Doug turned towards the exit, she dug in her heels.

"We need to find that file," she said, calmer now, her strength and will returning.

"I don't like the idea—"

"Did you find anything in the console?"

Doug's dark eyes searched her own.

"If you can't handle this, you shouldn't be down here."

A surge of anger rose up, but Loni quickly stuffed it down.

She took a deep breath in through her nose and let it slide back out.

"I can handle it. I just needed a minute. Now did you find something or not?"

Doug frowned, but let the matter drop.

"No. The console was fried. But if the grav unit is working, there must be power somewhere. This rock isn't big enough to generate this level of gravity. We'll have to search for a way down to the innards."

"Don't say it like that," Loni said.

Most of the rooms on the main level were slag or open to space. Thankfully, they didn't run across any more bodies. They were about to give up when Doug spotted a hole at the base of a wall.

"Looks like the shaft for a lift. But something tore it wide open," Doug said.

Loni examined the deep gouges in the impervisteel. "What would make something like this?"

"I have some guesses. Looks like the cables are still intact. We can climb down on those."

"Cables?"

Doug grabbed a cable, making his way down. Loni followed a minute later.

"Most of these fringe settlements use old tech harvested from stuff made back before the Terran Wars," Doug said. "It's cheap, as everyone wants anti-grav units. Mechanics are simple enough, but the motors are hard to find in good condition. Those who can't find them use a multi-man system to haul the cart up and down."

"Sounds exhausting."

"It is. They don't do it very often, which means not much is likely to be down here. But we'll see."

They reached the bottom and climbed up a short ledge into an empty hallway.

Loni checked her readouts. "There's limited atmo down here. Not enough to survive on for most humanoids, though. No bodies either, which is strange. People down here must have survived the attack and found a way out."

A crash echoed through the corridor. Loni brought up her weapon, holding the grip with both hands. Doug led the way, pistol in hand. They followed the passage to the far end where another hole like the first replaced a doorway. Doug motioned Loni against the wall and killed his ultrabeam before he peaked around the corner. He signaled her to follow and took careful steps inside.

Dim lighting illuminated an engineering room. Various large, engine-like devices and conduits filled the space. Off to the side, the crash, followed by a hollow scrape sounded again. Loni caught her breath at the sight of a pitch-black skeletal figure with two thick cables sprouting from its back, hunched over a console. The thing was easily twice their size. A large, beaked head, narrow like a spear, swiveled as it scrutinized components, its glowing, yellow eyes menacing.

"Don't fire unless I say," Doug's voice came over the com. He switched to his external speaker and raised his blaster. Stopping fifteen feet from the figure he shouted, "Drexx!"

The creature's head snapped up. Doug turned on his internal helmet lights, revealing his face. Drexx's beak opened, revealing rows of sharp spines.

"Ranger," the growling voice sounded over the com. It was strange, seeing as the creature had neither helmet nor any visible com unit. Stranger still was that its beak didn't move in sync with its words, it just sort of opened and closed languidly. "To what do I owe the pleasure?"

"Investigating some dirty deeds by the Empire," Doug replied, still on external speakers. "You find anything interesting?"

"That depends. What do you intend to do about my presence here?"

"Nothing. Unless you give me a reason to take you in."

Such was the ferocity of this creature, Loni expected it to laugh. It moved from behind the console and lumbered over, its taloned bird feet crashing loudly against the impervisteel floor, while its skeletal tail dragged behind. A clawed hand picked up a cylindrical power converter the size of Loni's head. It probably weighed a ton, but Drexx handled it like it was made of paper, his talons leaving behind deep gouges in the impervisteel. He towered over Doug.

Doug lowered neither his gaze nor his aim. Drexx swiveled its head toward Loni, and she sensed something hungry in those glowing eyes.

She wanted very much to be back in her ship, far too aware her heart was beating its way out of her chest. She kept her finger off the trigger, disciplining herself not to fire unless Doug gave the word.

"You must have doubled in size since the last time I saw you," Doug said. "You been diving into stins again? I told you that stuff'll kill you."

Drexx's solid, glowing eyes glared down at the Ranger. One snap of those jaws and Doug would be half a man, if that. Its head again swiveled toward Loni. It was all she could do to keep her aim steady.

A slight movement from Doug and the creature angled its head to find the Ranger's blaster pressed up against one of the joints in its spine.

"Careful," Doug said. "Unless you want to give me a reason to take you out instead of in."

Its beak opened and that horrible, gravelly voice sounded over her com.

"I didn't regenerate just to get killed by some pitiful ex-Ranger who thinks he's a bounty hunter. You sure you're not here to take me in?"

"You're not guilty of any crimes that I'm aware of, currently. Although you could do with disassociating yourself with the Pirates."

The beak opened wide and a deep, rumbling guffaw nearly deafened Loni.

"I wouldn't give up my position for the false promises of your petty honor. I was here searching for…scrap. I haven't found anything worth salvaging so you can have what's left. The computer core still has minimal power."

"That's mighty forthcoming of you," Doug said. "I must've done something to get on your good side."

"Don't press your luck, Ranger. Don't think I've forgotten the last time you killed me. I just have other priorities right now. There's someone I have a score to settle with. Be thankful she's a higher priority than you. Now if you'll excuse me."

Doug stepped aside and gestured toward the hall. The creature lumbered past, glancing those hungry eyes once more in Loni's direction.

"Drexx," Doug called out when the creature reached the doorway. Drexx paused and glanced over his shoulder. "Next time you threaten someone, be mighty sure you intend to make good on that threat. I do hate when someone goes back on their word."

Drexx's eyes narrowed, but he didn't respond, slipping away out of sight.

It was a number of heartbeats before Loni blurted out, "What —the space—was that!"

"Drexx, General of the Pirate conglomerate," Doug replied. "Regenerates each time he's killed. The longer he lives, the larger he gets, especially when he's on stins. Extremely dangerous and more aggressive than twenty Razorhulks hopped up on adrenaline. The fact that he's here and not one of his lackeys tells me the existence of that file we're after is known to him and it contains something extremely important."

"But you could have taken him down, right, if it came down to that?"

"Maybe."

"What?"

"C'mon, let's take a look at the computer core."

"What about my ship?" Loni said, glancing to the hall Drexx went through.

"He won't touch it. Either zero interest or the idea that I'm still a threat will keep him from it. Doesn't need it anyway. He's modified his own DNA to the point where he can exist in and travel through a vacuum. Don't know what he was before. Don't think even he remembers. Now let's get what we came for and get off this rock."

The search took some time. Minimal power meant everything was text-based with a keyboard.

Old tech.

They had to re-learn how to navigate the system before finding what they were searching for. And what they found was a string of data that would spell out a schematic when properly interpreted.

"What is it?" Loni asked.

"No idea. Whatever it is, it's big. Look at this measurement: three-thousand meters. Bigger than any transport ship or deep space hauler." He pulled a fob from his suit and plugged it into a port. "We'll download it and take it back to the *Blue Moon*. Maybe the computer can turn it into a schematic. One thing's for sure, this is why the Empire wanted this place vaporized. Guess they weren't counting on a sublevel with a backup computer core."

It was rather surreal for Loni to hear the Empire referred to as "them" after she'd been a part of it for so long.

They made their way back up to the surface and out to the *Barracuda*, Loni noting again the lack of bodies.

"Do you think Drexx…ate the bodies?" She could barely say the words without throwing up.

"Most likely. Try not to think about it."

———

They were on approach to the *Blue Moon* when they spotted Drexx's black form silhouetted against the outer hull. Even though his beak was incapable of it, Loni swore the creature smiled before he leapt off and disappeared into the void, his cables unfolding into bony wings. It reminded her of a scavenger bird.

"What was he doing?" she asked.

"No idea," Doug replied. "But it's doubtful it was anything good. How do I raise the *Blue Moon* on this?"

Loni tapped a button.

"Com is hot."

"Arch, this is Doug."

There was no response.

"Arch, you there?"

Nothing.

"Kill it," Doug said.

"Why wouldn't he answer?" she asked, cutting the link.

"Coms probably don't run throughout the ship. Knowing him, he's waist deep in some project or looking for a new place to setup shop. Let's do a scan for tracers once we're on board just in case."

"I thought you said that creature wasn't interested in us."

"Drexx is nothing if not conniving. I always expect a double-cross with him if he doesn't try to kill me outright."

Loni muttered the word *double-cross* to herself a few times before asking, "What do you mean, double-cross?"

"I mean I trust Drexx about as far as I can throw him."

"That doesn't help. Can you just speak plain basic?"

"I really need to take you back to New Texas some time, get you used to the lingo there."

"Maybe I should just take a course," Loni said.

They set down in the hanger bay and Loni ran a few tests on her own ship while Doug headed for the cockpit. Loni was just finishing up when Doug's voice came over the com.

"Loni, get up here. We've got company."

Loni raced up to the cockpit. On the way, she spied Arch in one of the crew quarters. His door was open and ear nodes were stuffed in his ears.

"Ten fighters inbound," Doug said as she slid into the pilot's seat.

"Any idea who?"

"Three guesses and the first two don't count."

"I don't think I can get us out of here in time," Loni said.

"Why not?" Doug asked.

"Because my brain is too slagged from all of your Earthean phrases."

"It means," Doug said with an annoyed edge in his voice, "that it's the most obvious answer. Space Pirates. I know that without even looking. Which is good, cause I still don't know where to look on this thing to find that info."

"You really are inept at flying a starship."

"Why do you think I was stranded?"

The ship shuddered as blaster bolts sizzled into the shields.

A voice crackled over the com. The connection was spotty, indicating a bad com relay or just really cheap hardware.

"Ug-aly ship." This garnered a glance between Doug and Loni. "You am have surrounded by us. All your database are belong to us. Transmit or destroy."

Loni made a face at the horrible grasp of basic as Arch bounded into the room.

"What was that—holy hand grenades of Antioch! Where'd all those fighters come from?"

"Drexx. He told us about the computer database so we'd find the info he was trying to steal," Doug said.

"Drexx? Who's Drexx?" Arch asked.

"A Space Pirate who's smarter than he looks."

"Pirates?" Arch yelled. "Now we have Pirates after us too? I should have never let you two into my shop. All you do is attract trouble."

"Can we blast our way through them?" Doug asked, ignoring Arch's comment.

"Probably. This ship has some punch and can probably match their maneuverability and firepower, especially with me behind the controls. But I'd rather not have to make repairs if I don't have to. We just got this bird."

"Well they're surrounding us on all sides, so we can't go to hyperspace," Doug said. "We'll both be torn apart. What did you have in mind?"

Loni smiled broadly and brought up a holo control.

"This bird has a few surprises."

"Oh," Arch said, hopping into the navigator's chair and strapping himself in. "I don't like the way she said that."

Loni switched on the com as her other hand entered a sequence before hitting a holo-button marked "activate." She lowered her voice a couple octaves, imitating the Pirate. "Stupid dumb Pirate, me am think you Basic very bad. Here am better Basic for you."

Her hand wrapped around a lever Doug hadn't seen her use yet as she returned her voice to normal.

"Suck my hyperdust!"

She pulled the lever and everything stretched into a field of white.

CHAPTER NINE_

"What the space was that?" Doug and Arch said in unison.

The star field returned to normal in the blink of an eye, leaving them intact and the Pirates nowhere to be seen. Loni was calmly checking systems while they both reeled from the feeling of their molecules being infinitely stretched across the cosmos.

"It's called a jump drive," she said. "It's another form of FTL. Very expensive. Not many are made. I'm surprised you haven't heard of it."

"You want to warn me before you do something like that?" Doug said.

"Not really."

"You mean to tell me we're light years away from those Pirates in the twitch of a whisker?" Arch asked, his claws still gripping the leather of the arm rests. "This is insane. Troopers, Pirates, jump drives. I think I'm gonna be sick."

"You better not puke in my ship," Doug said.

"Oh, excuse me, your highness. I thought there was only *one* princess on this boat." He retracted his claws and undid the straps. "I've had enough of this already. You two are gonna get me killed. You can let me off on the next rock."

He hopped down and bounded out of the cockpit.

Doug tapped his fingers on his arm rest, staring sidelong at Loni.

"Just how much did you get for my old ship?"

"Around forty million."

"Forty *million* credits?"

Loni gave a half-interested, "Uh-huh."

"How's it work, the jump drive, I mean?"

Loni's expression grew incredulous.

"I don't know. I'm not an astrophysicist. Some form of tele-portation. You enter the coordinates, wait for the drive to spin up and pull the activation lever. Then BLINK! You blip out of one space and blip into another, almost simultaneously. Its only flaw is similar to that of hyperdrives. You have to be outside a certain proximity from other objects or they'll jump with you. If you're too close to a massive object, say a planet or an Imperial cruiser, your ship and a portion of the object will be ripped apart. Also, you can't be in motion when activating. Same result. They're touchy things and delicate to calibrate. Probably also contributes to their rarity."

Loni continued her diagnostics. She made sure the drive worked properly and didn't negatively affect other systems, knowing full well Doug's eyes were on her.

After several lingering moments, he said, "I'm beginning to think you bought this ship just so you could have some new toys to play with."

Loni shrugged and tried unsuccessfully to stifle a grin.

"Uh-huh...At least you don't have a good poker face," Doug said. "We may have to work on that though if you're going to be my partner."

Partner? I thought I was just a pilot.

Loni's cheeks warmed.

"There's what looks like a conference room halfway down the

corridor to the bunks," Doug said, standing. "It has a table with a holo-display. That seems like a good place to review our little treasure. Meet me there whenever you're done…uh…doing whatever you're doing."

Doug walked out and Loni allowed the grin to spread across her face, the warmth in her cheeks intensifying.

Partner? To a Ranger?

She didn't know why that appealed to her so much, but she liked it. Shaking the thoughts away, she focused on the task in front of her.

———

"We'll need to get this decrypted," Loni said, staring at the floating, holographic display of garbled text.

"Afraid I don't know any slicers. We could always rent a decryption bot. They're expensive, but if my ship sold for that much, we should have enough to cover it."

"You're forgetting the price of this ship."

Doug opened his mouth to ask, but Loni beat him to it.

"Thirty-three million."

Doug gave her a wary eye but said nothing.

"Aren't you going to question my reasoning?" Loni asked.

"No. I'm starting to figure out that you know what you're doing when it comes to ships. And with what you said earlier about efficiency and needing things to be optimal, it makes sense why you'd spend that much. This must be a fine piece of hardware you bought. Everything I've seen so far matches up with that. I trust your judgment in this."

Loni's cheeks warmed at the unexpected compliment.

"Course," Doug added, "I still think you wanted a new toy to play with."

Loni playfully slapped him on the shoulder.

"Awful trusting of you. We did only just meet a week ago."

"You've proven yourself so far. I tend to trust in the general good intentions of most folk, unless they give me reason not to. I still keep an eye out, but people need to give more people the benefit of the doubt. Most folk aren't out to get other folk or trample them to get what they want. It's just those lousy few that ruin it for the rest of us."

"Well, mister trust, forgive me if I don't share your sentiments. As for the bot, don't bother. Remember that genius slicer kid I mentioned before? Bit of an eccentric, but he knows his stuff better than I know my ships. He'll be cheaper than a bot. Plus, he likes me."

"He likes you?"

"Puppy love. Don't think he's hit puberty yet."

"Y'know, I noticed you seem very reluctant to go to your family for help."

"I like being independent. They're there if I need them. But I'd prefer not to rely on them as a crutch. Financial or otherwise," Loni said.

"I like that. Alright let's set course for your slicer friend. Where's he at anyway?"

"Terra."

Doug's expression grew tight and he ran his hand through his hair.

"Something wrong?" Loni asked.

"Galactic Ranger headquarters is located on Terra."

"Oh. Well, uh, I'm sure we can find—"

"No, forget it. We'll head there regardless. We need this thing decrypted. I don't trust a transmission. Too easy to intercept. If this kid helped you before its likely he won't squeal on us. This is our best bet."

"What about the Rangers?"

"I knew my path would eventually lead me back there. I'll deal with the Rangers when and if we run into them."

Loni chewed her lower lip, but finally shut down the holo-table and said, "Oookaaay… I'll set course for Terra and let Lent know we're coming."

She walked away and Doug removed the fob from the table. He turned it over in his hand, apprehension roiling inside him.

You can't run forever, Doug, a voice spoke inside of him. *Sooner or later, you'll have to face them.*

He stared up at the viewport laid into the ceiling. Endless stars sparkled in the vast dark beyond. The scene encompassed him for a long while. Thoughts of where his life had been headed in the last six months bringing him back to the day men and women he respected had, seemingly of one mind, turned against everything they stood for.

"Knew this was coming since that day," he mumbled. "May not be the last either. Well, whatever you want. Just be with me."

The stars suddenly streaked and exploded into the brilliant colors of hyperspace. He rubbed at the stiffness in his neck from staring at the ceiling. Shoving the fob in his shirt pocket, he headed for the firing range.

———

Terra's surface was a mix of rocky terrain and lush forests in a constant state of daylight thanks to the twin suns on opposite sides of the planet. The capitol, Unity, was a sprawling mega-lopolis encompassing both desert and forest.

Loni piloted the *Blue Moon* down to a space port on the outskirts. The rocky desert stretched infinitely before them, the nearest city a smudge on the bright horizon. Loni set the ship on a landing pad of flat rock jutting from the side of a tower of sand-stone making up the whole of this particular space port.

"Y'know you don't have to come with me," she said, powering down the controls. "You could just wait here until I get back. It's a simple visit."

"You going alone to that part of Terra with a bounty on your head?" Doug said, checking the charges on his blasters. "No thank you."

She shrugged. "Suit yourself."

They met Arch in the docking bay, the massive door open to the outside. He was standing in the hatchway of his ship, focused on the bright orange Terran sky, a cool breeze ruffling his fur.

"Where you headed, Arch?" Doug said, grabbing his attention.

"Not sure yet. Found a couple promising spots."

"Well, let us know if you need anything else."

"From you two? I'm just as likely to get a bounty on *my* head for my trouble. Besides, with the credits from the sale of those shells, I should have enough to setup shop anywhere I like. I'll be fine."

He slid into his craft and closed the canopy. Doug and Loni exited the ship, rented a local air speeder, and took off for the distant slums.

———

The flight down to the slums was brief, but long enough for Loni to admire the cityscape. Towering structures rose high into the bright, orange troposphere. Numerous craft zipped through the endless city sea, actual traffic lanes farther below. Up here, the flying was open and free, just the way she liked it. She took her time, circling around, enjoying the view and the feeling of flight.

"You lost?" Doug's voice came from beside her. She forgot he was there.

"Just enjoying flying. But you're right. We should really get on track."

Before Doug could say any more, Loni shoved the yoke forward, headed straight down at breakneck speed, shoving him back in his seat. Everything flashed by in a blur, their stomachs lurching into their throats. The ground below rushed up at them. She hit reverse thrusters and leveled out with a quiet hiss of air. They hovered just above the permacrete street, surrounded by the old permacrete structures that made up the slums, miles below the glittering towers of the city.

"You," Doug said, sounding like he was going to throw up, "really need to warn me."

"Nope," Loni said, and pushed the throttle forward, taking in every sight they passed.

"Never been to Terra?" Doug asked.

"No reason to. Who uses stone anymore except ancient civilizations?"

"Well, that's basically what Terra was. The first colonists arrived after getting themselves lost in hyperspace, had no vector back to their solar system, or even their own galaxy, and wound up settling on Terra with minimal supplies. They basically had to start over with whatever technology they could salvage from the colony ship."

"C'mon, Cowboy. You really believe that old story?"

"What's not to believe?"

"All of it. A hyperdrive malfunctioning and not shutting down or sending them hurtling into a stellar body? And do you know the likelihood of coming randomly out of hyperspace near any habitable planet? It's astronomical."

"Facts are facts."

Loni shook her head. The shimmering buildings grew sparse, replaced by more derelict structures and ancient ruins.

"And if the hyperdrive was malfunctioning, how did they

manage to come out of hyperspace and then fix the thing when they were supposedly billions of light years from home?" Loni asked.

"There used to be an indigenous species to this planet that helped them repair it," Doug said.

"Uh-huh, and where did they disappear to?"

"Killed off in the Terran Wars and Alien Wars after that, from what I gather."

"Well, how convenient."

"Not so much for them."

Loni fell silent, realizing how irreverent her attitude was to a species that may have been completely wiped out. Even if she didn't believe the stories, they *could* be true.

Twenty minutes later they landed on the flat roof of an old, concrete apartment building. Surrounding the building were others of similar make-up, some half collapsed and many just piles of rubble.

"The old New Colony District?" Doug asked as they got out. "This place has been practically abandoned since the Terran Wars."

"Don't ask me. He chose the place. Likes the seclusion, I guess."

Loni led him down three floors to room six-zero-five and knocked. The sound of a lock clicked before the door cracked to a face wearing thick goggles.

Loni grinned.

"Hey, Lent."

"Hey, Loni! Just a second."

The door closed, a few more clicks, then fully opened. A teenage boy stood in a dark brown overcoat, dirty shirt, and pants. He pulled the goggles up to his forehead, revealing a twitching left eye. Doug winced at seeing it.

"Come on in," Lent said, gesturing them in.

The inside of the apartment was a cluttered nightmare. But at least some of the floor was visible.

"Please excuse the mess," Lent said, picking up random piles of trash and shoving them into other piles. "Oh. Uh, who's this with you?"

"Lent, this is Doug Lancer, Galactic Ranger."

Doug offered his hand. Lent took it, awe melting to concern. "Oh. Uh, nice to meet you. Doug Lancer. That sounds familiar. Are you, uhm, is he you're, uh, boyfriend?"

Loni let out a chuckle. "No."

The boy relaxed and shook Doug's hand more firmly. "Oh. Okay, good. Nice to meet you, Ranger. You're not here to arrest me, are you?"

"No, son, I ain't. Just make sure to keep your work legal and we'll be fine."

"Legal. Yeah, sure. No problem. Law abiding, that's me."

He was still shaking Doug's hand. Doug forcibly pulled his hand out of the boy's grip and felt grease on his palm.

"Loni said you could help us decrypt a file," Doug said, wiping his hand on his pants.

"Sure, sure, of course! You got the fob?"

Doug handed it over and the boy moved to a strange conglomeration of wires, computer monitors, and holo-projectors all connected to a large, black box in the corner. He sat down in a chair in front of the tech and plugged the fob into a port.

The same holo-image of garbled text appeared over one of the projectors.

"Hmmm," Lent said as he tapped furiously at keyboards and holo-controls. The image flickered and shifted, Lent mumbling to himself all the while. "Triple dead man's encryption. With a back-loop redundancy string? That's like Federation tech."

His fingers stopped mid-motion and he gave a wide, twitchy-eyed stare at the two of them.

"Is this a setup?" he asked, his voice cracking. "Are you trying to catch me at slicing a restricted Federation file?"

"It's not a setup," Doug said. "Official Ranger investigation."

Lent didn't appear convinced.

"It's okay, Lent," Loni reassured him. "Nothing's going to happen to you. Go ahead."

The kid was motionless. His twitching eye never fully settling on either Loni or Doug. His fingers started to move before the rest of his body. Mind made up, he resumed his tapping. The image shifted one more time to text in plain Basic.

"There you go," Lent said, shutting down the monitor and handing the fob back to Loni. "Now, if you don't mind, those things have a way of being tracked, so…"

Loni knew he didn't want to ask them to leave.

"Thanks, Lent. We don't want to bring you any trouble. We'll get out of your hair. What do we owe you?"

"Oh, huh, nothing. It's my pleasure, Loni."

"Thanks a million, Lent."

They turned to go and Lent called out, "Hey, wait."

They turned back and he shrank a little, his face growing red.

"Uh, I was just wondering, uh, Loni. M-maybe your friend can take the info to the Rangers and you could, um, maybe stick around?"

Loni smiled sweetly.

"That's sweet, Lent. But I can't stay. There's a bounty on my head right now and we need to get things cleared up."

Lent deflated at that, but then immediately perked up.

"Bounty? That's what it was. Doug Lancer. There's a bounty on his head."

"What did you say?" Doug asked.

"Yeah!" Lent slid into his seat,t apping out a few keys. "It came out the other day on public channels."

One of the monitors flashed showing a bounty page with Doug's picture on it and a price of one-hundred-thousand credits.

Anger burned in Doug's eyes.

"Doug?" Loni asked. "You okay?"

"Yeah… yeah, I'll be just fine."

"You two better get as far away from Terra as you can. This place is one of the Ranger's headquarters. Oh, you probably knew that. So, never mind. But, yeah, you should go. I'll keep an eye on any alerts and see if I can stifle or redirect them. I'd cancel the bounties, but those are Federation and Ranger set. I don't dare slice into their systems."

Loni laid a kiss on Lent's cheek.

"Thanks, Lent. Talk to you soon."

Lent melted out of his chair, a euphoric smile on his face. He gave a lazy wave as Doug and Loni walked out.

———

Doug fiddled with the fob, holding it up in front of him as they flew back to the space port.

"What has you so occupied?" Loni asked, her tan skin more cream in the light of Terra's sun.

Doug put the fob in his shirt pocket.

"I was just thinking."

"About what?"

"About the Empire, the Federation, the Rangers. What made them turn? What was it that changed in the Federation to turn them into the Empire? And what has the Rangers so spooked they felt the need to jump into bed with them?"

"I think lots of people feel that way. Even the pilots in my squadron were questioning why the change, even though from our perspective there wasn't much. We just took on more enforcement jobs."

"Imperial Law has become stricter," Doug said. "They've actually started policing the galaxy, whereas before, each system or planet was left to govern themselves with the Federation maintaining overall peace between autonomous governments, making sure there were no civilian casualties, no space shattering events, no collateral damage, things of that nature. It was the Rangers that enforced the laws set forth by the major systems, those that the majority of other systems approved. But now they've folded into one and using soldiers like you as enforcers."

"What's so unusual about that? Not that I approve, but it seems pretty normal for a regime when it goes totalitarian to absorb any independent organizations that exist."

"The problem is, the Rangers are supposed to have authority to arrest even the highest Federation official. The Federation and the Rangers were supposed to keep each other in check. We keep them honest, they keep us from gaining too much power. For the Rangers to come under the rule of the Empire goes against every principle the Rangers were founded on. We should have fought against it and made some arrests. Instead, we just folded. Doesn't make any sense. I'm wondering if this file is the key to understanding all this."

"The key to understanding human nature? Good luck with that," Loni said.

"I don't believe in luck."

Loni glanced over. Doug was staring straight ahead, his eyes distant, but determined. Here was a man who believed in what he did and followed it with conviction. He was seeing something, a pattern, maybe, to everything she couldn't. There was a lot going on behind those dark eyes and Loni's admiration for the man rose a notch. She couldn't stifle a grin as they passed out of heavier traffic and banked up toward the upper levels of the space port.

The speeder landed on the pad with a rush of air. Loni popped the canopy and they stepped out to find two Rangers on the pad, their focus undoubtedly on them. For a moment, Doug was thankful he left his badge and duster on board the ship. Until he recognized one of the men.

If he was a cursing man, he'd have cursed himself out for leaving the ship.

"Doug Lancer," the man said, a wide grin on his face. "I didn't expect to find you here."

"Stenson," Doug greeted him.

"Something I can help you Rangers with?" Loni asked.

"Just doing some patrols of the spaceport, Miss…"

"Lieutenant," Loni replied. "Lieutenant Colonel Taraska. And we're here on official Imperial business. So, if you gentlemen don't mind?"

The two men made no attempt to leave.

"Are you aware, Lieutenant, that your companion is a fugitive?" Stenson said.

"I'm aware that you Rangers think you can go wherever you like and order people around. Now I'll ask you gentlemen one last time. Clear out before I burn you out with my back thrust."

"Loni," Doug's voice was calm, but he kept his eyes locked on Stenson. His posture was relaxed, but Loni could sense the tension underneath. "Get the ship ready for lift off. Don't worry about me. I'll be with you momentarily."

Loni was about to object, but instead raised her chin, turning her eyes from the Rangers and sauntered beneath the ship, unhooking cables as she went. Stenson nodded at the younger man who gave some distance but kept his eyes on the standoff. Doug figured him for a Deputy training under Stenson. Poor kid.

"This isn't smart, Doug," Stenson said, brushing back his duster and revealing a blaster pistol. "You could just come along quietly."

"I've committed no crime," Doug replied. "If anything, I should haul you in for abandoning the code."

"You can try, but I've gotten a lot faster since you saw me last."

"I told you before, Stenson. Speed ain't all there—"

The air in front of Doug's face lit up as a high-intensity blaster bolt passed within millimeters of him. A split-second of residual heat made him whip his head to the side in time to see the bolt strike Loni in the chest, sending her tumbling to the ground. Doug immediately pulled his blaster and turned the opposite direction. Another bolt struck the transport just as he ducked behind it.

"Stenson! Call off your man!"

"He's not mine, Doug," came Stenson's voice from across the way as more bolts peppered the landing pad. "Scum must be after the bounty."

Never mind you're likely the scum that ordered it, Doug thought. But the shot wasn't for him, at least not him alone. He looked to where Loni lay sprawled on the permacrete and cursed his lack of observation. He should have seen the assassin. Grief and anger threatened to well-up inside him. He wanted to run to Loni's side, do something to somehow save her from her fate. He stuffed those feelings down.

Later, he told himself. *Survive first. There'll be time enough for everything else.*

"Well, don't just sit there, fire back!" Doug said, popping his head up long enough to see his target. He ducked back down as a slew of bolts chewed up the transport. "He's twenty meters up, due east."

Doug heard the return fire from Stenson's blaster. More bolts, but farther away. The assassin must have seen Stenson as competition. Doug popped up and fired. His bolts struck the ledge over which hung the elongated barrel of a sniper rifle. His bolts sparked, but did little else as the barrel swiveled back in his direction. He ducked down, bolts sizzling by so close they burned the sleeve of his shirt.

Doug sprinted across the bay, firing off his pistols at the distant sniper. Blaster bolts trailed his heels and he threw himself behind the crates where Stenson and his protégé waited. The bolts rocked the crates on impact.

"I always knew you were stupid," Stenson said from beside him.

"How's your jaw?" Doug asked.

Stenson's brow furrowed.

"My jaw?"

Doug right hooked him, knocking him back.

"That's for getting my pilot killed," Doug said. "You and I can settle up later. How's your charge pack?"

"You gonna shoot me if I tell you?" Stenson asked. He nonetheless checked his charge. "Green. Tin here is green too, aren't you?"

The boy was pale as a ghost, sweat rolling down his wide-eyed face, his back flat against the crates.

"First gun fight?" Doug asked.

Stenson grimaced.

"No. You know you hit like a sissy?"

"Didn't want to knock you out of the fight."

"Yeah, sure."

Both of them rose up on either side of the crates and let loose a volley toward the cliff face. The bolts either sparked harmlessly on the rock or struck without fanfare as the range was too far. They ducked back down when another hail of sniper fire chewed up the edges of the crates, one of them searing Doug's arm.

"G'ah! Scum must be firing something illegal to have that kind of heat and range."

"That's not a surprise," Stenson said. "We're not going to do anything at this distance. We need to find a way to circle around behind him."

"Ain't no circling around behind him. He's on a tower of rock. Probably got up there by a personal flyer."

"If one of us can get to the docking bay, we can commandeer one from the lower levels. They have them for rent there."

"Go ahead. I'll draw his fire. It's me he's after anyway," Doug said.

"You don't have to tell me, twice. Tin, stay here and keep an eye on the detainee."

The kid just nodded, his eyes staring into nowhere. Doug rose up and fired off volleys from both barrels as Stenson sprinted for the interior. More bolts came at Doug and he was forced to duck back down.

"This is getting old fast," he said. "Kid. Hey, kid! You ever fire that sissy pistol?"

The boy shook his head. Doug checked his arm. The burn was bad and would fester if he didn't get it some attention.

"Where you from, kid?" he asked.

"W-we're going to die, aren't we?"

"Hey, Tin, is it? Relax. We ain't gonna die."

The boy shook his head and scrunched his eyes shut.

"Listen to me," Doug said. "You know Stenson. I've served with him a long time. He's always good in a fight. Don't you worry, he'll come through. We just need to sit tight until he gets around behind the—"

THUNK!

Doug peered around the corner of the crate. A device with a blinking light clung to its side. He shot to his feet, grabbed the kid by the back of his shirt and threw him away from the crates. He'd barely made it two steps himself when the crates exploded in a fireball. Doug tumbled to the permacrete, his mind spinning and ears ringing. He barely registered that he was coughing in the thick smoke around him.

Someone was talking in his ear. All he could do was cough

and hack in reply. His arm burned white hot. Through the muddle and the pain, he crawled forward, not sure where he was going, but knowing he had to get out of the open.

The kid. Gotta make sure the kid is all right.

The world was spinning. Black smoke stung his eyes. One of the crates must be burning off some kind of petroleum. Forcing himself up on unsteady feet, the black smoke thickened, blinding him and he gagged.

Doug stumbled forward out of the cloud and into clearer air. He attempted to get under cover, but managed only to lean over, trying to breathe. Movement forced him to glance up. A humanoid completely clad in armor was walking toward him. The figure's face was concealed behind a dark-visored helmet. Doug knew the armor type and its capabilities. It was bad news. He watched in slow motion as the figure pulled the charge pack from his rifle and reached for another, revealing a jet pack on his back.

Doug's hand found his holster empty and he gritted his teeth. He went for his other, but he was slow. A red blaster bolt slammed into his shoulder and he went down. He drew and fired, his aim off. The shots sparked on a personal force field.

Get up! You're slag if you don't get up!

The hunter aimed his rifle. Smoke drifted across his vision.

Doug rolled, his limbs screaming at him with blaster fire following him back into the heavy smoke. The moment he was enveloped, he got to his feet and stumbled in the opposite direc-tion. He held his breath until he could get clear. Even so, he came out the other side coughing. He spun toward movement in his peripheral and fired, grimacing at the pain in his shoulder. The hunter, hovering in the air, returned fire. Doug stumbled away, switching his gun to his good hand, bolts sparking at his feet.

Probably can't aim right while he's hovering. I can use that.

He ducked under his ship and hid behind a landing strut,

trying to catch his breath. Remembering his com, he tried to raise Arch.

No response.

From his vantage point he could see the spot where Loni's body lay, except it wasn't there. He scanned the area, doing his best to stay behind cover. There was nothing but the empty docking platform. Even the kid, Tin, was nowhere to be seen.

What in space is going on?

No, he couldn't focus on that now. He had to deal with this bounty hunter first.

"Hey," Doug said, still keeping an eye out. "I hope you realize you're hunting a Galactic Ranger. And you just executed an illegal contract."

There was no reply.

"You ain't getting paid by the Empire or the Rangers. I can guarantee you that."

Movement.

A blaster bolt struck his gun before he could pull the trigger, knocking it from his hand. Another bolt struck the hunter's shield from his left. Tin was shooting from behind another strut. The hunter turned, caught off-guard. Doug tackled the bounty hunter, sending his rifle clattering away across the deck. Spying a holstered blaster pistol, Doug grabbed it. But the hunter grabbed his wrist, clamping down and forcing him back with inhuman strength. Doug's ligaments strained, pain shooting through his arm. The hunter slammed his helmeted head into Doug's face, sending the Ranger falling backwards.

Doug lay dazed on the permacrete, something warm and wet on his face.

Dust, but he hits hard, his muddled brain thought.

The hunter stepped into his vision, the rifle aimed squarely at Doug's chest. A whirring sound drew both of their attentions. Doug craned his neck just in time to see one of the *Blue Moon*'s gun emplacements fire off an enormous bolt of blue energy. The massive bolt slammed into the hunter's shields, sending him flying from the landing pad and careening over the edge toward the ground miles below.

Doug stumbled to his feet and sprinted for the now lowered ramp.

"Thanks for the help, kid! Better get clear!"

He ran up the ramp, slapped the close button, and sprinted through the ship. His lungs were on fire and his injuries burned white hot. But he pushed himself until he reached the cockpit.

"Loni!" he said, squeezing through the still opening door. "Get us—"

He stopped short. Arch stared back at him from the co-pilot's seat.

"Well, come on!" Arch said. "Let's go! That bounty hunter ain't done yet."

"I ain't leaving without Loni. Where is she?" Doug said, nonetheless sliding into the pilot's seat and wiping his face. His hand came back crimson but he ignored it.

"Relax, she's here. I dragged her in myself. Now come on. No, no! Thrusters first. Blue switch over there. Aw, criminy!"

Arch hopped up onto the console and helped Doug get the engines started. Doug pulled back on the yoke, throwing Arch from the console with a yelp. The ship rocketed away from the space port. Arch scrambled back into the co-pilot's seat.

"You better be glad my species almost always lands on our feet."

Doug leaned back in his seat as the atmosphere gave way to the darkness of space. He was spent. His clothes were soaked with sweat. He felt like crawling into a cold dark hole and going to sleep for a year.

"I thought it was always," he said, pulling a handkerchief and wiping the blood from his face.

Arch shrugged. "Nobody's perfect."

"Where'd you put Loni's body?"

Arch stared at him and although his facial muscles weren't capable of a smile, Doug could see the amusement dancing in his eyes.

"She's in the med bay. Go see her. I can get this tub into hyperspace."

Despite his fatigue, Doug was out of his chair and running. He arrived to find Loni lying on an angled bed, an oxygen mask over her face.

"Loni," Doug called from her side.

Loni's eyes opened halfway. She reached up a lethargic hand and pulled open her jacket. The blaster-resistant under-armor beneath had a hole burned in it the size of Doug's fist, a testament to the intensity of the assassin's bolt. But something glinted underneath. He pulled the suit down to reveal a silvery plate, likely duranium, blackened, scorched, and pocked with holes.

She was trying to say something, so Doug pulled the mask down.

Her voice was a coarse whisper, "You look terrible."

Doug smiled despite himself.

"Told you…I'd be fine," Loni said.

"I'd say you're far from fine. But I'm glad to see you're not dead."

"Still penetrated. Armor…took the brunt."

Doug glanced at the readouts. It showed some minor internal damage to her lung, but her heart was intact.

"You rest up. We'll get you to a med center ASAP."

Loni gave a slow nod and closed her eyes. Doug replaced the oxygen mask, covered her with a blanket, and stumbled to the cockpit on shaky legs. Arch was perched on the console, the brilliant colors of hyperspace streaking past outside the canopy.

"Never gets old," he said as Doug collapsed into the pilot's seat. He winced at the injuries to his shoulder and back. One too many tumbles on the rock.

"What made you come back?" Doug asked.

"You commed me."

"Come on, Arch. I know I was in the middle of a firefight, but I'd have noticed your ship flying into my hanger bay."

Arch was silent for a long moment, his golden eyes fixed on the multi-colored waves before him, his tail swishing.

"You two are in a lot of trouble," he said quietly.

Doug didn't know Arch all that well, but one thing he did know is that Arch *never* spoke quietly.

"Yeah?" Doug asked.

"I heard on the public com. There's a bounty out on both you and your friend. One from the Rangers, the other from the Empire. I contacted some people I know that are up on Pirate movement. Guess who else is gunning for you?"

"Yeah, tell me something I don't know."

"I decided you two would need some help, especially parked out in the open on Terra. Whose bright idea was that instead of staying in orbit, or better yet, finding some other place to get in trouble? You had to go right to the heart of the beast."

"It was kind of both of ours."

"Stupid. That was stupid, Doug. She could have been killed. You *both* could have."

"You didn't seem to have a problem with it before."

"That's cause I didn't think about it. Doesn't make it any less stupid," Arch said.

"You ain't wrong."

"Course I'm not wrong. And I'll tell you something else. Those Pirates aren't after you for nothing. You got something they want. What is it?"

Doug padded his clothing, fearing the fob had fallen out in the firefight. But he found it right where he left it. He inserted it into a port and hit the display button. The rendering of the schematics in holographic text written in Basic was smaller and not as clear as it was in the conference room. Arch gaped.

"What in the nine hells?" he whispered. "Doug, this is a gun. A really, *really* big gun."

"You sure?" Doug asked, sitting up a little straighter.

"I know my firearms, Doug. This is definitely a weapon. There's some detail here I'm not familiar with. An engineer would be able to render it into an image. But the parts I do understand spell out this thing is packing some serious firepower."

"How much power we talking?"

"Enough that they'd need several Sovereign-class destroyer anti-matter cores just to power the thing."

"That makes it what, a planet–killer? That's nothing new. Folks been trying to come up with those since the Terran wars. The Xiktri almost succeeded. It's only cause the Terrans finally united and overthrew them that their device and their race was wiped out."

"This ain't no planet killer. This is something far worse."

Arch pawed the image, causing it to scroll.

"The energy modulation and output is all wrong," he said, pointing a claw at a line of text. "It would take a sustained blast to break up something as dense as a planet and there's no way they could maintain that. This is an energy disruptor. Think of it like an anti-grav gun, only much, much bigger. Something you'd aim at a solar or gravity well. This thing could disrupt the magnetic and gravitational forces of an entire solar system, maybe two, and send the planets spinning off into space, condemning everyone on them to a slow death."

"Obliterate the core…" Doug mumbled to himself.

"Where'd you find this?"

"That asteroid field in the Diltan sector. My guess is whoever had it, smuggled it from the Empire. Loni's team was sent to destroy any trace of it. The Empire isn't just going totalitarian, they're planning a total takeover. They really are turning into an Empire."

The bright waves of hyperspace rippled across the cockpit while the weight of their discovery sank in.

"We gotta take this to someone," Arch said, breaking the silence.

"I know. But right now, Loni is our priority. I take it we're on route to a med center?" Doug asked.

"Yeah. Out near the far point of the galactic ring. Safe from the Rangers and the Empire. Too out of the way for Pirates."

Doug nodded. "Good. Maybe when she's all settled, you and I can see to that. I don't want her getting in harm's way again."

"You gaining some feelings for her?"

"Nothing like that. She's a princess, and a pilot, and she was almost killed for standing up against the Empire. She's no lawman. Neither are you for that matter. You don't need to be involved in this. Might be best—"

"Aw, shut your pie hole, Doug. I can't just walk away now that I've seen this. This may be the dumbest thing I've ever done, but I'll stick around long enough to make sure this gets in the right hands."

Arch hopped down from the console.

"I'm gonna go catch some Z's. Com me when we're ready to dump out of hyperspace and I'll initiate the shutdown."

Arch padded out of the room, leaving Doug to his thoughts.

CHAPTER TEN_

Doug watched through the window, sipping on a drink while surgical bots worked on Loni. Patching up blaster wounds to lungs was a relatively simple procedure. He had confidence in its success. His own injuries had been easily and quickly tended to. He didn't even have phantom pains.

"I thought you wanted to go after they patched up your shoulder," Arch said from one of the waiting seats. He had his foldable blaster disassembled, cleaned, and was now piecing it back together.

"I just want to see her through this first," Doug replied, her condition weighing on his conscience as he unconsciously rubbed his shoulder. "Once they're done working on her and she's resting comfortably, we can take off. I'll contact her family and let them know where she is."

Doug noted the precision of the bots and their cleanliness.

"I'd forgotten this place existed," Doug continued. "Federation tried to bring this world into their fold several times if I'm not mistaken. But all they managed to do was convince them to sell their medical technology to other worlds."

"Aw, they're a bunch of isolationists. Freaks, if you ask me.

But they know their stuff, and they're smart enough not to turn down a Tarsekian princess."

"Being injured helps. They don't take visitors unless one of them is."

"What was that you mumbled before about obliterating the core?" Arch said.

Doug related Loni's story.

"That's some heavy stuff," Arch said. "The Federation going after the core? That's insanity."

"They're not the Federation anymore."

"Federation, Empire, whatever. They can't be planning to actually use it, unless on an uninhabited system as a demonstration. Using it on a habitable system, especially any of the core systems, would destroy the very people they need to support them. I would say it has to be just an empty threat. Except, you don't build something that big unless you plan to use it."

"How else could they use it?"

Arch licked his paw and rubbed his ear.

"Well, they could disrupt a fleet's shielding array, I guess. Even linked shielding wouldn't stand up to it. Might even completely de-power them."

"Except there is no fleet other than the Empire and Tarsek fleet. But they're not big enough to warrant something like this," Doug said.

"Maybe there is," Arch said.

Doug finally tore his eyes away from the window. Arch had paused in his reassembling and was tapping a short metal tube against his thigh.

"Maybe they're prepping for something that's coming, something only they know about."

"I'd be more inclined to believe that if they hadn't gone all totalitarian," Doug said. "Besides, the Federation I know might try to hide something like that from the general populace, but I doubt they'd try to kill over it, much less one of their star fighter pilots and a Tarsekian princess. Something just doesn't add up about all this."

"You don't think it's to obliterate the core?"

Doug sighed.

"I don't know. It's not like the core is a single place. Core systems are scattered throughout the ring. Let's see. There's Terra, New Texas, about a dozen other mostly human worlds. Come to think of it, there are several core systems that have at least one human world in it."

"You humans do have a reputation for survival. I read what you accomplished in the Terran Wars and the conflict you had with the Xiktri. Incredible that you lot not only survived and defeated them, but scattered them across the stars and robbed them of their tech. I wouldn't have believed it if it hadn't been so recent. Hey, you think the Xiktri are behind this? You said yourself the core is mostly made up of human worlds."

"I doubt it. Like you said, they're pretty scattered. Rest of the galaxy doesn't much like them either and were happy to see them get their tails kicked. Federation is mostly human with a few other species. It's unlikely, way I see it."

The bots finished their work and moved away from Loni's bed which detached from the wall and hovered on its own out of the surgery room.

Doug turned to see Arch almost done re-assembling his blaster. "You got any spare blasters? I lost mine in that last firefight."

"Seriously? What kind of Ranger loses his guns? Yeah, I might have a couple. The case I grabbed before I left contains some essential parts and credits. If I don't have what you need, I'll know where to get it."

A bot came in, hovering a few inches above the floor, its sleek, silvery body reflecting everything around it.

"Princess Taraska's wounds have been healed and she is in stable condition. She is resting comfortably and will be conscious within the hour if you wish to see her. Please allow three local rotations for complete recovery and restrict diet to plants high in subderanial elements. This will aid in both healing and comfort."

"Any lingering affects?" Doug asked.

"If guidelines are followed, there will be none."

"Thank you."

The bot spun and hovered out of the room. Arch clicked the last piece of his blaster into place.

"Come on," Doug said, tossing his drink into a receptacle. "Let's get going before she wakes up."

Arch pressed a button on the rifle and it collapsed in on itself. He attached the small square to his belt and followed after Doug.

"You think she'll try to follow us?" Arch asked.

"I've only known her a little over a week, but, yeah, she strikes me as that type."

———

"Well, you think you can fly it?" Doug asked, leaning over the edge of the cockpit of the *Barracuda*.

"Sure I can, if I knew what any of these switches did," Arch said, examining the controls from the pilot's seat. "None of them are labeled. Seriously, I got as much chance of flying this and not crashing as you."

"We gotta get it out of here somehow. I ain't taking her ship from her."

Arch ducked beneath the console, his tail in the air and rear in Doug's face.

"Maybe there's an instruction manual. Aha! There's a compartment down here. Let's see. Emergency rations, extra air tank, emergency beacon, some singularity shells. Woah! Nice blaster. Must be a Telek Seven. This is a rare model."

"Arch…"

"Right, sorry. I'm not finding anything down here."

"How about we tow it out with your ship?"

Arch came back up.

"Hey, y'know, I just had a thought. Maybe I can tow it out with my ship."

"Good thought," Doug deadpanned.

"You got any cables?"

Doug glanced around the docking bay.

"Nope. You?"

Arch stared up at the ceiling and gave an exasperated sigh, then he squinted.

"Hey, what are those?"

Painted on the high ceiling was a series of intersecting green lines running in different directions. They led him to the far back wall, converging at a large, mushroom-shaped device hovering just shy of the ceiling.

"I do believe, that is what we're looking for," Doug said. "C'mon."

They located the operating panel displaying unlabeled virtual controls, which was eye-level for Doug. Arch hopped up onto his shoulder.

"Dust, you're heavy," Doug said.

"It's the vest."

"Sure it is."

"Shut up and hit that button there."

Doug pressed the indicated button and a blue light shown around them. Doug felt himself lift off the floor.

"Ah, shut it off!" Arch yelled.

Doug hit the button again and they dropped to the floor, Doug barely catching his balance. Arch's claws dug into his shoulder as the Ikati attempted to catch himself. Once squarely back on Doug's shoulder, he retracted his claws.

"Next time, just fall and hop back up," Doug said.

"Hey, I may almost always land on my feet, but free-falling ain't an experience I relish. Try that one."

"Why don't they label these things?" Doug sighed.

After several tests, and more arguing, they got the mushroom-device positioned over Loni's ship. Arch ran over to make sure they had it lined up.

"Back this way more," he yelled across the bay. "Hey, how we gonna get it out of the bay once we get it to the edge?"

"The tractor beam should have a range far enough to place it outside the ship."

"Alright, that looks good. Hit it."

"I'd prefer you didn't," a familiar feminine voice said over the ship-wide com.

"Loni?" Doug called.

"If you two are done trying to backstab me, I'd like to get going."

Doug shared a glance with Arch and the two of them headed for the lift. They entered the cockpit to find Loni in the pilot's seat, looking tired, but otherwise alert.

"Loni, what are you doing out of bed?" Doug asked. "You should be resting. You trying to kill yourself?"

Loni attempted a scowl, but it seemed she didn't have the energy to hold it.

"Doctors said my healing was to the point where I didn't need to stay, though they recommended I do in order to get proper rest."

"Exactly my—"

"So I commed you and got no response. I get back here to find you two trying to abandon me on this rock."

Arch held out his paws plaintively.

"We weren't abandoning you. We were, just, uh…"

"We were concerned about your safety," Doug said.

This time Loni's scowl held.

"Safety?"

"Look, Loni. We got bounty hunters after us, the Empire, and the Rangers."

"And Pirates," Arch put in.

"And Pirates," Doug repeated. "I can't have your death on my conscience if something were to happen to you."

Loni rolled her eyes.

"It's not safe," Doug insisted.

Loni forced herself unsteadily to her feet. Doug moved to help her but she slapped him away.

"Stop treating me like I'm some damsel in distress! I'm a fighter pilot. You think impending death is anything new to me? You think this is the first time I've been burned by blaster fire? Why do you think I wear the armor in the first place? For style?

"You hired me to be your pilot. We had an agreement that I would join you on some of your operations. I don't recall getting shot at being a deal breaker. Suddenly I get injured and you can't handle it? This isn't about me, Doug. It's about you. You and having your conscience salved. Were you worried when we were facing those Pirates? When we were facing down Drexx?"

"Yes, I was!" Doug calmed himself before continuing. "I couldn't do anything about those situations. It's getting too hot for me."

"For *us*, Doug! I don't see you kicking Arch off your ship."

"Hey, hey," Arch said, holding up his paws. "I got my own reasons for sticking around. Besides, you two clearly have some issues to work out, so I'll just—"

He hopped off the seat only for Loni to grab him by the scruff of his neck.

"Hey! Hey!" Arch squirmed impotently. "Put me down!"

"You're just as guilty, Arch," she said, shaking him. "Did you utter one word of objection about this? Huh?"

His eyes danced around, his forelegs hanging limply.

"Well, I, uh…"

"Loni, we're just trying to protect you."

"I don't need your protection, Doug! Not like this. What I need is your respect. This isn't honorable, it's insulting."

She set Arch down on the seat.

"Now, if you two don't mind, I'd like to get this ship in the air and find out why the Empire is so eager to kill me. So kindly extract yourself from my cockpit before I give each of you a cockpit of your own."

Doug and Arch glanced at each other before trudging out with their heads hanging.

Loni lay in her bed, reading a data-pad when the chime for her room sounded. She glared at the door, sighed, and tapped the panel by her bed. The door swooshed open, revealing Doug. He seemed rather surprised the door opened on its own. His hat was in his hands and when he gained back his composure, he was rather chagrinned.

"Yes?" Loni said.

"Uh, can I talk to you?"

"Sure."

"Can I come in?"

Loni rolled her eyes. "You have to be so spaced honorable, Cowboy? Yes, come in."

Doug entered, allowing the door to slide shut behind him.

"Look, I, uh, I wanted to apologize for…"he fiddled with his hat, clearly searching for the right words.

"For treating me like an inferior invalid?"

His expression soured and he wandered around the room.

"I really don't like the idea of you working with me after almost getting killed."

"*Are* we working together? Cause whatever this hang-up of yours is, it's not us working *together.* It's you working solo and me just tagging along. That's not going to fly with me."

"I did name you my partner," Doug said. "Look, this is all new to me. Back in the Rangers, someone got injured, they were given leave until they were better. My last pilot was a Karklorian, big rock fella. Hard to injure. You're…"

Loni raised an eyebrow, daring him to continue.

"More…delicate," Doug finished. "Look, it's all fine and dandy until someone gets hurt. I ain't comfortable with it."

"Well, maybe I should have thrown Arch against a wall and kicked you in the—"

"Look, Loni—"

"No, you look," Loni slammed her datapad onto her bed. "You're being an idiot. I don't think this has very much to do with me getting hurt. You know what I've been reading? The Ranger's guidebook. You know what it says? Here. I'll read it for you."

She picked up her datapad and scrolled.

"You don't have to—"

"'Females of any species should not be put in danger,'" Loni read aloud. "'They are to be protected and under no circumstances to be put in harm's way. Blasters or other weapons are to be provided them—" she slammed the datapad back onto her bed, "—*only* if the Ranger is incapacitated and *only* as a last resort.' That is antiquated insanity, Doug."

"Ain't nothing wrong with wanting to protect a lady."

Loni fumed, getting to her feet.

"You sexist, piece of space—"

"Have I ever prevented you from carrying a blaster?" Doug raised his voice. He wasn't shouting, but his anger had been kindled. Loni crossed her arms, not answering. "What were we doing on Tapolas? Cause I seem to recall you purchasing some shells for a rather destructive weapon. And before you jump to any more conclusions, it's not because you're a Tarsekian princess."

Loni tried to rationalize the words through her own frustration. It was true he'd never said a word to her in opposition to her carrying a blaster or firing her singularity gun. In fact, back on the colony, he had *told* her to keep her blaster ready.

"A lot of those precepts," Doug continued in a calmer tone, "are just strongly encouraged guidelines. Rangers don't have to abide by them. Most of them come from an old Earthean wild west honor system, at least what we can piece together.

"Rangers were formed by two men: Phil Dro and Jason Cals. They were both supposedly lawmen back on Earth, Dro being a self-proclaimed expert on the old west. Turns out he only had a partial knowledge. The rest he pieced together from old non-holo films, dramatizations of what actually happened. Since then, Rangers have done what we can to iron things out and make more sense of them, but a lot of the old influences are still there. Like you said, antiquated. I do believe in protecting the innocent and those who can't protect themselves, people not like you. And for the record, there are a few women Rangers and I happen to respect them a great deal."

Doug gestured to the datapad and shook his head.

"Stuff like that there, I don't follow."

"What is this, then?" Loni asked, most of her irritation abated. "Cause this isn't making sense to me."

Doug's posture relaxed a bit.

"It's rather… personal. Yeah, it's partly cause you're injured. Something like that happens, tends to get under my skin. And the way you practically run right into danger doesn't help things.

"I do want you to stick around. You're a good pilot, got a

good head on your shoulders. Not many people I've found in the galaxy are like that. And I do want to work together. Just the fact that you're trying to understand is a step up from my last partner, and I want you to know it's appreciated. I just need you to be patient with me in this. That is, if you're willing to stick around."

Loni sighed and glanced around, trying to decide. She stared into those dark eyes, humility and hidden pain lurking in them.

"I'll think about it," she said, sitting back down and returning to her reading. She said no more and after a few quiet moments, Doug walked to the door.

"You'll at least come up when it's time to dump out of hyperspace, won't you?" Doug asked.

Loni saw an opportunity, holding the datapad so it hid her face, and her smile.

"Maybe," she said, keeping her tone light.

Doug leaned into her line of sight. She quickly adjusted her datapad, her body shaking slightly from a repressed laugh.

"You're messing with me, aren't you?" Doug asked.

Loni made a display of clearing her throat.

"Right," Doug said.

She heard the swoosh of the door and found herself in an empty room.

He doesn't like it when I mess with him. I'll have to make a point to do it more often.

CHAPTER ELEVEN_

The *Blue Moon* popped out of hyperspace over the planet of Tellus Four, a gray-and-brown mottled orb spinning lazily before the cockpit.

"Moving us into orbit," Loni said.

"You sure there's someone down there that can help us?" Doug asked.

"A lot of Federation ship designers started or retired here. I'll do some digging into the local net to find someone who's not on friendly terms with them while you two are en route planet side. You have a plan on how to get down there?" Loni said.

"You're not coming?" Doug asked.

"You shouldn't need me on this one and I'd rather rest. Despite what I said, there is some truth to what you said before. I can be of more use to you in a pilot's seat."

"In that case, no, I really don't have a plan. Unless you can show me how to fly your ship."

"That would take too long, and you'd need several test flights before you got the hang of it anyway."

"We could always take my ship," Arch said, checking his

blaster's charge pack and then collapsing the gun into its flat square. "That's what I plan on taking."

"Thanks, but I don't really care to be stuffed in that fish bowl again."

"Well, I'm not taking this bird down some place where we can get ambushed again," Loni said. "So unless you want to call and wait for a shuttle, which would draw more attention…"

Doug glanced between them and sighed.

"Alright, let's go. Keep your eyes peeled, Loni. Way things are going, I expect trouble to show up at some point."

The door to the cockpit slid shut and Loni scrunched her brow.

Peel her eyes?

———

Arch's pod flew over the multi-faceted landscape of a vast city. Every structure was of a different design, the next more alien than its neighbor. Air-speeders were like ants running intersecting lines far below them.

"Interesting place," Arch said.

Doug adjusted, trying to get comfortable in the spherical area behind the pilot's chair.

"Tellus Four is mostly made up of engineers and schools. It's where the Federation and other systems get most of their designers and builders, those that can afford to live here anyway. It's a Federation world which means we need to be extra careful."

"Sure, no problem. Coordinates just came in. Looks like ten Kilometers port. Guy by the name of Lis…Lister…"

Doug craned his neck to see the display.

"Listernk Klaktoo. Probably a native. Brilliant engineers, these Tellusians. He should be able to give us the info we need."

"Says here he's over three-hundred cycles old," Arch said.

"Tellusians live a long time. That's just hitting elderly for them. He's been around long enough to see the formation of the Federation. Probably not too keen on seeing it go Empire. Good news for us. Means he won't be likely to turn us in."

"I prefer absolutes."

Arch banked and headed for the coordinates.

———

Arch landed on top of a parking tower for speeders and small spacecraft and powered down. Doug stretched the second he squeezed himself back into freedom.

Arch hopped out and locked the craft, sizing Doug up.

"You sure you wanna be wearing that coat and badge? Makes you kind of stand out."

"He'll be more likely to trust us and not betray that trust if he knows where I stand as far as the Rangers."

"Okay. But hey, plausible deniability. Just throwing that out there."

"Do you even know what that means?"

"Aw, shut up and let's go."

They took a turbo-lift to the thirty-seventh floor and entered into a hallway filled with aliens and humans alike, most of them young adults by Doug's assessment.

"What is this, some kind of youth mind wiping facility?" Arch asked.

Doug noticed the words printed on the doors in Basic and Tellusian.

"It's a university. Listernk is probably a professor here."

They made their way through the crowd to a wall panel marked "information." Doug tapped the panel, bringing it to life and stated Listernk's name. The screen changed to display the pathway they would need to take to find him.

Multiple *oohs* and *awws* came from some human females as they passed. One tried to pet Arch, to which he drew his blaster.

"Hey, hey! No touchies!" Arch hissed.

The girl yelped and took off into the crowd.

"Boy, I'll be glad when we're done with this place," Arch said, collapsing his blaster.

"Don't like people petting you?" Doug asked.

"Threats and firefights I can handle. But touching is where I draw the line."

They found the room and other younglings poured out of its doors. When there was a break in the flow, they slipped in. A few students still milled about a huge room with holo-stations. A large holo-display table sat off-center with a desk at one end of the room. Standing by the table was a human girl talking with a seven-foot-tall insectoid with six arms. He resembled some of the youths wandering the halls, but with skin that was yellower and more stretched. His bovine head was wrinkled, but his yellow eyes were clear and attentive to his charge.

"Do not be discouraged, Mitesa. Your designs are quite brilliant. You only lack patience and forethought. Take your time. Do not rush."

Doug and Arch waited to one side for him to finish. After a few more words, the girl thanked him and walked away, revealing a face full of freckles and stunningly bright, crystal blue eyes. Listernk turned calmly toward them, his six limbs folded regally behind his back. Doug held a palm toward him, speaking in clicks and guttural sounds. Listernk smiled at the greeting and inclined his head.

"I appreciate your greeting, Ranger, but there is no need to be so formal. I am Listernk Klaktoo."

"I'm Doug Lancer, and this is my companion, Ar-Chitak."

"An honor to meet you both. How may I be of service?"

"We have a schematic we'd like you to take a look at if you have a few minutes. It's most important," Doug said.

Listernk waved one of his many appendages. "I have already communicated to the Empire many times that I will have nothing to do with their new designs. I am retired. Leave me be."

"We're not with the Empire," Doug said in a quiet voice.

Listernk's eyes darted to the badge on Doug's chest, then to Arch. "Is that so?"

"Oh, trust me, it's so," Arch said.

Listernk glanced around the now empty room and motioned with two of his arms.

"If you will come with me."

Doug and Arch followed him into a back room. Listernk promptly locked the door. The room was cramped with old, unused equipment covered in sheets. Listernk pulled a sheet off a table similar to the one in the main room and powered it on.

"There are no listening devices in this room," he said. "I request that you tell me what your business is and what this schematic has to do with it."

"We believe the Empire is building a super-weapon. We've obtained some plans that seem to spell out its construction but we need an engineer to read them," Doug said.

"And what do you intend to do with these plans once your suspicions are confirmed?"

"Stop them from becoming a reality, any way we can."

Listernk eyed them each a second time, then gestured to the table. Doug pulled out the fob and inserted it. The scrolling text appeared in holographic form. Listernk's eyes narrowed and one of his lobster-like hands rubbed his chin while another tapped some buttons on the console. The text flickered and shifted to a garbled mess, then to a more garbled mess, and finally to a rotating, three-dimensional model of a series of rings surrounding a long cylinder. Listernk tapped a few buttons and measurements appeared.

"Three-thousand kilometers long, with a diameter of each ring of one-thousand kilometers. Each ring is forty kilometers thick."

Silence filled the room.

"What did I tell you," Arch said into the quiet. "It's a super weapon. The damage this thing could do."

"It is not just a weapon," Listernk said. "It is a ship."

"A ship?" Doug and Arch said in unison.

"Yes, quite so. There is a secondary schematic here, though the rendering is incomplete. It shows components of hyperdrive engines within its design."

"Makes sense actually," Doug said. "The core worlds are scattered all throughout the Galactic Ring. If you wanted to destroy them, you'd have to be able to move the thing."

"This is dire news," Listernk said. "This shows the Empire is not just a name, but the first indications of a regime bent on galactic dominance."

Arch's head twitched toward the door.

"Listernk, do a bunch of your students wear heavy boots?"

Listernk opened his mouth to answer, but his reply was cut short by a barrage of blaster fire shredding the wall they came through. Doug and Arch ducked behind the table, both drawing their blasters.

"Guess the Empire tracked us down," Doug shouted over the blaster fire. "Must be the tracker the slicer kid was talking about."

"Tracker?" Arch said. "You didn't say anything about a tracker!"

"Must've slipped my mind. Listernk, is there another way out of here?"

Doug turned to find the aged Tellusian lying motionless beside him, cauterized holes in his chest.

"Aw, Dust."

"Doug, the fob!" Arch said.

Doug reached around the table, fumbling for the fob. A bolt struck the console, sending smoke and flame into the air, obliterating the evidence. Doug yelped at the sudden heat and drew his hand back.

"Princess," Arch called into his com, "The Empire's got us pinned. We need an evac. Princess? Princess!"

"She ain't answering?"

"Interference. They must be jamming us."

"Guess we're on our own. Hope she made it out okay," Doug said.

"My guess is she's sticking around. Can't scare away a dame like that too easy."

"We need a way to signal her where we are, or get to your ship."

"I have a method for both," Arch said.

Arch slapped the side of his gun and the barrel widened, aiming at the back wall. The gun bucked as a projectile launched in an arc and exploded, sending debris and heat flying at them."

"Don't say it," Arch warned.

"I ain't complaining," Doug said, and they sprinted toward the opening.

The hallway was thankfully empty on the other side. They took off.

"Beat feet," Arch said, following exit signs.

"What?" Doug asked, right behind him.

"Nothing. Just calling my ship."

Doug spied a passing sign and took a sharp left.

"This way."

Arch scrambled back after him just before blaster fire filled the hallway. They reached an intersection that opened into a wide space, connecting to an adjacent hallway on the other side. A series of lifts within that rectangular area were laid into both sides of the walls. A rather large plant with thick, feathery leaves was the only sad attempt to break up the stale, metallic environment.

Doug hit a button on one of the lifts nearest the plant and ducked behind the planter. He took one of his blasters and fired it at the other, blowing the end off the barrel.

"How long till your ship is here?" Doug asked, willing the indicator light on the lift to move faster.

"No idea, ain't got a tracker. It's just a call sign. It'll signal me when it's within a hundred meters, though."

Doug checked their orientation to the outside. Floor to ceiling transparasteel along the halls running parallel to the lift area gave him a good view of the outside. And the drop was deadly.

"If there's a wall in the way, will it crash through it?" He asked.

"It's not armored transport. Though it'll blast the wall down if I tell it. Otherwise, we'll have to find a way to access it."

"What about transparasteel?"

"Uh… yeah, it can crash through that if I disable its stopping protocols."

"Do that."

"I don't know what you're planning, but it better not get me killed," Arch said. "Full throttle."

Their pursuers arrived, along with the whine of several high-powered weapons. Doug fiddled with the settings on the now damaged blaster.

A synthetically enhanced voice boomed in the corridor, "Enemies of the Empire, come out with your hands up."

The lift's doors slid open. Arch tensed to make a break for it, but Doug held him in place.

"Alright!" Doug said, "I'm throwing my blaster and coming out with my hands up. Don't shoot!"

He slid his good blaster toward the elevator and it stopped in the open doorway, keeping the lift from closing. The other he put on the surface of the planter, hiding it from the troopers. Doug raised his hands above the plants thick leaves, slowly standing up.

Seven Armored Corps Troopers aimed their rifles at him. They were covered from head to toe in uniform gray armor, their helmets possessing a bulbous "T" shape for a viewport. Doug noted slight movements from most of them, indicating their surprise at seeing a Ranger.

"Now, you boys mind telling me what has you firing a full volley of high-intensity blaster bolts at a Galactic Ranger?"

"Identify yourself, Ranger," the trooper with sergeant's markings said.

Doug committed the name emblazoned on the sergeant's armor to memory.

"Doug Lancer."

"We'll have to confirm your I. D. with the Ranger corp. Stand by."

"You could do that, but I can tell you what you'd find," Doug said. "Rangers have gone turncoat and claim I've been ousted from their organization. The claims you'll find are that I've gone against the code, turned my back on the Rangers."

Doug focused on each of the troopers individually, committing names to memory. Some shifted. Perhaps uncomfortable aiming their blaster rifles at a Ranger. One trooper undulated slightly. Good, they were telling jokes over their private com. Just maybe they would see past the lies their superior no doubt rattled off.

"Confirmed," the sergeant said. "I don't know much about how the Rangers work as an organization. Frankly, your internal politics are not my concern. What is my concern is the signal we received from a sealed Imperial file accessed in this facility. You wouldn't happen to know anything about that, would you?"

"Actually, I would. It's a file containing plans to build a super weapon by the Empire."

The troopers shifted almost imperceptibly at the word *Empire*.

"Some kind of weapon to use against the core worlds," Doug continued. "Unfortunately, your errant blaster fire destroyed both the console and the file."

"Standard protocol, Ranger," the sergeant said. "We get a signal like that, we go in guns blazing. Even a Ranger shouldn't have access to a file with such high alert status. Where did you get it?"

"A fighter pilot whose squad was summarily executed for knowing too much. She had a slicer friend retrieve the file and barely escaped with her life."

Their helmets turned from one trooper to the next. A few even adjusted their holds on their weapons. There was definitely an argument going on across their coms.

"What was the name of the ship your pilot was stationed on?"

They already knew. Loni, the *Dominator*, the deaths. Doug could easily guess at the bogus story they were likely fed. That Loni's squad were all shot down in a Pirate raid or died from an infection of White Scars. They just wanted confirmation.

"The *Dominator*," Doug replied.

"Ranger, we'll have to take you into custody until we can confirm all this and straighten things out," the sergeant said.

Doug felt a paw tap his leg and he nudged Arch twice with his foot.

"You want me to make a break for it?" Arch whispered through their coms.

Doug nodded, a shape beyond the troopers and behind the transparasteel wall catching his attention. He resisted a smile.

"You take me in and I'm good as dead, "Doug said. "And so are the core worlds. I need to handle this in official Ranger fashion. Now."

Arch darted for the lift, and two rifles jerked their aim after him. In the same moment, three troopers turned to face the windows. Two others fired stun blasts at Doug. He barely managed to dodge, grabbing his damaged blaster in a sideways dive. He only needed one shot.

The unfocused blast hit all seven troopers. It didn't drop them, but did succeed in sending them into a momentary state of confusion, amplified by Arch's ship smashing through the transparasteel.

Arch darted out of the lift after the ship, shouting something into the com. The ship slowed and Arch jumped inside.

"Keep going!" Doug shouted, chasing after the craft.

No blaster bolts came after him, thanks to the wild energy spike from Doug's blaster temporarily disabling the troopers' weapons and armor.

Arch's ship smashed through the windows at the opposite end of the hall. Doug reached the edge and jumped, grabbing onto the back of the craft just before it banked out of view. They flew through the city, Doug dangling, until they were under the cover of another building. Arch slowed to a hover, allowing Doug to climb inside the cockpit.

"That's got to be the craziest escape plan I've ever witnessed," Arch said as they took off into the atmosphere. "You're insane, Doug."

"At least it worked. And we may have gained some allies."

"Allies? Have you been inhaling blaster fumes?"

"Later. Right now we need to get back to the ship. See if you can get Loni on coms."

CHAPTER TWELVE_

Sergeant Dole Ati watched the craft fly away, his sealed armor protecting his ears from the howling wind. His armor booted up. Text scrolled across his visor—*systems check.*

"Sergeant Ati, do you copy?"

It was Waters on overwatch.

"I'm here, Waters."

"Sergeant, I have the craft in my sights. Shall I take the shot?"

"Negative, Waters," Ati replied. "Let them go. But track them."

"Copy. What's going on down there? I couldn't raise anyone on coms."

"I'll go over it in debrief."

"Yes, boss" Waters said.

Sergeant Ati turned to his men.

"Everyone booted up?"

He got confirmed acknowledgements from each.

"What in stages blazes was that?" Q asked. He was the short, incessant questioner of the group. "I turn my back for one second and everything goes dark."

"Specs, what do you have for me?" Ati asked.

"Checking now," Specs said, his voice a deep rumble across the coms. "Yeah, my recording shows he modified his blaster. Looks like he blew the end off. Probably did it before we arrived."

"What does that mean?" Q asked.

"Most hand blasters need the full barrel to get a focused, compacted energy blast," Ati said. "By cutting off the end, he effectively made a wide-beam, unstable blast."

"Its energy was unstable, spiking and throwing our electronics all out of whack," Specs said. "Improvised EMP."

"Exactly. Specs, take Tolso and inspect the room they fled from. See if you can locate that file. Or at least what's left of it. Everyone else meet back at base for debrief. I'm contacting Central. I want to know what all this mess was about."

"Understood, Sir. Sergeant Ati out."

The holo-image of the Admiral blinked off. Ati stewed before the projector, suspicions roiling in his mind. He'd called the matter in to his captain, but the Admiral of the Terran sector came on instead, ordering him and his squad to turn over any relevant material. Except they didn't have any, at least none that he was aware of.

Since the Federation officially transitioned to the Galactic Empire, the Armored Corps had been increasingly used as enforcers and escorts. Sergeant Ati and his squad, Titan Squad, were no exception. While Captain Brainard seemed to embrace every move the Empire made, Ati and his men were increasingly disillusioned.

Sergeant Ati pulled his I.D. chip from the projector and stalked back through the complex that was their base of operations in Ha-chic city to the data reclamation room. Or "the lab" as the boys called it. He joined Specs who was nose deep in a console.

"Tell me you've got something," Ati said.

Specs shook his head. In his armor, he looked like any other standard Armored Trooper. Out of his armor, his appearance was nothing like the data nerd he was. It always threw Ati for some reason.

"Nothing," Specs said. "The whole thing was fried, just like the Ranger said."

"So much for standard procedure."

"What'd Cap have to say?"

"I didn't talk to the Captain. Admiral Traik came on instead."

Specs raised an eyebrow.

"Ah, this whole thing stinks. Something's up," Ati said.

"Careful, boss. That's treason talk."

Ati smirked at his friend.

"You always did keep my focus."

"Somebody has to. What did the admiral say exactly?"

"To keep an eye out for the Ranger. We've been given leave to shoot to kill on sight."

"Were those his exact words?"

Ati thought for a moment.

"His exact words were, 'I want your men on constant patrol for this renegade Ranger. You have leave to shoot on sight.' Blazes, we're a special ops squad, not some local militia…"Ati glanced around the room. "Where's the rest of the team?"

"Rec room, I think."

"C'mon."

Specs shut down his console and they made their way to the rec room. Most of the squad was gathered there, relaxing in standard issue undersuits. The crisp *pik-pok* of ping pong mixed with the electronic sounds of vid games and the voices of casual conversation as each relaxed in their own way. They were technically off-duty, but could be called upon on a moment's notice.

All attention went to Sergeant Ati.

"Boss, what'd Cap have to say?" Q asked.

"I would rather not repeat myself. Where's Bot?"

"Where do you think?" Drawl said in his New Texan accent.

Ati smirked and tapped a com node on the wall.

"Bot, report to the rec room."

Barely a minute later, a trooper in full kit walked in.

"Good, now that you're all here, here's the situation: I commed the Captain, but got Admiral Traik instead. He wouldn't deny or substantiate any of the Ranger's claims. He didn't even address them. He basically told us to keep vigilant. I think he expects us to shoot on sight and deliberately kill anyone who has evidence against the Empire. But we're not going to do that."

"Sergeant, isn't that defying orders?" Bot's synthesized voice was level.

Ati knew Bot was neither threatening nor challenging him. It was a subtle way of letting him know they all knew where this was headed and they were with him.

"Not at all, Trooper. In fact, I plan to follow Admiral Traik's orders to the letter. He ordered us to remain 'on patrol' and keep a look out for this Ranger. I plan for us to do exactly that. We're a special ops team, so we have leave to take our missions off-world if that's where our orders take us.

"But I'm more interested in finding out if what the Ranger said was true. Despite Admiral Traik saying we have leave to shoot on sight, he did not order us to do so. Specs, see if you can track this Ranger down. Waters, did you get a good look at that craft he took off on?"

"RTX-7. Old craft made for smaller species. I don't think it was his. Maybe the Ranger's pet cat."

"That cat was no pet," Specs said. "It had on a tactical vest and bolted at the Ranger's signal. I'd say it's sapient."

"Alright, you two see if you can find any info on that ship and its intended destination. Don't just check the spaceports, check orbital surveillance as well," Ati said.

Waters set down his ping-pong paddle and followed Specs out of the room.

"Bot, see about securing us some off-world transport in case we need it."

Bot nodded and walked out.

"Vid, find out what the *Dominator*'s path has been for the past week. The rest of you, get kitted up. We're going on a hunt."

CHAPTER THIRTEEN_

"Alright," Doug said to Arch and Loni seated on the circular couch in the conference room. "We may not have the schematic anymore, but we know what the Empire is planning. We need to get this information into the hands of someone that can do something about it."

"And who would that be?" Arch asked. "I mean, the only law enforcement out there was the Federation and the Rangers. Now they're both the Empire. That don't leave us with many options."

"We have Loni's family," Doug said.

Loni nodded, for once agreeing that was an option.

"The Tarsek system has a fleet. It's a small one, but our ships are tough and pack some serious firepower," Loni said. "It's enough of a threat that the Pirates never made a major strike against us, and would be enough to cripple the Empire if it came to all-out war. Though we'd lose in the end."

"But if we informed them of the Empire's plans, would a warning to cease all efforts be enough of a threat to make the Empire think twice about building their death ship?" Doug asked.

Worry filled Loni's eyes.

"Maybe. It's a tenuous thing. Could also put our system in a dangerous position. My parents may not go for it."

"Would you?"

Loni raised an eyebrow. "You have to ask? Of course I would. But I'm not my parents. They have years of experience that I haven't even begun to train for."

"Then we'll need a backup plan," Doug said.

"Or an alternative one," Arch said.

"Isn't that the same thing?" Loni asked.

"No, no. I mean something else we can do at the same time," Arch said.

"Hmm… We could give the plans to local governments," Loni suggested. "The Empire would lose support. Maybe several worlds could cobble together a secondary Federation."

Doug shook his head.

"Most worlds capable of that are core worlds already in the Federation. By the time we could convince them to believe us in the first place, and defect, then organize, build and mobilize their own Federation fleet, the Empire would have their weapon built. No, the only other option I can see is not one I relish, and it's a long shot anyway."

"The Rangers?" Loni asked.

"Ah, no. Big no!" Arch said. "You're crazy, Doug. Don't they want you dead?"

"No, just want me to throw in with them. But there're good people in the Rangers. They've just been duped. If I can convince them of this threat, especially the Marshall, maybe they'll turn and do the right thing."

"Or they'll side with the Empire and blow you to space debris," Arch said. "Not a good idea."

"You have a better one?"

A soft growl burbled inside Arch, his ears flattening against his head.

"All right then, that settles it," Doug said. "I think in order for this to work, we need to get another copy of those plans. Loni, you know where we can find a copy?"

"No, but Lent could probably find it for us, if I can convince him. He'd be putting himself at risk, and he's technically one of the 'innocents' you're so bent on protecting."

Doug let out a hard breath. "There's more at stake here than just a small group of outlaws. And this thing is way bigger than just me. We'll make the danger clear to him. It'll be his choice and I'll just have to let that choice be his if something happens."

Loni's coy smile made Doug want to shift his stance, but he held his ground. "What?"

"I think that's the first time I ever heard you refer to yourself as an outlaw. I like a man who can admit his faults."

"I can admit my faults," Arch said.

"You're not a man, kitty-cat."

"You say that like it's a bad thing." Arch flicked his tail at her dismissal. "Y'know, you bi-pedals have some kind of crazy, running around like you're an army of transformed Ikati trying to take down the Empire. You're just two weakling humans. That's crazy hero stuff and I ain't no hero." Arch glanced between them, their expectant stares making him squirm.

"All right, all right! Quit staring at me like you expect better out of me. I'll tell you right now you ain't getting it."

Even as he said the words, he knew them to be hollow. He sighed.

"You two do have a way of rubbing off on me, you don't gotta twist my paw. I'm in. I have other reasons for saying yes too, so don't think it's just cause of you. But if you get me killed, I'm desecrating your graves in my third life."

Doug raised an eyebrow.

"*Third* life?"

"Ikati humor," Arch replied, hopping down from the table. "I better go see about assembling some more blasters. I have a feeling we're going to need them, especially since sheriff outlaw here keeps losing his."

Loni glanced at Doug's empty holsters. Doug shrugged. She rolled her eyes and headed for her room.

———

"You don't have to do it, Lent."

Lent rubbed a nervous hand through his hair, Loni's image on the screen in front of him.

"I-I don't know. I mean, I like you and all, but this is the Empire we're talking about here. The Federation was bad enough, but have you seen what they do to people who are considered enemies of the Empire? It's horrendous."

"I know the cost, Lent. My whole squad was executed for knowing too much. I'm too involved in this to walk away, but you're still able to. I wouldn't ask if I knew any other way."

"W-would you still like me if I said no?"

Loni opened her mouth to reply, but immediately closed it, hanging her head.

"Lent, I'm sorry. I guess I've been stringing you along. You're a nice guy and all, but I just don't think it would work between us. I like you, but as a friend."

Lent slumped in his chair.

"I'm really sorry. I never meant to hurt you," Loni said.

"It's okay," he mumbled, and sat a bit straighter, doing his best to put on an uncaring air. "It's fine, really. I mean, you're an ace fighter pilot and I'm just some kid slicer. I get it."

"It's not that. It's just—"

"I can't help you at any rate. I mean, I could, but then I'd be on the run and I don't have anywhere to go."

"You could stay with us. You'd be a useful member of our crew."

Lent considered it. Staring into Loni's beautiful face, those bright blue eyes that seemed to call to him…

He wrenched his eyes away.

"No, I-I couldn't do that. Not when…I-I'm sorry, Loni."

"I'm sorry too. Take care of yourself."

"Hey, uh, Loni!"

"Yes?"

"I can't help you with this, but if you need anything else from me, something that, y'know, won't make the Empire want to hunt me down. I'll be glad to help."

Loni smiled and his insides melted.

"Thank you," she said in that angelic voice. "I'll definitely hit you up. Do you think you could at least give us the name of someone who could locate the file for us?"

"Oh, I can locate the file no problem. I just can't retrieve it without making myself a target. But a simple search…"

He worked his keyboards, watching information flash by on several monitors.

"Just give me, give me one second…"His hands worked like never before and in less than a minute, he had it. "Looks like there are only two copies. I'll send you their locations."

"Thank you, Lent! I could kiss you."

He turned beet red, and in a small voice said, "I-I wish you would."

"How's this?" Loni moved close to the holo screen and mimicked a kiss. Lent quickly hit the screen-capture button.

"That'll, that'll do," he said, his face hot as a skillet.

Loni smiled and signed off.

Lent brought up the screen capture and another of her just smiling. His smile faded the longer he stared at her. His hand moved to the delete key and tapped it twice.

The images vanished.

———

An elderly man with a badge on his button-up shirt and a thick mustache appeared on the holo display. He straightened when he recognized Doug.

"Well, I'll be dusted," the old man croaked.

"Howdy, Marshall," Doug said. "How've you been?"

The man shrugged, his hands fiddling with a pen.

"Just fine and dandy, Doug. Would be better if you were here with us."

The man's eyes flicked to something off-screen.

"Who's in there with you? Stenson? Dalk? Doesn't matter. Don't bother tracing. I ain't gonna be on long enough for you to find me."

The Marshall sat back in his chair.

"If you're not contacting me to turn yourself in, why *are* you calling?"

"Empire's building a super weapon, planning on wiping out the core worlds. Thought you should know."

"Is that a fact? And you know this because?"

"An ex-Imperial helped me uncover a schematic taken from a file with an Imperial seal. You hear about that mess on Tellus Four?"

"That was you?" the Marshall asked.

"I was getting it rendered when an Armored Corps squad tried to play target practice with us. File was destroyed."

"Well, I can't say I blame them. Stolen Imperial property is no light matter. That's a dangerous file you poked your nose into. You have an extra copy?"

Doug studied the Marshall's face through the holo-image.

Even though the man's eyes stared steady and calm, something about what he said bothered him. As if he already knew.

"I might," Doug replied.

"Well, bring it in and we'll see what we can do about this."

"Really, Marshall?" Doug said. "Bring it in instead of just transmitting the blasted thing? You trained me better than that. You have no intention of doing anything about this. I think the really disappointing thing is that you would stoop to lying to me in order to draw me into a trap."

The Marshall lowered his head, his wide brimmed hat covering his eyes. "Look, Doug—"

"Save it. I'll figure this out on my own." He cut the transmission.

Rage boiled within him. Doug grabbed the edge of the holo-table, flipping it in a horrible crash of metal and clutter. A violent kick sent his chair careening across the room. Searching for something else on which to take out his frustration but finding nothing, he paced, his hands wringing.

The remains of his outburst were a sad reflection of his current state of life. He hated it. Moreso, he hated himself for losing control. He breathed deep, attempting to quell his temper. But the more he paced, the more the anger just turned cold. He retrieved his chair, slamming it onto the deck and plopped down, his head in his hands.

It wasn't just the Marshall's betrayal. His allies were becoming enemies, and he was slowly being backed into a corner. The more he trusted, the more he tried, and the further he fell. Worst, the more those around him turned against him. It was as if the universe itself was trying to crack him, to compromise the only path to success, and twist him into something he didn't want to become.

"Lord, help me to know what to do," he mumbled.

Doug sat there for some time, head in his hands and eyes closed, allowing his emotions to cool.

"Hey, you awake?" Arch said, sitting on the floor in front of him.

"Yeah, I'm here." Doug rubbed his face.

"What were you doing? Sleeping, praying?"

"What if I was?" Doug snapped.

Arch's ears flipped backwards and flattened.

"Sorry," he said sarcastically. "Next time I won't interrupt your brooding."

"No, I'm sorry. It's not you."

"Rangers?"

"Marshall."

Arch licked his paw then rubbed it against the fur on his head.

"Ain't that the same thing?"

"Marshall is the head Ranger. The current one is the man who took me under his wing and trained me. Taught me everything I know about being a Ranger."

"Let me guess, he's pretty much chucked all that out the airlock and you don't know how to deal with it."

"Something like that."

"You, my friend, need a stiff drink. Forget all your troubles for a few hours."

Doug stood and walked out of the room, Arch on his heels.

"A stiff drink is about the last thing I need," Doug said. "What I need is to get this whole mess solved. Forgetting my troubles ain't going to do me a lick of good."

"Naw, but it sure feels good to get plastered. Not so much the next day, but at the time—"

"You talk to Loni?"

"I think she's still talking to her slicer friend. Hey, y'know, I know a few slicers myself if this kid doesn't work out."

"I'll keep that in mind."

They arrived at Loni's quarters just as her door slid open and she stepped out.

"Lent won't do it. He wasn't too keen on being a fugitive from the Empire. I tried to offer him a place here, but he turned it down."

"I'd have thought he'd jump at the chance just to be closer to you," Doug said.

Loni glanced at the floor. "I had to level with him. Told him I wasn't interested."

"What?" Arch blurted out. "Why in the nine hells would you do that? You could have strung him along at least enough to get the file, then broke it off afterwards."

Loni scowled. "Maybe that's okay for someone like you, Arch, but where I come from, that's a pretty heartless thing to do to a person."

"Oh, cry me a river. You know you bi-pedals need to learn that it's a predatory galaxy out there. If you don't do what you need to survive, sooner or later someone's gonna come along and have you for breakfast."

"I'll take my chances, furball. Thanks," Loni said.

Arch's ears flattened and he looked away.

"You did the right thing, Loni," Doug said. "I wouldn't have been comfortable putting him in that position anyways. Arch says he knows some slicers. Maybe we can get one of them to locate it for us."

"Well, Lent was able to get me the two locations where the file is being kept. Maybe Arch's contacts can retrieve it for us."

"I should have added 'if you have the credits to pay for it,'" Arch said. "They cost a pretty credit, especially for a premium slicing and recovery job like that. There's only one person I know of who could pull that off and would do it just for the thrill of it, and I only know *of* him. Never made contact myself."

"What's his name?" Doug asked.

"Jack. Everyone in the slicer circles refers to him as Wild Jack, on account he takes some insane risks, but can do things with computers that no one else can."

"Alright, maybe we can track this Wild Jack down and get him to help us. Think you can gather some intel from your hacker contacts?" Doug said.

Arch opened his mouth, but Doug beat him to it.

"Just get me a price and I'll figure out a way to pay for it. Just don't let them overcharge us."

"What do I look like, an amateur? I broker guns for a living. I'll see what I can dig up."

Arch tapped his com, bringing up a holo display in front of his face. He tapped the display and a moment later said, "Reggie, it's Arch. How's my favorite hacker doing?"

"What'd your parents say?" Doug asked Loni.

"They weren't thrilled at the news, but weren't all that excited about taking on the Empire. They have some things they can do to put pressure on them, but that's about as far as they're willing to go."

"Every little bit helps. Tell them we appreciate whatever they can do."

"I already did. They just need a copy of the file to back up their actions."

"Hopefully Arch can come up with something."

"Not likely," Arch said, killing his holo controls. "According to my source, Jack disappeared off sensors six months ago. No one's heard from him since. Reggie and his fellow slicers have tried to contact him in their own ways several times. Nothing."

"Looks like it's up to us, then," Doug said. "Where are the files located?"

"Ifdil in the Trasent sector and the other is in Grandus," Loni said.

"Both places are information hubs for the Federation, and

they're heavily guarded, "Doug said. "We're gonna have a time getting in either one,"

"I take it the Rangers aren't going for it?" Loni said.

Doug shook his head. "I think we're on our own on this one."

Loni smirked.

"You make it sound like we're a team who's been at this for a while."

"Maybe that'll be the case. I certainly wouldn't be opposed to it."

Loni and Arch shared a glance, but neither said a word.

"Ifdil is more sparsely populated," Doug continued. "While Grandus has a large city surrounding it. Let's go for Ifdil. The security might be more lax there."

"What if…what if we tried to find Jack?" Loni said. "I mean, just because he's disappeared, doesn't mean he's unreachable. I'm just concerned about getting caught trying to sneak in."

"I've no intention of sneaking in. I plan on using my Ranger credentials. Let's just take the quicker option for now. If we're denied access, we can see if we can track down Jack. Agreed?"

Loni didn't appear convinced, but nonetheless nodded.

"Sure, I'll set course for Ifdil."She started to move away.

"Hey," Doug said, halting her. "This may be my ship, but I'm not treating us like my word is law. If you're not comfortable with something, or feel strongly about another course, we can talk about it further before settling."

Loni smiled. "Thanks, but I think you're right. It would save time if they let us just walk in."

"Me, not you. You're wanted by the Empire. They run your identity, it'll immediately red-flag you. I'll need you to be on standby here where you can do the most good. I don't suppose this ship has a cloak?"

"Unfortunately, that's one thing I didn't think of," Loni said.

"Alright. Well, let's get to it."

They parted ways, leaving Arch glancing between their retreating backs.

"Arch, what do you think of this plan?" he asked himself. "Oh, I'm so glad you asked. I think you bi-pedals are both space crazy and you're going to get yourselves and me killed. Ugh, humans."

CHAPTER FOURTEEN_

Doug stepped out of the transport. A cool breeze rustled his duster, bringing with it the smell of moisture threatening a storm. He craned his neck toward the overcast sky and the towering structure before him.

The driver raised his voice, grabbing Doug's attention and waved a device. Doug scanned the credit chip, transferring the payment.

He touched his hat in thanks.

"Much obliged."

The man rolled up his window and drove off. A little too eager to get away from the area, Doug noticed.

Does he know something I don't or is it just this place?

The pyramid structure, wrapped in an unseen forcefield deterring both physical and digital intruders, lit up in strips of iridescent light. Marines, though they weren't fully fledged Armored Corps Troopers, were sparsely posted around the facility. Doug wagered he could probably handle two or three at a time before they converged on him but instantly scolded himself.

Stop thinking that way. Just do what you came here to do.

He climbed the stairs to the entrance, approaching the Marines guarding it. Their visored half-helmets hid their eyes, making them look uniform as they held up hands, halting him. Their movements were not the sharp movements he was used to seeing from soldiers of the Federation, indicating they were either tired or bored.

"State your name and business," one of them said rotely.

Boredom, Doug decided.

"Galactic Ranger Doug Lancer. Official Ranger business." They probably didn't care what his business was as long as he gave them a legitimate reason for his visit.

"We'll need to scan your I.D."

Doug pulled back the edge of his duster, revealing the gleaming badge beneath. One Marine ran a scan over the badge. He stepped back and showed his companion the results, whispering too quiet for Doug to make out. Their mannerisms and speech were casual, their guns remained pointed at the ground, and their trigger fingers didn't twitch toward the trigger.

The Marine nodded and said, "Ranger, you are permitted to enter. You understand that everything you search for will be monitored and no access will be granted to certain files without authorization."

"It's a good thing I'm a Ranger then, huh?"

The speaking Marine didn't smile, but Doug caught the hint of a smirk on the other.

"I understand and will abide by the laws set forth by the Federation," Doug said.

"You'll have to leave your blasters here."

Doug drew his blasters and handed them to the Marine, grips out. The man stuck them in a storage locker on the wall, not even bothering to lock it, and tapped in a sequence on an unlabeled panel. The steel doors slid open.

Doug tipped his hat, noting neither one corrected him when he said "Federation."

Arch perched in his usual spot on the console, the gray planet of Ifdil far below his only focus.

Awful place.

Between its overcast skies and the constant drizzling rain it was known for, Arch was glad to be stuck on board the *Blue Moon*.

"You ever been down there?" he asked Loni.

"Can't say I have," she said, checking systems.

Arch swiveled his head toward her. She'd been doing that since they settled into orbit an hour ago.

"Haven't you checked those systems enough?"

"I don't like to sit still. If I'm not doing something, I need to be reading something. Just a personal hang-up of mine."

"I don't think it's a hang-up," Arch said.

Loni's focus settled on him with a smile.

"Thanks."

Heat rushed along his skin, bristling his sleek fur. Arch quickly turned away, not quite knowing what to do with his paws. His tail twitched uncertainly. Was he moving it too much? He started to wrap it around himself. No, that was stupid and weird. What was wrong with him?

He needed something to distract himself and said, "You know, you were wrong before."

"About what?" Loni asked distractedly.

"About the NK-47. Its range is only twelve-hundred meters. And the reason they don't make them anymore is because people who used them all died from the fallout. They just don't work as weapons."

Loni sat back in her seat, system checks forgotten.

"Really?"

"Yeah. They tried everything from shortening the barrel to adding rocket propulsion. Things just aren't viable weapons."

"What about the NK-49s?"

Arch made an odd sound somewhere between hissing and sputtering. "Those pieces of junk? They're even worse, designed by some idiot that thought he knew of an alternative way of containing the radiation." He stretched his paws forward, extending his claws in a cat-stretch. Tension flowed out of him, easing his nervousness. "Which reminds me, despite what Mister I-keep-losing-my-blasters said, there's plenty of radioactive material. Problem is, it's too powerful. Needs a high yield energy field to keep it contained, and that kind of equipment is enormous. That's why it's only used on the engines of larger star-ships. The radiation always leaked out when they tried to make them into weapons, ruining the weapon and killing the owner."

"But they *were* effective weapons," Loni said.

"Not if they kill you before you can use it. I like my weapons to be stable and reliable. I only had the forty-seven in my shop as a piece of memorabilia. I would never have used it personally."

"What's your preference then?" Loni leaned forward, interest peaked. "I noticed your custom blaster."

"My Arch Blaster?" Arch indicated the flat square. "The fold-up mechanics makes it convenient, but it don't got a lot of storage. I prefer a mounted heavy repeater, something along the lines of a Raltek Nine. Those are sweet pieces of hardware. I haven't really found a handheld that satisfies. Nothing is high yield enough. I need something with some punch behind it, so for now, my Arch Blaster fits the bill."

"Punch. I like that," Loni said.

"If I had my choice, I'd take your singularity gun. Of course, I'd never be able to fire that fine piece of art."

Loni leaned away, her smile fading.

"Yeah, I know how it really works and why only your family

has it," Arch said. "But you can relax. You're a princess. My kind highly regard royalty, even if you are bi-pedals. And knowing your pension for weapons and such makes me respect you even more. I ain't gonna say nothing."

"Thanks, Arch. That's sweet."

Arch's whole body warmed again, this time with the beginnings of a purr bubbling up. He pushed it down and jerked his head back to the viewport. Movement in the vast star field drew his attention and he padded a little closer.

"Hey, what's that?" He asked.

Loni turned to face the viewport, then swiveled back to her controls.

"Uh-oh."

———

Doug's boots were loud on the polished marble floor amidst the stacks upon stacks of data towers. The vast amounts of information here, from every known species in the galaxy, made him appreciate what the Federation accomplished. It simultaneously rubbed his inner wounds, deepening his sadness over their turning into the Empire.

He found a holo-terminal and activated it. It took some time to locate the file. It was buried deep in the Federation records. At least, he assumed this was what he was looking for. The file was marked "Classified."

Sure hope this works.

Doug scanned his badge.

The screen flashed red lettering in Basic—ACCESS DENIED.

Doug scrunched his brow and scanned his badge again—ACCESS DENIED.

His face soured and he was about to try a third time when a scratchy voice rang out.

"You won't get access, Doug."

Doug looked up, meeting the Marshall's eyes. The elderly man was flanked by two others, Stenson, and another by the name of Rilt. Doug didn't know much about Rilt, but Stenson he knew. What concerned him, however, was that they all leveled their blasters at him.

"You seem to already know what file I'm searching for," Doug said, his hands drifting to his sides on instinct, only to remember the Marines had taken his blasters.

How the Marshall and his lackeys got in with theirs said something about their level of access. More results from bedding with the Empire. Doug's stomach turned at the thought.

"I know all about it, son," the Marshall said. "From the moment you—"

"Don't call me son, sir," Doug said, menace in his voice.

The old man's eyes flashed hurt.

"I'm sorry it has to be this way, Doug."

"So am I."

Doug kicked the console as hard as he could. The cover folded in with a pop and spark of electricity. Alarms blared, the lights shifting to red, momentarily distracting the three Rangers. Doug bolted for a walkway between two data towers. Blaster bolts struck the marble and towers around him, taking out chunks of the latter.

The clomp of boots told him the Marines were on the scene. A voice in the distance shouted, "Drop your weapons! On the ground, now!"

"Hold it!" the Marshall shouted back. "We're here—"

"On the ground! Now!"

A bolt fired, followed by a barrage of blaster fire that faded as

Doug fled further into the complex. That wouldn't last long. His fellow Rangers would make short work of those Marines.

Doug turned at every intersection, hoping he hadn't been noticed slipping away and praying the entire facility hadn't gone into lockdown yet.

———

Loni pulled the yoke left and right, rolling and swerving to avoid the blaster fire from the interceptors coming their way.

Arch slammed his paws on the firing controls from the co-pilot's seat, the shot peeling too far to the left.

"Will you quit swerving so much? I can't get a lock!"

"And let them hit us? No chance."

Loni dove, doing her best to put distance between the *Blue Moon*, the massive cruiser, and the interceptors before they managed to geta lock.

"Loni Taraska," said a voice over the com. "You will—"

Loni switched off the com.

"How the space did they find us?"

"You tell me, Princess. You're the former Imperial. Ha! Got one! We need to get word to Doug."

"That place is shielded. Transmissions don't get through. We'll need to lose these guys first."

"If you have any ideas, I'm open to them."

The cruiser initiated a micro jump. This was playing out exactly as it had before when she'd barely escaped with her life. She wasn't about to make the same mistake twice.

She spun the ship, heading directly into the oncoming fire of the interceptors. Despite her best attempts to dodge, blaster fire impacted the shields. Arch managed to take out one more before the rest scattered. That left six.

"Hey, where are we going?" Arch asked. "We're not going toward it are we?"

"Reroute power to the engines."

"Oh, I hope you know what you're doing."

So do I, she thought.

When they were close to the carrier, she banked along the Y axis. The *Blue Moon* angled down, barreling toward the main body of the massive ship.

Arch's claws sunk into his arm rests.

"Loooooniiiiii!"

The cruiser grew in size. The *Blue Moon* shook against the amount of raw energy from blaster fire it had to absorb. Arch's fur stood on end, his eyes wide, and a feline yowl exited his throat. They were close enough to see the lights on the viewports and people moving about inside.

At the last second, Loni pulled on the yoke, sending the ship skimming meters above the carrier's surface. Arch's scope alerted him to another downed fighter, smashed into the carrier. But he was too busy trying to hold his bowels together to notice.

Loni held the position a moment longer before diving down toward the planet. The interceptors pursued them, but soon broke off as the *Blue Moon* entered the atmosphere.

"Princess! Princess, the re-entry burn!"

"I know. I know," Loni said through gritted teeth.

She held the shaking yoke in her gloved hands. Streaks of fire blazed past them in a brilliance of red and orange across the viewport. They shot through the cloud cover into the rainy world beneath. Loni eased back on the engines and hit reverse thrusters, slowing their descent. The flames vanished.

She angled the ship toward the complex and shot away.

———

Stenson crept through the complex, taking care on corners. Doug had hidden himself somewhere in these catacombs. Maybe he'd find him and make this place his grave. Then he'd be rid of the boy scout and he and the rest of the Rangers could focus on the future.

The edge of a brown duster peeked out from behind a corner a distance away. He stalked the still object. The duster shifted and he adjusted the grip on his blaster.

Finally, he'd end the one man holding them back.

Stenson set his blaster to its highest setting. A few more steps. He rounded the corner, pressing the barrel to the back of the coat. It collapsed under its own weight, having been hanging from the corner of a data tower. Stenson spun in time to catch Doug's fist wrapping around his blaster hand.

The blaster fired. Stenson lost his grip, pain shooting through his wrist. He tried a backhanded swing. Doug dodged, retaliating with a right cross to Stenson's jaw.

Everything went black.

———

Doug shook out his fist as Stenson crumpled to the floor.

"Now who hits like a sissy?"

Doug took Stenson's blaster and examined the settings, then eyed the deep burning hole in the now dead data tower. "You never did like me much, did you? Didn't think you'd stoop to this level though. You should be ashamed of yourself."

The unconscious Ranger didn't respond. Doug relieved him of his badge and com, threw on his own coat and headed for the exit. Two Marines stoically guarded the entrance, not seeing him from his hiding place.

He had no idea how to get past them, so he stayed hidden. Something would eventually come. Doug spotted a nearby holo-terminal. He crept over and activated it, initiating another search. Once he found the file, instead of scanning his own badge, he scanned Stenson's.

AUTHORIZATION ACCEPTED.

"Stenson, you dirty traitor," Doug mumbled.

Doug slipped a fob into a port and downloaded the file. Once downloaded, and the fob safely in his coat, he paused. He entered a quick command then closed down the terminal.

Boots approached. Doug slipped further out of sight.

Their mumbling voices caused him to peak around the corner. The Marines and the Rangers were grouped in front of the doorway, looking a little worse for wear. He activated his stolen com and made his way around the side of a tower to get a better listen.

"…still somewhere in the facility," one of the Marines was saying. "Shoot on sight if you see him."

"One of our own is missing," the Marshall said in his craggy voice. "He may have been taken out by the outlaw."

"Uh, Sergeant?" another Marine said. "How do we know the outlaw when we see him? No offense, but all you Rangers look alike."

"Scan his badge," the Marshall replied. "He won't have the clearance to exit the building."

The Rangers and some of the Marines marched off. Doug peeked again. Two Marines were once again left to guard the doorway. He waited several heartbeats then turned the corner and walked up to them. They immediately trained their rifles on him.

Doug threw up his hands.

"Easy, boys. Just passing through."

"Let's see your badge."

"Alright, alright. Easy now, don't shoot."

Doug kept one hand in the air as he approached and pulled back the top of his duster. One Marine stepped up and scanned the badge. It beeped and he nodded at his partner. They both lowered their rifles.

"All right, you check out. Go ahead."

The Marine opened the door. Cool, moist air blew in from outside.

Doug lowered his hands.

"Much obliged."

Doug walked confidently past them, when a voice came over his stolen com.

"All units, be advised. Outlaw is carrying a stolen badge. Repeat: Outlaw—"

Doug didn't hear the rest. He spun, stolen blaster drawn, and fired off two quick stun blasts. The Marines grunted and stumbled, their limited armor absorbing most, but not all of the blast. Doug dropped the blaster and drew the hand blasters the Marines had holstered at their sides. He pressed the barrels against their exposed sides and pulled the triggers. Both Marines crumpled to the floor and Doug dropped their weapons next to them.

"Sorry, boys," Doug said as he retrieved his blasters from the storage locker and holstered them. "I know you're just doing your job, but I need to be moving on."

He shut the door behind him and walked down the steps into a drizzling rain. He kept his pace casual so as not to arouse the suspicion of other Marines.

Another alert came across the com and Doug ducked behind a pillar. Red blaster fire sizzled the rain droplets around him. He tried his own com.

"Loni, do you read me?"

Nothing.

"Guess I got to do this the hard way…"

He studied the rate of fire of the military grade blaster bolts. At the right moment, he popped up and fired two stun blasts of his own. Direct hits. Doug charged down the walkway, reaching the two guards while they recovered, already raising their weapons. Doug dove toward one and fired, his barrel close enough to avoid the armor and hit the man's exposed side. The Marine crumpled.

Doug rolled on the wet ground, switching one of his blasters off stun. He came up on a knee and with the stun-disabled blaster, fired on the Marine's weapon, disabling it. Two swift strides and Doug was on him, firing a stun blast into the man's side.

More fire came from atop the structure and other stations around it. Doug had no intention of killing anyone if he didn't have to, so he switched the blaster back to stun.

He sprinted for the pillar he'd ducked behind before.

"Loni, do you copy? I need extraction."

Still no reply. Doug leaned out and fired off a round, temporarily disabling an approaching Marine.

The door to the facility opened. Rangers and the remaining Marines poured out, a barrage of blaster fire coming for Doug. He ducked back in time, the many shots sparking against the pillar.

"Doug," came the Marshall's voice over com. "I know you can hear me. Come out with your hands up and your guns on the ground, and no harm will come to you."

"Interesting proposition," Doug replied. "Here's my answer."

He fired blindly around the corner and was rewarded with a grunt over the com.

"That wasn't smart, Doug," the Marshall said through the cacophony of blaster fire.

"Why don't you just end this little dance of ours and declare me a full outlaw. Give your Rangers full permission to dust me."

"You know I'm not going to do that."

"Too bad, Marshall," Doug said, a fireball in the sky catching his attention, transforming into a familiar blue crescent the closer it came. "Cause the only way I'm going along with your plan is as a corpse."

Doug pulled the com from his ear, tossed it into the air and blasted it to nothing. The *Blue Moon* came in hot, five large gun emplacements trained on the group firing on Doug, who turned the focus of their blasts on the ship.

A female voice resounded over the *Blue Moon*'s external speakers, rebounding and echoing off the structure.

"Drop your weapons! Get on the ground!"

The response was an increase in blaster fire easily absorbed by the *Moon*'s shields.

The ramp lowered. Its cannons let loose a salvo, obliterating the blaster fire around them and slamming into the shields of the main complex. Doug sprinted and leapt. A searing pain burned through his leg .He landed hard on the steel ramp, writhing as the ship rose into the sky.

CHAPTER FIFTEEN_

Loni pushed the throttle forward, her other hand gripping the yoke so tight her fingers tingled. The world outside spun as she barrel rolled. Bolts from two interceptors streaked past. Arch's claws threatened to cut through the arm rests. He glanced over and saw a smile on Loni's face.

"Unbelievable. You're enjoying this," Arch said.

"This ship handles like a dream."

"Not from my perspective."

"Learn to have some fun, Arch," Loni said as she swerved.

"There's an old Ikati saying, 'If we were meant for flight, we'd have wings.'"

"I heard some do."

"Not my point!"

She barrel rolled again and Arch let out a feline yell. The horizon and ground spun in a dizzying dance, the *Blue Moon* rocketing out toward space.

"I think I'm gonna be sick…" Arch said.

"You could always man the turrets again."

"That would be worse."

They vanished into the dense clouds, Loni already planning to hit hyperspace the second they broke through the atmosphere.

But when the *Blue Moon* broke atmo, a full squadron of interceptors was waiting for them. The ships opened up. Several bolts slammed into the shields, absorbed with green flashes. Instead of dodging, Loni pushed the throttle all the way forward, pushing her and Arch into their seats. She hit the firing controls, setting off every turret on the ship. Three interceptors were blasted to vapor and several more scattered.

"Calculate for hyperspace," she said.

Arch's response was retching on the floor.

"Uck! Nevermind."

Loni moved for the calculation controls. Her whole body jerked hard against her harness. Pain ripped through her shoulder. Alarms blared and warning messages flashed in holo across the viewport.

IMPACT.

"That carrier just rammed us!" Arch said.

"Space heads probably micro-jumped to catch up. What is *wrong* with them? Do they want us dead that badly?"

"Apparently."

"Stupid commodore is going to get everyone on that carrier killed."

"Better them than us. Are we venting?"

"Doesn't look like it," Loni said. "But the shields are gone and we won't be able to jump to hyperspace until we get clear of them. No jump drive either. There's a tactical room near the engine compartment, right about in the belly of the ship. Think you can figure out the controls?"

"Yeah, I'm familiar enough with those types of systems."

"I'm going to need you on them."

"That I can do." Arch unstrapped and bounded out of the room.

"Keep them off our tail until we can get clear of the capitol ship," Loni said over the ship-wide com.

Arch slid into the tac room and jumped into a chair. He tapped several buttons on the arm rest. Control grips came online, and a full holo-display with several reticule displays appeared. Arch selected the center one, orienting the ships gun defenses there. He swept his view across the stars, honing in on the interceptors. Target locked, he pressed his thumbs to the triggers. An overwhelming barrage of high-intensity blaster fire tore through the enemy ship.

"Haha!" Arch shouted in triumph. "I love opposable thumbs!"

He caught glimpses of the carrier as they flew around it like a fly bothering a cat, numerous blaster bolts sizzling past them as the craft rolled.

"Ugh," Arch groaned, shifting his view. The ship shook with connecting blaster fire.

"Arch, what are you doing?" Loni said over the com.

"Sorry."

He switched the other guns to auto-target, letting the A.I. pick its targets, leaving him to focus on his own. Another interceptor exploded and he caught a glimpse of a third going up in flames. Loni's voice came back over the com.

"We're clear. Jumping in five, four, three, two—"

The ship shuttered against another connected shot just as the familiar pull of jumping to hyperspace engulfed them.

"Ruin my fun," he muttered, shutting down the firing program. He hopped down and padded toward the cockpit.

He just reached it when the door slid open and Loni rushed out in a panic. Arch glanced into the cockpit. The brilliant colors of hyperspace rippled by…sideways? He gave chase after Loni, following her to the crew pit and gingerly jumping down to join her.

"What's—oh!"

The smoking hole in the engine compartment told him everything. Almost everything.

"What does this mean?" Arch asked as Loni rushed around grabbing tools.

"It means we're hurtling uncontrolled through hyperspace. If I can't get these engines shut down quick we could wind up in another galaxy or out in dead space."

"How can I help?"

"Do you know anything about ship repair or hyperdrives?" She ripped a panel open, inserting a tool.

Arch's feline nose picked up the smell of perspiration wafting off her, despite the cool air of the compartment.

"Uh, not really."

"Then you can help by staying out of my way and praying."

Arch raised his paws in the air, stamping his feet, and began a caterwaul, his wail becoming louder with every stomp.

"Somewhere else!" Loni snapped.

Arch ceased his display and crossed his arms, silently mocking Loni's outburst. He hopped back up the ladder and out of the crew pit. Best he find Doug anyway.

The Ranger lay prone by the ramp. At least he was breathing.

"Lying down on the job, I see," Arch said. "Did you manage to keep your blasters this time?"

"What happened?"

"We got rammed by the carrier," Arch said, moving to examine Doug's injured leg. "Took a couple direct hits without shields and now we're flying uncontrolled through hyperspace headed for certain oblivion. No big deal."

Doug grunted as he sat up. "We need to get down to the engines and see if we can help Loni."

He struggled to his feet, his sweat-coated face a mask of pain. Arch wrinkled his nose and shook his head.

"You bi-pedals. Always think you can do more than you can.

Unless you know about ship repairs, we can't do anything to help her. She nearly tore my head off for trying. She'll have to handle it on her own. C'mon, I'll carry you to the med bay."

Doug scrunched his brow.

"I'm stronger than I look," Arch said. "I got the princess to the med bay on my own, didn't I? Now quit being all proud and get down here."

Doug slid to his rear. Arch grabbed his arm and hauled the human onto his back, grunting in surprise.

"And you say *I'm* heavy."

Arch managed to half-carry, half-drag Doug to the med bay without much strain, though he was panting by the time he got there. Doug pulled himself onto the bed. The ship bucked. Doug grabbed the sides of the bed before he was thrown back onto Arch.

"I'm gonna go check on the princess," Arch said. "You good here?"

"Yeah," Doug said, laying back. "I'll be fine."

Arch bounded down the corridor to the crew pit and poked his head into the hole. Loni knelt before the now dark and silent hyperdrive engines like some ancient worshipper pleading with her god. She gripped the engine's housing, her forehead pressed against her hands, breathing deep.

"Did you get it?" Arch asked.

Loni nodded, then stood on shaking limbs, wiping her face.

"We need to get Doug and then find out where we are."

"I already took care of the cowboy. He's in the med bay. Let's just figure out…"

He trailed off as Loni scaled the ladder and wormed her way around him, trotting toward the med bay.

"Oh sure, Arch," he said. "Nevermind me. Thanks for your help. Nevermind the strain of carrying that bi-pedal."

Arch continued grumbling all the way to his quarters.

Wriggling out of his vest, he left it there on the floor and moved to the case he took from his shop. He removed guns and tools, a box containing credit chips, and finally, a small wooden case. He opened it up and retrieved the palm-sized holo-projector inside. Thumbing it on, an image of a feline with wings on her back appeared, with another younger one beside her. They held each other, mouths open in what passed for a smile of their race.

"You never ignored me," Arch said. He sat down on the simple foam bed, memories of a time long-forgotten rushing back. "I'm sorry. I'm sorry I couldn't save you."

A tear trickled into his furred face as he thought of her, thought of all he'd lost. His life was so empty now. He couldn't say where he was going, or what he was doing selling weapons and hanging around with a couple of humans. He should be back home.

Back with them.

He turned his mind from them, to their deaths, and the holocaust that caused them. The fur on his back stood on end and his lip curled up, revealing his fangs. He closed his eyes, forcing his emotions back down.

Opening them again, at least they were still there in the image, smiling back like nothing ever happened.

"I'm sorry it took me so long," he said. "Don't worry. They're gonna pay. I'll make sure of it."

He licked the image, causing it to flicker, then closed it down, and buried himself in the covers.

CHAPTER SIXTEEN_

"At least we're still in our galaxy," Loni said, checking her instruments. "But we're pretty far into the outer edge. Not much around."

They were on the edge of the Outer Dark. Vast blackness hung outside the viewport before them. Galaxies dotted the expanse as tiny as Doug's pinky nail. The starry band that made up one arm of the galactic ring was far in the distance.

And somewhere out in the Outer Dark was the galaxy humans came from. The Milky Way, was it?

"Three hundred years," Doug mumbled.

"What's that?"

"Nothin'. Just thinking about how long it's been since humans left Earth and we still haven't found our way back."

"Earth? You mean Terra."

"No, I mean Earth. Our home planet in a solar system somewhere in the Outer Dark."

He waved his hand to indicate the endless black void beyond the viewport.

Loni rolled her eyes and went back to her instruments. "Wherever your mythical planet is, it's not here. But there is a semi-habitable planet not far from here. Looks like a rogue. Should be stable enough to set down for repairs."

"Arch told me what happened. You did good getting us out of that."

"Yeah, well, not good enough. Got your bird all banged up."

"Aw, don't be too hard on your—"

"Save it, Cowboy. Let's just touch down and see what we can do."

Doug hobbled around the co-pilot's seat and dropped into it with a grunt of pain. He stayed silent during the approach to the planet, reflecting on Loni's mood. She loved her ships. It was obvious in the passion she put forth in keeping the craft in excellent condition. Even though she was attempting to appease him, *she* chose this ship, and allowing her craft to get severely damaged must be weighing on her conscience.

Doug knew it wasn't healthy to beat yourself up over a screwup, no matter how responsible you were for it. He needed to find a way to improve her mood without antagonizing her. Maybe he could help her on not being so hard on herself for things that weren't necessarily her fault.

The rogue planet appeared as a red-brown sphere abandoned in the darkness of space. An unfrozen, semi-atmosphere encircled it. An odd feature since there was no nearby star to warm the surface. Loni angled the ship and they headed in. No turbulence. Though that could be the advanced tech on the ship compensating.

They touched down in a valley of dust surrounded by the only thing they could make out in the perpetual night—tall structures of red-brown rock. Doug considered the possibility that life may still thrive on this dead world.

Loni checked her instruments and her eyebrows rose.

"What?" Doug asked.

"Atmospheres almost breathable. Though there's too much

methane and some unidentified particles. But just the fact there's any breathable atmosphere at all is surprising. All indications say this is a dead world."

Doug peered out the viewport as if he could see the invisible properties of the air. What he did see, right at the edge of the *Blue Moon*'s landing lights, was the unmistakable remains of an enormous statue.

"You ever been to any planet on the edge of the Outer Dark?" Doug asked.

"Can't say I have. Furthest my assignments took me was the Outer Belt," Loni said.

"Funny thing about these planets and those in the Mid Dark, they're real wild space. Especially the interference cloud territory. I know a few people that have been to these worlds. Strange stuff, strange aliens."

"Everyone's an alien," Loni commented off-handedly.

"Not like this. In the Ring you get mostly humanoids, with a few species that aren't such, but still intelligent like the Ikati. There's a clear line between sentients and beasts. Out here, aliens can be truly alien. Stuff that makes your head itch, makes you question what you know about how the galaxy works, stuff the human brain can't quite comprehend."

"Are you trying to dissuade me from going out there? Cause it's not working," Loni said.

"Not at all. Just want us all to be prepared."

Loni shut everything down but life support and headed for the ramp. Doug followed with a hobble. On the way they met Arch just coming out of his room.

"We touch down?" Arch asked.

"Yeah, but we're in wild space," Doug replied. "Atmos got too much methane in it too."

Arch's ears went flat against his head and he turned back into his room.

"I'm coming anyway."

Doug peeked in from the doorway, "Thought you didn't have a suit."

"I bought one back on Terra. Once I decided to stick around, I figured I'd need it. Go ahead, I'll meet you at the ramp."

Doug caught up with Loni. She was already suited up in one of the suits that came with the ship, her under-armor having been compromised by the hunter's sniper bolt back on Terra. She was checking it for a proper seal, her singularity gun holstered at her side.

"That chambered?" he asked, taking off his gun belt.

He reached for his own suit and stumbled. Loni caught him. Doug blushed and she smirked.

"I have no idea what's out there," she said. "After what we've encountered so far, I don't trust a simple blaster rifle to do the job."

Loni helped him into his suit until he indicated he could do the rest. Doug locked his helmet into place, checking the seal when Arch arrived. He wore an orange and black suit made for his species. Loni hit a button sealing them inside the airlock and vented the chamber with the outside atmosphere.

The ramp lowered, exposing them to the dark surface, illuminated only by the *Moon*'s landing lights. The hard ground crunched beneath their feet in the still silence of the dead world. Doug watched the perimeter, not convinced it was as dead as it appeared. Arch did the same.

"You see something out there?" Doug asked over com, knowing Arch's eyesight was more suited to the darkness.

"No. But I don't like this place. Something's not right here."

Loni ignored them, leading them around and shining a light on a section of the ship where the shiny impervisteel exterior had been ripped away. A string of quiet curses came over the com.

"Whoa!" Arch said, turning away from their surroundings.

"Suddenly I'm not so afraid of what's out there. That mouth could kill a Razorhulk."

"Stow it," Loni shot back, her arms crossed in defiance to the damage.

"I'm sorry…" Arch said.

Doug and Loni both turned toward him.

"Oh, both of you go jump in a vortex," Arch grumped.

Loni turned back to the ship.

"This definitely needs to be repaired, but I can't do it here. It shouldn't prevent us from flying, but the hyperdrive… That's another story. It'll take me a few hours to diagnose and fix whatever's wrong with it."

"What about the jump drive?" Doug asked.

"We're so far out into the Outer Dark, I can't get a fix on our location. Jump drives require precise coordinates of where one is and where one is going. With nothing on the star maps to tell us where we are, we can't operate the jump drive. At least with hyperdrive we can jump a certain distance until we get close enough to pinpoint our location." She tapped some buttons on her arm console. "I'll have the *Moon* scan for any abandoned tech that might be on this world. Who knows, there may be something we can use."

Doug turned back to their surroundings still not convinced this was a safe place to be when he noticed Arch was gone. "Arch?"

"Don't shout. I have sensitive ears," Arch said, flashing a light. "I'm over here."

The light led him out to the edge of the *Blue Moon*'s landing lights. To the remains of the massive statue Arch was now inspecting. The shape was difficult to make out. Erosion had likely rounded the edges, but there was enough still there to assume it was a pair of arms reaching into the sky. What might have been a head lay on the ground, though it seemed too big for the body.

Loni came up beside him.

"Whoever lived here sure knew how to make ugly statues."

Her console beeped and her brow furrowed.

"You find something?" Doug asked.

"Maybe. Readings are inconclusive, which means there is tech about, but it's so alien from standard, the *Moon*'s A.I. is having trouble recognizing it as such. Actually, one of the readings is coming from this statue."

Arch padded forward, then backed away. "Yeah, I'm not touching that."

"Scaredy cat," Loni said with a smile, approaching the statue.

"Oh, ha-ha. Laugh it up, you—"

Loni paused and turned back to face him.

"Go ahead."

"No, uh, nevermind," Arch said.

"Something bothering you, Arch?" Doug asked.

"No. Yes. I mean… Aw, criminy. This whole place has me creeped out. Can we just get back on board and get out of here?"

"I'm not stopping you," Loni said.

"No, I mean, can you…" he degraded into mumbling.

"Oookaaay," Loni said, now inches from the statue. "Let me just see if I can find some tech in this thing and—"

Arch's head shot up.

"No, don't touch it!"

Loni's hand rested on the stone and she went rigid with a sharp breath.

"Loni? You alright?" Doug asked.

She didn't answer.

"Lon—"

The statue shifted. Stone grinding against stone vibrated the air around them. Doug hobbled up, grabbed Loni and pulled her away. Doug called to her but she was unresponsive, her eyes distant.

The assumed statue-head lifted into the air and returned to its place on the shoulders. Malformed, glowing red eyes appeared in the aged sockets. Doug hustled faster, pain shooting through his leg as Arch came over to help, lifting Loni's legs.

The stone creatures raised arms dropped, slamming against the ground with such force, it knocked the two companions off their feet. Doug scrambled up, getting his hands under Loni's arms.

The statue rose four stories high on two previously hidden legs.

Arch pulled his blaster, unfolding it to its shoulder-mounted version, and let loose a lethal volley. Doug drew his own blaster and fired while still trying to drag Loni toward the ship. The bolts sparked harmlessly against the ancient stone, leaving scorch marks but doing little else.

"We need to get back to the ship!" Arch shouted, still firing.

"Loni's out cold and our blasters ain't working against this thing. We need to think of something else or we're gonna be part of the scenery before we reach the ramp!"

"Like what?"

"Anything!"

"Oh, real helpful! I guess I should just transform into a giant hellcat and—"

The statue's foot crashed to the earth, throwing them off their feet once again.

"Aww, nine hells, forget this!" Arch said, bounding back toward the ship. "Get the princess to the ship, I'm turning the main gun on this freak of nature!"

The thing took another crashing step toward Doug and Loni. It reached down a knobby arm and Doug realized it was after her.

He grabbed Loni and yanked her out of the way just in time. The rounded end of the statue's arm hit the dirt.

The *Blue Moon*'s main gun whirred to life. A massive, blue energy bolt launched from its barrel and slammed into the statue's chest. The creature paused, as if confused. Doug took advantage of the lull to drag Loni a few more feet. They were almost at the ramp. Another bolt fired, but the statue batted it away like a fly bothering a human.

Doug cycled through options. He couldn't make it to the ship as long as that thing was stalking him and he doubted Arch's distraction would last long. His blaster didn't even dent the thing and neither was the main gun. He spied Loni's singularity gun.

Worth a shot, he mused, drawing the glinty, silver weapon. He aimed it at the monster and pulled the trigger.

Nothing. The statue raised its knobby arm. The end convulsed and cracked. With the sound of tumbling rocks, three long fingers jutted out.

Doug took Loni's hand, wrapped it around the grip and forced her finger down on the trigger.

Still nothing.

The thing reached down again, ignoring the constant fire from the ship's gun. Doug threw himself on Loni to protect her, but he was tossed aside like a rag doll. The thing picked up Loni and stalked away.

Doug pushed himself to his feet, forcing himself to follow the statue on shaky, limping legs. He ignored the alert of a tear in his suit. The atmo leak wasn't too bad. Abandoning Loni to that stone creature was out of the question. The statue continued unabated as several more shots fired. Then all the *Moon*'s gun emplacements turned and fired a relentless barrage on the statue.

And still it stalked away.

"Arch," Doug called into his com. "Forget it. The thing's

impervious. We need to follow it, see if we can somehow get Loni free.”

“I’m right behind you.”

The ship’s engines started up, lifting from the ground and rotating.

Are you kidding me? Doug thought, hurrying after the rock monster.

The *Blue Moon* floated overhead toward the fleeing creature. A green tractor-beam shot out of the open hanger bay. The creature stuttered in its steps, struggling against the power of the beam. The engines strained against the statue’s strength, the whine vibrating the air around him. The *Moon*’s thrusters fired on full burn. The statue did a motion, something akin to shrugging, and an explosion ripped through the hanger bay. The beam disappeared and the *Blue Moon* hurtled backward out of sight.

“Arch! Arch, talk to me,” Doug shouted, keeping up his pace after the creature. He hoped the Ikati didn’t crash. “Arch!”

“Woah, that was close,” Arch replied. “I almost slammed into a mountain.”

“Look, don’t try anything else.” He was getting a bit winded, reminding him of the atmo leak in his suit. He continued on regardless. “This thing is obviously more powerful than any tech we have. We’ll have to find another way to free Loni. Just bring the ship around and keep close so we can jet out of here right quick when I get her free.”

“Copy.”

The creature stopped at a large pool filled with a glowing substance of swirling blue and sea-green. With Arch hovering the *Blue Moon* just above, Doug moved around until he saw Loni. She hung limply in the thing’s featureless arms.

It raised its non-fingered hand and sprouted three more fingers, wrapping them around Loni’s helmet.

“No!” Doug shouted, dizziness overwhelming him and his

chest tightened. He was helpless to do anything as the thing ripped Loni's helmet free.

The statue waded into the middle of the pool and bent over, dropping Loni into the luminescent waters.

Doug's mind was becoming muddled, making it hard to think straight. He held onto one thought—Loni. He had to save Loni.

Doug hobbled to the pool's edge. His suited feet landed on solid stone and he found himself on the other side. He whirled, trying to understand what happened. That brought another wave of dizziness and he stumbled. He shook his head, trying to clear the fog. It hurt to breathe. He caught sight of Loni and tried to enter the pool again, only to find himself back where he started.

Loni's body sunk beneath the waters and the creature waded out, lumbering away.

"I can't get to her, Arch," Doug said, struggling to form the words. "Can you...lower the ship?"

"I'm trying, but there's something blocking the ship's movement. Some kind of energy field or something. Criminy, I can't understand these readings."

Arch's words faded into indistinct murmuring as Doug watched the placid waters of the pool, his mind too clouded to think clearly. He had to save Loni. But how?

"Please, God...don't let her die," he croaked.

Alarms in his helmet flashed and wailed, fading even as they sounded. Doug stood on the bank of the pool, his body going numb from lack of oxygen. Silence engulfed him. His legs grew weak and he collapsed to his knees.

No. Please, God, no, his muddled brain thought. *This can't happen. Not again. Please.*

His silent cries melted into despair, his will leaking out like so much vented oxygen. Doug's world faded into a sea of heartache.

Movement from the pool roused his barely open eyes. A

figure emerged. Doug forced himself back to his feet, gasping for air, his mind working to catch up with what was happening.

He tried to call Loni's name, but his lungs wouldn't work.

Blue liquid ran off her in rivulets. Her brown and gold hair hung in wet, curly locks around her tan face. Her blue eyes were a glowing blaze focused on him.

He stumbled back as she stepped onto the embankment, his legs giving out. She grabbed his helmet, keeping him on his feet. His weak arms slapped helplessly at hers. Her hands hit the release switches and yanked the helmet free. What little strength he still had disappeared and his lungs collapsed.

And then her lips were pressed to his, the liquid between.

The dam in his lungs broke and he could breathe again. Loni's eyes closed and she collapsed. Doug caught her before she hit the ground.

He stood there, dumbfounded, his mind and strength fully restored and his breathing calm and rhythmic.

"Uhhh," came Arch's voice, "what just happened?"

"I have no idea. Land the ship. I need to get Loni inside."

"Coming down."

Doug hefted Loni's limp body and carried her inside, belatedly realizing he was no longer limping. He laid her on a bed in the medical bay, and he and Arch worked to get her suit off. Though the liquid evaporated off of her suit, it still coated her skin. The vitals readout showed everything normal.

Doug scratched his head. He noted Arch fixing him with a hard, golden-eyed stare, the Ikati's lip curled up slightly.

"What?" he asked.

"Did you kiss her?"

There was a tone of anger in Arch's voice. Doug wasn't sure what to make of that. He could only assume it was Loni's honor Arch was concerned with, his species revering royalty.

"*She* kissed *me*," Doug said. "I didn't kiss her back. She was in some kind of trance. That pool did something to her. When our lips touched, I could suddenly breathe. You can relax. I wouldn't think of violating her honor. I ain't interested in her like that."

"What, she ain't good enough for you now?"

"What's your issue, Arch? Doesn't seem like it has to do with her honor as a princess."

Arch turned his head away. "It's nothing. I'm sorry. I just got concerned."

"Listen, Arch. If there's something—"

"I said it's nothing!"

"Will you two stow it?"

Loni's blue eyes were open and staring at the ceiling.

"Are you alright?" Doug asked.

"Fine," Loni said curtly, sitting up. Doug and Arch both reached out to help her but she slapped away their efforts. "I said I'm fine. Neither one of you listens very well."

"You have any idea what happened to you?" Doug asked.

Loni was silent a moment, before speaking in subdued tones. "No. All I remember is touching the rock and feeling...a presence. Next thing I know I'm waking up here. But I feel calm."

"Must have been something in that pool," Doug said.

"What pool?"

Doug opened his mouth to reply, but she held up a hand.

"No, y'know what? Nevermind. I need a shower and then I need to get working on the hyperdrive. You can tell me all about it while I work."

She shuffled off the bed and stood like she was more stable than she had ever been, her posture screamed stability and strength. She turned to Arch whose head was down. Her brow furrowed as she stared at him.

Arch looked up and he reared, eyes widening. "What?"

Loni turned away without a word and walked out of the med bay, leaving Doug and Arch to give each other curious glances.

CHAPTER SEVENTEEN_

"Something's bothering Arch," Doug said as he leaned against a wall in the engine compartment. Across from him, Loni worked, her jacket off and her hair pulled back into a ponytail. "He says nothing's wrong. But he's been acting funny, and it's elevated now, ever since Ifdil. That's what we were arguing about when you woke up."

Loni wiped her brow and took a swig of water.

"He's attracted to me," she said matter-of-factly.

Doug's brow furrowed.

"He is?"

"Well, he didn't say as much," Loni said, resuming her work. "When I woke up, I got this sense from him, like a bunch of feelings pouring off him all at once. It got harder to sift the longer I focused, and I know there was affection for me amongst everything else. But… I don't think that's all there is to it."

Loni spoke so casually about it, as if this was everyday normal stuff for her. It gave Doug a moment of pause. What in space was in that blue water?

"Is this ability something you've always had?" he asked.

"Nope."

She didn't offer any more, and Doug began to wonder…

"You ever hear of the Awareness?"

"It's something that lets you see the future, right?" Loni said.

"It's not as clear cut as that, it's somewhere between a sixth sense and clairvoyance. Someone with the Awareness can tell what's about to happen, but only a split second before. They can also sense things around them, and some can do other minor things with it like block out sound or sight. But it's all internal. You can't use it to float rocks or anything. And it only seems to occur in women. No one knows why, or what causes it. The women who have it have no common traits as far as anyone can tell. It's completely random. I'm just wondering if you gained it from that pool."

"Well, I don't have that," she said, wiping her greasy hands on a rag. "When I woke up, everything was clearer than it's ever been. The minor scars left over from the surgery were completely healed and I could sense Arch's emotions. But it's all faded now. Everything seems normal. I'm even getting tired."

"You've been at this for hours. You almost done?"

Loni tapped a button and the engine lit up with a blue glow. She smiled at Doug.

"Yup."

Doug helped her gather her tools and reassemble the housing for the engines.

Loni's expression became subdued and she said, "Don't tell Arch what I said. He'd probably prefer those feelings remain private. I shouldn't have said anything."

"I've already forgotten."

"Hey," Arch called down. "You two want to get some grub? I'm starving."

"You two go ahead. I want to get this bird back to some place familiar," Loni said. "Then I need to wash up and get this grease off me. Where was that Ticksar? The one you recommended to fix my ship, before I geared us to Eisen Ro."

"Lavtak Three," Doug replied.

"I'd like to head there if it's alright with you and get to repairing things. We'll need to pick up some parts too."

"We still got credits?"

"Some. Enough for that and a nice meal. After that we'll need to come up with some," Loni said.

"Good thing we got plenty of food stores on board. I'll call ahead and let him know we're coming. See if you can put a list together."

Doug studied Loni, thrown by how still she was.

"Doug!" Arch called down. "You coming?"

"In a minute. You go ahead," Doug said.

"Suit yourself, slo-mo."

"Something else on your mind?" Doug asked Loni.

"I also saw your memories and thoughts from the planet. I must have gained them when I kissed you."

"Uh, about that…"

Loni held up a hand and shook her head.

"I know you don't have any feelings for me. It's fine. Just, thank you for caring enough to come after me."

Doug smiled.

"Anytime."

Loni gave a sincere smile of her own and said, "I know. You're a good man, Douglas Lancer."

Doug stared at the floor, embarrassed, but also honored. The words felt good to hear.

"I do what I can," he said. "But if you don't mind my saying so, you should talk to Arch."

"I will. Just want to get in the air first."

———

Arch backed up from the wall where he'd placed the display rack. He tilted his head then jumped onto a crate for a better view. All it needed was the blaster rifle. If they touched down in the right location, he'd be set.

"Hey, Arch."

Arch twisted to look behind him.

"Hey, Princess. What do you think? Is this even?"

"Yeah. Looks good." Loni glanced around at the brackets sticking out of the wall of this particular cargo hold. "What are you doing in here?"

"Since I'm going to be hanging around you two bi-pedals for a while, I figure I might as well setup shop and make some credits. Just need to purchase the inventory, which I should be able to do with the emergency credits I snagged from my shop."

"You ask Doug about this?"

"He'll be okay with it. If he's not, tough hairballs. It's cause he brought you to my shop that I lost it in the first place. We on our way to Lavtak?"

"Should be there in half-a-day."

"Swell. So, what can I do for you? I assume you came in here to talk to me about something."

"I just wanted to thank you for trying to protect me down there."

Arch flattened his ears and rubbed a paw on his arm.

"Oh, sure thing, Princess. It was nothing."

"And I wanted to ask you what you were going to say before I touched the statue."

"Uh, I, uh…y'know, don't worry about it," he said, waving it away. "I mean, you're safe and not maimed or nothing—"

"Arch…"

Loni's gaze held him captive, and it took everything in him to turn away.

"Can we talk someplace more private?" Arch asked.

"You're not going to try anything, are you?"

"Oh, please. Pardon me while I retrieve my eyes from rolling into the next room. We're completely different species. It's not like that. Ships just tend to have ears, y'know?"

Loni shrugged. "In that case, sure, lead the way."

Arch hopped down and padded to his quarters, Loni following. He closed and locked the door, then padded over to his bedside table and activated the holo-display. The image of two cat figures with their mouths open appeared. The larger one had beige fur and a pair of wings folded on her back. The smaller one was a grayish color.

Arch sat on the bed, Loni joining him, and he placed the display in his lap.

"My wife and son. You hear of the Ikati massacre on Mao?"

Loni nodded. "It happened ten years ago. Space Pirates firebombed the planet and your people were nearly killed off. Those of you that were left were scattered to the stars. My family sent relief efforts to the Ikati once we heard."

"And we appreciated it. I personally benefitted. All native Ikati owe the Tarsek system and the royal house a debt of gratitude. The Federation sent aid too, but what we really wanted was for them to go after the Pirate scum that caused it. They made some efforts, but as far as I know nothing much came of it. Uh, I'm getting off track…

"My wife and son were caught in the initial blasts. I was working underground in a mine when the Pirates struck. I raced home through the flames as fast as I could. They were long dead by the time I got there."

He touched a paw to the image, his opposable thumb bending, revealing a hairless scar.

"I swore I'd track down the Pirates responsible and make 'em pay for what they did. Then the Armored Corps came and chased the Pirates off. Never did find out why they hit us. When the

Armored Corps sent rescue troops down, I hopped on board one of the ships and told them to go after the Pirates, but…"

"They wouldn't do it," Loni surmised.

"Oh, they wanted to. Those troopers are ready for a fight anytime any place. They were just as upset about it as I was. But Federation orders kept them from chasing the scum down. I tried to grab one of their blasters, get them fired up enough to disobey orders, but you know we Ikati don't have opposable thumbs, so all I wound up doing is making a fool of myself and drawing their sympathy.

"I had surgery done so I could go after the scum myself. I started my shop to make money and fund my efforts. I chose Tapolas in order to make some connections, find out what I could. I haven't forgotten, just got sidetracked I think with the buying and selling.

"Anyway, I was so consumed with the whole mess, I never gave much thought to romance. I didn't see many Ikati on Tapolas. Like I told you before, the few females that entered my shop were dumber than a dead slug. But when you came in with your singularity gun and your knowledge of weaponry, you really grabbed my attention. And I like your no-nonsense attitude. You're a little crazy for my liking, but I can overlook that."

Arch shook his head with a nervous laugh.

"Criminy, I ramble a lot. What was I saying? Oh, yeah, we started talking weapons, and with how we Ikati feel about royalty, and you were saying those nice things…well, I-I started to like you even more. Like, more than normal." His eyes became solidly fixed on the holo image. "But I didn't want to betray Nala. Besides, we're different species. It would never work between us. I tried to dismiss the feelings and remind myself of that stuff, but every time I look at you…"

"Is that why you tried to stop me from touching the statue?"

Arch shrugged.

"There was something I sensed from that thing. Y'know us Ikati have sixth senses. Something wasn't right with that whole planet and I wanted off that rock. But I didn't want to leave you out there, even if Doug was with you. Maybe especially cause Doug was with you. We're a very territorial species. We're a little bit beyond peeing on things to mark our territory, but a lot of the old instincts are still there. When he kissed you, ho, that really boiled my blood. It's a good thing he was holding you or I might have landed the ship on him."

Loni chuckled.

"So, yeah, I like you," Arch said, shutting down the display before placing it on the table. "No matter what I do I can't deny it. I didn't want to make it awkward for you, and I didn't want to betray Nala, so I didn't say anything. I know I need to get past that. She'd want me to be happy and not consumed with anger. She was always chiding me for that."

He sat with his paws on his legs, staring at the floor, feelings of loss flooding through him.

"I miss her."

And then he felt it, a gentle scratching behind his ears. A purr bubbled up and he closed his eyes, pleasure coursing through him. After a minute, Loni stopped and Arch opened his eyes. She was smiling, those blue eyes shining.

"I'm glad you're all right," he said.

"I'm glad I have a valiant Ikati to watch my back. And if you ever want to talk weapons, I'll be happy for the conversation."

Arch opened his maw in an Ikati smile and hopped off the bed. He bowed, one paw on his chest and the other swung out to his side.

"It's an honor to serve, your majesty."

CHAPTER EIGHTEEN_

Sergeant Ati examined the scorch marks dotting the previously polished marble floor. Several data banks had smoking holes from blaster fire and the whole place smelled of ozone. It was a complete mess.

"And you have no idea where they went?" Ati asked the Ranger standing before him.

"If I did, I'd be after that traitor myself."

"How does that work, exactly? If one leaves your organization, is he automatically labeled an outlaw?"

"Well, no."

"So why is this particular Ranger an outlaw?"

"Because he turned his back on the Rangers. Went rogue. We don't take kindly to that."

Ati nodded, though he wasn't convinced.

"Thank you, Ranger. We'll do what we can to find them."

The Ranger grumbled something about soldiers and walked away. Specs approached, his boots crunching on the debris littering the floor.

"This is a big, rotten mess, Specs," Sergeant Ati said. "A shootout between Rangers and Marines, then those same two groups combining to hunt down a Ranger that, as far as I can tell, hasn't done a thing to deserve this kind of hunt."

"Except attempt to access the same Imperial file that alerted us back on Tellus Four," Specs said.

"Attempt?"

"His access was denied. But he used another Ranger's badge to get around that."

Ati crossed his arms.

"Rangers have certain authority. Really no file from the Federation should be off-limits if he has a warrant pass. For his access to be denied, he'd either have to be truly ousted from the Rangers or there's something else at play here. Maybe both. Were you able to access the file?"

"No, boss, he sort of…"

Specs trailed off and glanced around at the Rangers and Marines still milling about. Ati got the hint. It was something Specs didn't want to say around everyone else. They started walking.

Even though their voices were inside their helmets, transmitted via a specific, unsliceable net, discretion was always the wiser course.

Ati thought about accessing the file himself. Specs knew some slicers that could do more with computers than he could, but doing so would be an act of treason. He didn't trust the Empire or the Admiralty, but he was still a soldier who respected rank. He wasn't about to go traitor, not to the Federation at least.

"What were you saying," he asked Specs over com.

"He deleted the file."

Ati opened his mouth to reply when his com chimed. Captain Dekler. He answered.

"Go for Ati."

"What's your status, Sergeant?" Captain Dekler said.

"We're on the surface and have just wrapped up investigation of the events that transpired, sir."

"Very good. Rendezvous on the *Dominator* and prepare for debrief. I need to be caught up to speed."

"Yes, sir."

"Dekler out."

Ati turned to Specs.

"Captain's back. Wants a debrief."

"Think he'll tell us to call it off?"

"Hard to say. If we present it right, he'll give us the okay." Sergeant Ati keyed in the squad com and said, "All units report to drop zone. We're heading back."

"Captain back?" Came Q's voice.

"Are you listening in on my transmissions, trooper?"

"No way, boss. Just noticed the incoming shuttle, tapped into their flight logs—"

"Alright, fine. Yes. Captain's back. Have you and Bot finished checking the perimeter?"

"Yeah. Nothing but blaster marks. What happened here?"

"I'll explain it all in debrief. Ati out."

———

Ati pressed the chime button and a voice bid him enter. He marched into the office with Specs trailing behind. They stopped in front of the desk and saluted the officer seated behind it, their bodies rigid with attention.

"Ati and Gennart of Titan Squad, reporting as ordered, sir," Ati said.

"At ease, Sergeant," Captain Dekler said, giving his own crisp salute. "Let's hear what you've found."

"Sir, Titan Squad, currently stationed on Tellus Four, responded to an MCS from a restricted Imperial file being accessed at a terminal in an engineering school on said planet. We responded in standard protocol and cleared the building before opening fire on the slicers. The suspects fled. We pursued and cornered them to find a Galactic Ranger and an Ikati. The Ikati's ship attacked from the rear and the Ranger fired an unstable blast from a damaged blaster in order to disable our gear long enough for both of them to escape.

"We were subsequently ordered by Admiral Traik to patrol and keep eyes out for the Ranger. In light of those orders, we began a search. When the MCS triggered a second time, we rendezvoused with the *Dominator* which was en route to this location. Our investigation revealed the Ranger was trying to access the same file here. He was also being hunted by his fellow Rangers and the Marines stationed here. There are no leads as to his current whereabouts."

The Captain nodded thoughtfully.

"What is your assessment of the situation, Sergeant?"

"Sir, I believe this Ranger to be hunting some secret the Empire doesn't want getting out. I believe his fellow Rangers have turned on him because he refused to fold into the Empire. He needs to be hunted down in order to find out what he knows, per Admiral Traik's orders."

"A fine assessment and a correct one. As you know, the upper brass are having all captains trained in new Imperial standards. I will be here on the *Dominator* training and thus cannot oversee your operation. I am placing sole leadership of the squad in your hands, Sergeant."

"Sir, all due respect, we need you on this mission," Ati said.

"I agree, but the Empire needs me here and this will be advantageous for all of Titan Squad," Dekler said. "I have to report to my superiors what my subordinates report to me if I am not there to witness for myself, especially in this matter."

"Yes, sir."

"Follow Admiral Traik's orders. Find this Ranger. Find out what he knows. Report relevant information back to me. I'll grant access to anything you need from the *Dominator*. Work in the best interests of the Federation."

"Do you mean the Empire, sir?"

"Yes, the Empire. Still getting used to the term. Very good, Sergeant. You'll do well in my absence. Dismissed."

Ati and Specs saluted. Captain Dekler saluted back and the two exited the room. Once in the hall, Specs gave Ati a sly smile. The Captain's words clicked for Ati then and he smiled too.

"We'll need a transport and a pilot," Ati said as they walked down the hall. "But I can't say I trust anyone on the *Dominator*."

"Bot's a pilot."

"That's right, I tend to forget that. Did you find anything more on the Interceptor squad?"

"Yeah," Specs said. "I didn't even have to be secretive. Lieutenant Colonel Loni Taraska. Best fighter pilot on the *Dominator*. Heir to the royal house of the Tarsek system and leader of the now spaced Spearhead Squad. She's been labeled a fugitive and extremely dangerous. Infected with White Scars. Shoot on sight."

"Like the rest of her squad. If she was infected with White Scars, I doubt she'd be running. At any rate, she wouldn't have survived this long. The Ranger definitely has her and an Ikati helping him. Any word on him?"

"Lieutenant Taraska was spotted by a squad of troopers on Tapolas and was attempted to be apprehended. The shop they were pinned in exploded and they escaped. The shop was supposedly owned by an Ikati arms dealer named Ar-Chitak, a survivor of the Ikati massacre on Mao."

"Well, that explains his hostility."

They reached the training room, coming out on a short balcony overlooking the converted cargo hold. When the squad left the surface with no action, the troopers were so wired, they needed to burn off their energy.

Drawl lead the team through a maze of walls. Ati put on his helmet and tuned in to their frequency.

Silence.

Drawl held up a fist, halting the troopers behind him. He spread his fingers and they fanned out. Each carried a CS-41 short-form blaster rifle made for close quarters combat. All except Tolso, their explosives expert, who wielded a training SAB.

Ati was pleased with their exercise so far. Drawl didn't have a higher rank than anyone else, but he'd been on the team the longest and they respected him. In contrast, Bot was relatively new, though had already proven to be a focused soldier through and through. Ati honed in on Q, the non-stop questioner that was a little short to be an Armored Corps Trooper, but he meshed well with the others.

Holo-images of targets appeared and were subsequently cut down by the members of Titan Squad. A tagged holo-image Bot took out reappeared from behind, taking the trooper by surprise. It tagged Bot on the side before being taken out by Q. Q pointed to Bot's simulated wound. Bot's pause in movement was enough for Ati to know the trooper was checking the visor readouts. After a moment, Bot gave Q the thumbs up and they proceeded forward.

They were nearing their target, a holo-image of a Blarsek strapped to a chair behind two sets of walls. Drawl, alongside Tolso, made their way down the center isle toward the target. As they approached a large, open area before the first wall, a group of ten men with blasters appeared. The troopers didn't hesitate, opening up on the group and picking off targets in controlled, precise actions.

No sooner had the shots started, Bot and Q emerged from a passageway on the left. Waters, their sniper, and Vid, who spent more time playing holo-games than anything else, approached from the right. With the pincer attack, the assailants were cut down in short order. Only minor simulated impacts to the troopers' armored suits was registered.

Sergeant Ati was again pleased. It might be like pulling teeth to get Vid off his bum during off-time, but when it came to combat, he was right up there with Bot for focus and reaction time.

They proceeded to the door, taking breach positions. Tolso pulled a flashing orb from his belt, meant to simulate a fragger. Drawl counted down on his fingers, then kicked the door open. Tolso tossed in the fragger. Before it went off, Bot was already moving, charging in and taking out targets. The rest filed in, lending their fire to clearing the room.

Once the room was secure, they charged the second room, taking out two guards. Drawl put a disc on the floor beneath the image of the Blarsek while the others took up watch positions. A countdown appeared above the Blarsek's head. When it reached zero, the image vanished.

"Mission complete," a feminine voice announced.

The troopers relaxed.

Drawl removed his helmet, addressing Bot.

"You gotta stop charging in like that," he said in that New Texas accent that granted him his nickname. "Could have walked right into a blast zone. That fragger was meant to clear the room. You wait for it to detonate, *then* rush. Don't be in such a hurry. Haste makes a waste of your skull. Understand?"

He poked Bot's helmet for emphasis. Bot's head bobbed an affirmative.

"Okay," Drawl continued. "Let's reset and run through another one."

"Maybe later," Ati called from the balcony. "Right now, we have a Ranger, a rogue featherhead, and a sapient cat to hunt down. Bot, get us a transport you're comfortable flying that's large enough to stow some gear. Tolso, you're on weapons detail. We've been cleared to acquire any ordinances and supplies we need. Everyone else, gather supplies. Please note, Vid, I said *need* and not *want*."

"Spoiling my fun, boss," Vid complained.

"I want sharp eyes on this op, troopers. This is a Galactic Ranger we're talking about. He may be friendly, but we need to be in control of the situation. Understood?"

"Hooah!"

"Where are we headed, boss?" Q asked.

"Grandus."

CHAPTER NINETEEN_

Redneb tsked as he moved over the torn section of the *Blue Moon*. The Ticksar's four, extra-long limbs propelled him more agilely than any human could manage. Loni's nerves frayed, watching him swing around, afraid he was going to fall off. It wasn't *that* far off the ground, but enough to potentially break a limb. It grated on her nerves so badly she forgot about the intense heat beating down on her from the twin suns overhead.

"Hum, ubub jib," Redneb said, poking a hairy hand inside the workings. He turned his attention to Doug and Loni. "Cu dub hub a drub?"

"He wants to know if the hyperdrive was damaged," Doug translated.

"Yes, but it's been repaired," Loni called back.

"Hum, yub," Redneb muttered, and swung underneath with one arm.

Loni tensed. She nearly had a heart attack when he let go and flipped in the air, landing on the ground before them in a cloud of dust.

"Yub. Hudle drub."

"He says he can fix it," Doug said. Redneb continued to

jabber on in his native tongue while Doug translated. "He would like to examine the hyperdrive. He can also supply spare parts for it. The price for the parts and the labor…Ubjer?"

"Club du."

Doug grimaced.

"What?" Loni asked, tugging on the loose shirt she wore and fanning herself, remembering the heat now that the Ticksar no longer swung about over their heads.

"Wub a kloo?" Doug asked.

"Ubi jub."

"It'll cost ten-thousand credits. I asked him why so high, apparently because it's a new model, especially the chassis, the parts are expensive."

"You sure he's not scamming us?" Loni asked, eyeing Redneb.

"Ubi! Hobi—"

"Can you speak Basic?" Loni shot at him. "Like, at all? You can obviously understand it."

Redneb's dust-colored face reddened. He spoke slowly, "Usa hardu meu talka busic."

"It's fine, Red," Doug said. "Order the parts. Don't worry about the hyperdrive. That's good to go."

"Hum jub." Redneb loped off.

"That's more than we have," Loni said once Redneb had gone.

"We'll have to see if we can find a bounty to haul in. I'll check the bounty net for anything local."

Doug noticed Arch standing on two legs at the base of the *Blue Moon*'s ramp. A human clad in leather approached, pushing a large crate of repulsors. Arch greeted the man, though they were too far away to hear their exchange, and they walked on board the ship, the crate in tow. The scene seemed odd to Doug, but he dismissed it, not wanting to pry into Arch's personal business. He checked his feed.

"Anything?" Loni asked after a minute.

"Nothin' local. And Red doesn't allow payments. Normally he wouldn't even order the parts until he received payment. He makes an exception for me 'cause he knows I'll pay. Let's head into town. There's a temporary work place we can check out."

They retrieved water canteens from the *Moon*, and Arch declared he would not be joining them. Doug preferred that someone remain with the ship anyway.

The walk to Jindar took a couple hours. By the time they reached it, they'd sweated through most of their clothing. It wasn't a rich area, but neither was it poor. The town had a 'scavenger town' feel to Loni. The kind of place you could probably find aftermarket versions of just about anything for the right price.

Doug led her to a booth made of the red, sandy stone native to the planet. A large Uglug stood behind the counter, sorting through data on a fritzy holo-display.

"Begging your pardon," Doug said.

The Uglug didn't look at him as it tapped away at an analog keyboard large enough for its beefy hands.

"Yeah? Waddaya want?"

"Work."

"No more worka for today," he said, waving Doug off. "Come backa tomorrow."

"Unfortunately, that's not an option," Doug countered. "We really need the work today. If you could just look in your database—"

The Uglug slammed a beefy fist onto the counter, causing the holo-screen to fritz.

"I saida…"He trailed off as he took in Doug's appearance. "A Ranger?"

Doug nodded.

The Uglug shrank slightly, his hands nervously fiddling with the counter.

"Looka. I do nothinga. I cleana now. You no hunta me no more!"

"Relax," Doug said, holding up his hands. "We just want some work."

"Justa worka?" The Uglug's large, round eyes darted between Loni and Doug. "Why you wanta worka? Rangers hunta baddies."

"Just need some extra credits to fix our ship."

The Uglug scratched his blue-beige arm, obviously not sure this wasn't some kind of trap.

"I really don'ta have any more worka for today. You have to go to Cantina Dusta Bucketa. They sometimes have worka or extra bounties nota ona bounty neta. Downa thata streeta. Take a righta ata the wapma shopa. You'll see ita."

"Much obliged," Doug said, moving on.

"You think he's guilty of something?" Loni asked when they were out of earshot.

"Maybe. More likely he was before and has since gone straight. But lawmen still make him nervous."

They found the cantina, a building situated half in the ground. The cool air washed over them as they entered. Loni sighed in relief to be out of the oppressing heat. They made their way past the few patrons to a man behind the bar. He leaned against it, preoccupied with a datapad.

"Howdy," Doug said.

The man set his datapad down. "Afternoon, folks. What can I get for you?"

"Looking for some work," Doug replied. "The Uglug at the employment booth said we could find some here, maybe some local bounties."

"Well, I'm afraid there's not much right now, Ranger. But

requests come in throughout the day. If you want to have a seat, I'll let you know when something comes in."

"Much obliged," Doug said and moved to a nearby booth.

Loni was just thankful to sit down.

A blue-skinned Hassa came over with two drinks on a tray, not bothering to look up when she set them on the table.

"Compliments of the house. Bill says to pass on his thanks to the Rangers."

"Tell him it's much appreciated," Doug said.

The Hassa raised her head, her eyes growing wide.

"Douglas? Douglas Lancer?"

She threw herself at him, Loni having to dodge the flying tray. She kissed him full on the lips. The sweet scent of spring flowers surrounded him at her closeness. The tenderness, her warmth—it reminded him of another woman from many years ago. She'd been a wave of calm delight. The Hassa pulled back and Doug mentally shook himself.

It couldn't be... Recognition flashed across Doug's confused face.

"Arta?" he asked.

"Yes!" She smiled wide, her braided tendrils swaying with her head bob. "You remember me."

"Well, yeah, but..."

"I'm not red anymore, I know. I turned forty-two last cycle."

"Oh, right. I forgot that's something that happens at that age. It suits you nice."

Her skin gave off a slight glow. "Thanks."

Arta noticed Loni and her skin returned to normal. Her smile dropped and her hands went to her hips, though she remained perched in Doug's lap.

"And who is this?"

"Oh, uh..." Doug was suddenly all too conscious of Arta's closeness and Loni's curious stare. "This is Loni. Loni, Arta."

Loni smiled and waved.

Arta focused on Doug, her face somewhere between angry and pouty.

"Is she your girlfriend?"

"No, no. She's my partner."

Arta reared, blue hands covering her chest. "Your partner?"

"Not *that* kind of partner, a business partner. She's my pilot. She helps me track down and capture bounties."

"Oh, well, I guess that's okay." Arta eyed Loni. "What are you doing on Lavtak? Did you come all this way to see me?"

Doug smirked. "I'm afraid not, Arta. I didn't even know you were here. Last I saw you were back on Drisdil."

"There were too many people there that knew me as—" she gave a quick glance at Loni, "—as what I did before you rescued me. I had to find work somewhere else. I caught a transport as far away as I could get. I wound up here and now I work waiting tables. It's not glamorous, but it's clean and I make enough to survive and even have a little spending money left over. You know it's just me, and cost of living here is low, so my expenses aren't high." She shrugged. "It's a life. But it can get lonely sometimes."

The last bit she added with a flutter of her eyes. Loni's eyebrows went up and she looked at Doug as if to say, "Seriously?"

Doug's legs were starting to go numb from the pressure. He cleared his throat. "Yeah, well, I'm sorry to hear that, Arta. But we're in the middle of a pretty big job, honest. We just stopped off here to make some repairs and a few extra credits."

"Oh! Did you come here to find work? You should have said so in the first place. There's this Tarbadan two doors down from me that keeps harassing me, trying to offer me stins. I've looked him up on the Bounty Net. There's a bounty out for him for dealing stins, but it's not very high and it's not on the regular channels. The only bounty hunters that come in here aren't inter-ested because the hassle of dealing with a Tarbadan isn't worth the reward. But you could take care of him, Doug. I know you could."

"A Tarbadan is nothing to mess with, but yeah, of course I'll help."

"Great," Arta exclaimed, maneuvering off him. "I'll let Bill know and then we can leave."

She trotted over to the bar, a spring in her step and leaned against it, talking with the bartender, one leg in the air.

Loni crossed her arms, eyebrows raised, trying very hard not to smile.

"Arta was in a less than honorable profession when I met her," Doug said. "I saved her from some low-life trying to force her into a speeder, then convinced her to leave her profession and got her a decent job delivering supplies. She's had a kind of thing for me ever since."

"*Kind* of thing? Oh, it's a *thing*, Douglas."

Loni scrunched up her face and shook her hands in mock imitation of the Hassa. Doug grimaced.

Arta trotted back over.

"All set." She bounced on her feet, hand-bag slung over her shoulder.

"I don't need you to come with me, Arta. Wouldn't want you to get hurt."

"Nonsense. You need me to show you where it is. The streets are confusing where I live. Besides, I wouldn't miss a chance for you to show off those Ranger skills of yours."

She winked at him and Loni rolled her eyes.

"All right," Doug said. "Lead the way."

———

A half-hour later, they were walking down a winding series of streets. Arta in her tight, brown leather pants and halter top leading the way, her calf-length, braided tendrils swaying behind her.

Loni mused what biological purpose the tendrils served. She reflected on all the species she'd come across since meeting Doug. She'd only met a few species during her time in the Federation and was a little shell shocked at the diversity there was in the galaxy, and even by how well Doug seemed to know each. She wondered what this Tarbadan was that it would give Doug concern.

Can't be worse than Drexx.

She shivered at the thought of the creature eyeing her with that hungry glare.

Arta stopped halfway down a quiet street and pointed at a door set into a series of connected hovels sunk half-way into the ground.

"That's Utcha's place," she said. "He doesn't usually go out so he should be home."

"All right," Doug said, handing his blasters to the two women. "You two stay here. Hide behind that crate. If he gets past me and comes after you, shoot him. Otherwise, don't fire and keep your heads down."

"You're going in unarmed?" Loni asked.

"A Ranger doesn't shoot an unarmed sentient, and Tarbadans don't believe in using weapons. They don't much need them anyway. Their neural systems are such that stun blasts have no effect. So if you shoot, make sure you're using a lethal setting and aim for the torso."

Doug took off his duster and hat and set them on the crate. Loni and Arta ducked behind the crate as Doug walked up to the door.

"He's so brave, isn't he?" Arta said.

Or stupid, Loni thought.

Doug banged on the metal door with his fist.

"Galactic Ranger! Open up!"

An indistinct baritone voice came from inside. Doug pulled the badge from his shirt and held it over the lock panel just to the right of the door. He kept it there until the door slid open. Doug replaced his badge and walked inside.

Loni steadied the blaster on the crate, aiming at the empty doorway. She'd brought her singularity gun, but didn't want to waste the shells if she didn't have to.

Doug came flying back out the door. He landed in the dirt and rolled a couple of times before getting to his feet. An eight-foot tall bi-pedal squeezed through the doorway. Its arms, legs and elongated torso rippled with muscles, its ape-like head glaring death at the Ranger.

It blurted out some phrase in its native tongue and took a swing at Doug.

Doug dodged, the thing's fist swiping air. It swung again and Doug barely got out of the way in time. The Tarbadan's fist hit the dirt and the ground beneath Loni vibrated slightly. Loni's eyes widened. One hit and Doug's insides would be jelly.

The Tarbadan shouted in pain, gripping his hand.

"Now, see," Doug said, keeping his distance, "you shouldn't go messing with a Ranger. You wind up just doing yourself more harm than good. Why don't you come along quietly now. I won't even add the charges of resisting arrest and assaulting a Ranger."

The Tarbadan shouted something in its alien tongue and charged. Doug was a hair too slow, and the hulking alien pinned him against a wall. Despite being crushed by the alien's strength, Doug managed a couple good swings striking it in its throat.

It backed off, holding its neck. Doug rammed an elbow into its hip. The Tarbadan's eyes widened and it stumbled away, gasping for air. Doug threw a roundhouse at its side. The thing barely moved and Doug grimaced, bouncing on one foot. The Tarbadan, however, fell to one knee, its good hand moving to its side, its face writhing in pain.

Doug hobbled up to it, breathing heavy and said, "Now, Utcha, is it? You're under arrest for—"

The thing's hand shot out and engulfed Doug's head, clamping down on his skull. It rose to its feet, Doug taking blind swings at its arm.

Something caught its eye and it turned a scowl toward the two women. It tossed Doug behind it and took a step toward them. Loni's finger moved to the trigger. The Tarbadan swung its fist, bringing Doug back into view holding onto its thick wrist. The Tarbadan turned toward the extra weightj ust in time to receive a kick from Doug's boot.

There was a wet *CRUNCH* and the alien cried out.

Doug dropped to the ground and kneed it in its spine. It tumbled to its knees and Doug leapt onto its back, throwing an arm around its neck. The creature's eyes bulged, its mouth opening in a vain attempt to draw breath. Its good hand tried to pry Doug's arm off, but its thick fingers couldn't get a grip. It slapped uselessly at the Ranger, unable to reach him. It tumbled sideways onto Doug, convulsing. Its eyes bulged larger before rolling back in its head and its body went limp, mouth hanging open.

Loni and Arta rushed over and pushed the large alien off Doug. He gasped for air as soon as he was free. He was a disheveled mess, dirt smattering his clothes. He winced getting to his feet, touching his back.

Arta threw herself at Doug, kissing him. He winced again, moving the Hassa off him.

"Are you alright?" Loni asked.

"Fine," Doug said, though he seemed anything but. "Though my back and skull might disagree with me."

"I can't believe you took that thing on. And Arch calls *me* crazy."

"Shouldn't have been so bad, but he must be on stins. That stuff'll make anyone twice as strong as they are and Tarbadans are already a tough species to fight."

Arta cupped his face in her hands. "You were so brave. I'm so glad you're safe. I thought for sure he was going to paste you."

"All right, Arta," Doug said, moving her hands off him. "Just help me roll him onto his stomach so I can cuff him."

―――――

"So, possessing and selling stins, assault on a Ranger, resisting arrest," said the insectoid behind the counter, tapping away at a datapad. "Anything else?"

"How about attempted murder?" Loni chimed in.

Doug nodded. It continued to tap its datapad as a Razorhulk appeared from a back room, its massive, fur-covered body dwarfing the Tarbadan. Doug removed the cuffs and the Razorhulk carried the prisoner away. The insectoid finished its tapping and ejected a credit chip from its datapad.

"Your reward is nine-hundred credits. Thank you for your service."

"Much obliged," Doug said, pocketing the chip.

They walked out of the bounty station into the arid weather. The suns were setting and the evening was already cooling off.

"Will that be enough?" Doug asked Loni.

"Barely," Loni replied. "We should try and find another bounty once we're in the air."

"You're not leaving already, are you?" Arta asked with a worried frown.

"Parts won't be in until tomorrow at the earliest," Doug explained, "so we'll be here for another day at least."

"And then you'll leave?"

She sounded to Loni like a child losing a puppy.

"Yeah," Doug said, not unkindly. "Like I said before, we're wrapped up in a pretty big situation. Don't know what kind of time table we have, but the galaxy isn't going to wait around for us."

"Can I at least walk you back to your ship?"

"It's a long way, Arta. We're over by Redneb's shop."

"Redneb? You mean that junker that lives out past the outskirts? That's at least a two-hour walk! You'll never get there before nightfall and you'll be half-frozen by the time you reach it. Come stay at my place for the night."

"Now don't fuss over us. We can always—"

"Nonsense! Don't be a fool, Douglas Lancer. You're both coming home with me and that's final."

She turned on her heels, her tendril braids swaying with her walk. Loni was again trying hard not to smile as she followed a chagrined Doug down the street.

———

Arta's door swished open and she set her bag by the door. In the short time it took to reach her home, the temperature had dropped significantly. Loni was glad the Hassa had been so insistent.

Ambient light illuminated the modest space and the attached kitchen. Colorful furnishings and glimmering decorations contrasted the dull, red landscape outside. Three large, colorful spheres occupied the center of the room surrounding a table with a holo-projector. Loni wondered at their purpose, especially the one that was more of a sideways oval.

"Make yourselves comfortable and I'll get dinner started."

"Now, Arta—" Doug said.

Arta spun, pointing a finger.

"Don't you dare say a word of objection, Douglas Lancer!" Her eyes were wet with tears. "You've saved my life and gotten me out of two horrible situations. I can never repay you, but I'll be spaced if I let you leave my home without at least serving you a decent home cooked meal!"

"All right," Doug said, holding up plaintive hands. "I'm sorry. I'd be much obliged for the meal."

Arta wiped her eyes.

"Good. Now sit."

Doug glanced at the sphere behind him. "How do I—"

Arta pushed him and he stumbled backwards into the sphere. It bulged, reshaping around him much like a plush armchair. Doug looked confused, but didn't attempt to get up. Arta nodded curtly and headed to a back room.

"You sure have a way with women," Loni said, sinking herself into the other sphere. The material was soft and warm, relaxing her muscles. "Wow. I need to get one of these."

"Arta's just appreciative. It's nice to receive that once in a while, but she's confusing it with affection."

"Affection? You mean love."

"No. I mean affection. Once we're gone, she'll be all right."

"I don't know, she seems to have it for you bad."

"You don't know Arta."

"I don't think you do either. What are you going to do if—"

Arta appeared out of the back hall, now dressed in a simple cotton shirt and loose, pink pants. "Do you like spicy or bland?"

"Spicy for me," Loni said. "I don't know what Cowboy likes."

"Spicy's fine." Doug's com beeped, and he answered it. "Hey, Arch."

"You two coming back to the ship? Temperature's dropping pretty rapidly out there."

"We're staying with a friend for the night. Go ahead and lock up. We'll see you in the morning."

"Can do," Arch replied.

"Can I give you a hand in the kitchen?" Loni asked, attempting to rise but couldn't get her feet under her.

"Punch the sides," Arta said.

Loni did so and she shot to her feet.

"Woah! That's fun."

Arta smiled and the two ladies went into the kitchen.

"What's it like being a pilot?" Arta asked, pulling out what Loni guessed to be fruits and vegetables. "Do you get to pilot large ships and fire off their guns at Pirates?"

"Nothing so grand. I was a fighter pilot for the Federation until they turned Empire."

"I heard about that on the holo-news," Arta said, handing Loni a tool and a strange vegetable. "Does that mean they're taking over the galaxy?"

Loni struggled with the tool. "From what Doug and I have discovered, it seems to be heading that way."

Arta corrected her grip, demonstrating how it was used. She went back to her own vegetable, biting her lip. Her next words came out quiet.

"Do you like him?"

Loni put a hand on her arm and Arta tentatively raised her eyes.

"No, he's all yours if you want him."

Arta smiled at that. She scooped her disassembled vegetable into a pan with a red slime and it began to sizzle.

"What's it like in the Federation, er, Empire? We're so remote here, we don't see much of them beyond the occasional Armored Trooper patrol."

Arta grabbed a small cylindrical container, sprinkling a yellow powder over the simmering pieces.

"Honestly, it's surprisingly human-centric. Being outside of it has given me a clue as to how many species there are in the galaxy," Loni said, shifting her chunks over for Arta to include in the dish. "I've never even heard of a Tarbadan, Uglug, or Hassa. And you change color at a certain age? I've never heard of a sentient species with that trait."

"We actually change color three times. Females are born black and males are green. At around twenty-two females change to red and males to blue. Blue is the ideal color for a Hassa and Hatchul."

"Hatchul?"

"Oh, that's what the males are called, named so after our homeworld. But females don't turn blue until forty-two. Males just slowly shade to a deeper blue as they age. And at sixty-five females become white. And if a Hassa lives beyond a hundred and thirty cycles, they change a fourth time to silver, which I think is beautiful."

"Then, that makes you, what, twenty in human cycles?"

Arta paused, sticking the stir stick in her mouth and glancing up at the ceiling.

"I did the calculations once. I think it's like for every cycle a Hassa ages, a Human ages one-point-six-two-five times."

Loni mentally worked out the calculations and said, "You're about twenty-five point-eight?"

Arta laughed, her voice echoing as if several voices layered on top of the other.

"I've never thought of my age in decimals before," she said, her voice back to normal. "But, yes, that's about right."

"That's good. I don't know how old Doug is, but he looks like he's about thirty."

Arta smiled, her skin glowing slightly.

They continued to talk through the meal preparations and separated it into three bowls. Arta carried Doug's only to find him snoring softly in his sphere. Arta and Loni giggled at each other.

"Poor guy. He's had a rough day," Loni said.

Arta set the bowls aside and grabbed a blanket, covering him up.

"I would like to be special to him. Do you think Doug…" She bit her lip and her skin glowed again, a little softer than last time.

Loni wanted to encourage Arta, but she wasn't sure about Doug's feelings. He was rather reluctant to accept Arta's affections.

"Arta, I think—"

Arta held up a hand, shaking her head and making her tendrils quiver.

"I know it's wishful thinking. He deserves someone better. Someone who isn't…trash." She hung her head, her body shifting uncomfortably.

"You are *not* trash. Don't ever think of yourself that way," Loni said. "And don't let anyone else make you think that way either."

Arta pressed a series of spots on her right shoulder. The blue skin disappeared, revealing an arm of shimmering, metal plates. Arta couldn't bring herself to meet Loni's eyes.

"It's a birth defect. No Hatchul wants a Hassa with only one arm. Though they didn't mind gawking at the rest of my body. That's how I wound up in that profession. Going from trash to filth…"

Arta's smile returned. "Then Doug came along and rescued me, encouraged me that I didn't have to live that kind of life. And when I explained about my arm, he bought me this, said I didn't need it, that I could do anything I wanted. I just needed to trust that I could and do my best.

"No one's ever been so kind to me. I knew right then and there he was a good man. And I've never met a man like him since. He really cares and he's doing his best to do the right thing. I really admire that about him."

She touched her arm, restoring the mirage.

"Arta, I know that voice inside that tells you you're not good enough, that you'll never make it. That's partly why I became a fighter pilot, to prove that I could and silence that voice. It's still there, but I've learned not to listen to it."

Loni smiled when a bit of hope filled Arta's eyes.

"Doug was right. If you're really going to listen to his advice, it applies equally to him. If there's something on your heart, you go for it. Don't let anyone tell you you're not good enough, especially yourself."

Arta smiled and threw her arms around Loni. They moved to the oval sphere and settled into it, chatting as they ate their meal.

CHAPTER TWENTY_

Was it her or was it twice as hot out as the day before? Loni gulped down the last of her water. The *Blue Moon* was a shimmering blue crescent three kilometers away towering above a squat, red building. She wished they'd had enough credits to rent a speeder. Arta offered her another water-boulb and she gratefully accepted.

When they reached the ship, cool air washed over them in the shade of its massive form. Doug eyed several speeders parked nearby. He guzzled down the last of his water, focusing on a couple of human males examining a pair of blaster rifles.

"When did you get this ship?" Arta asked, taking in the *Blue Moon*'s shiny exterior.

"Just recently. You want the tour?"

Arta perked up.

"Really?"

Doug glanced at Redneb applying the hull-plating to the damaged section. That would take some time.

"Sure, why not."

Arta smiled and took Doug's arm, a spring in her step as they walked toward the ramp. Loni followed, moving off to her quarters once inside.

Doug walked Arta through the ship as much to show her the different areas as to learn them himself. He couldn't quite place the expression on her face. Something like satisfaction. They crossed a hall and Doug overheard Arch making comments amongst several other voices.

Doug separated himself from Arta and strode forward. The noise brought him to one of the cargo holds, and a large group of people milling about, some human, others not. They were examining weapons mounted on the walls, or turning others over in their hands. Arch was talking with a couple, the human male shouldering a heavy repeating blaster. The female, a Sersec, held a sniper rifle in her transparent tentacles, looking down its scope.

"…blast the wings off a flea from a kilometer away," Arch was saying. "Only nine-thousand, seven-hundred credits. That's a steal for a rifle of that quality."

Doug marched up to Arch. "Can I talk to you in private?"

"In a minute, Doug." Arch waved him off. "Since you already bought the Delter, I'll even knock it down to an even nine-thousand."

"*Now*, Arch."

Arch turned to Doug and bared his teeth, before turning back to the couple. "Please, take your time to consider and check out all the features. I'll just be a moment."

He padded after Doug out into the hall.

"What is the matter with you?" Arch quietly hissed. "I'm trying to make a sale here."

"Why are you trying to make a sale in the first place?"

"Hey, I gotta make a living, Cowboy."

"No one ever said anything about setting up shop on my ship. You didn't ask permission."

Arch crossed his arms over his chest.

"Yeah, well, nobody decided to warn me you were bringing a fugitive into my shop back on Tapolas. I lost one-hundred percent of my inventory because of you and her royal highness. You owe me for that. The least you can do is donate a cargo hold and allow me to operate out of it. You won't miss it. Besides, I sealed off the rest of the ship so no one can go wandering. And I keep a dampening field on, so no blaster fire on board."

Doug wanted to say more, but he had no argument. Arch was right. He did owe him and it wouldn't hurt to have him run his shop out of his cargo hold.

"All right," Doug said grudgingly. "Just keep a tight lid on things."

"Aw, keep your shirt on. I've been doing this for ten years. I know what I'm doing." He glanced at Arta who was trying to remain invisible. "Who's this?"

"Arta. She's an old friend, the one who housed us for the night."

Arta gave a wave.

"Nice to meet you," Arch said. "Now, if you'll excuse me." He trotted off without waiting for Doug to answer.

"You okay?" Arta asked, her face a mask of concern.

"Yeah, I'll be fine. Just between him and Loni, people think they can do whatever they want with my ship."

She smiled.

"What?"

"I just think it's honorable of you." She slipped her arm into his. "You kept your cool, mostly, and admitted when you were wrong. It's a very admirable trait, Douglas Lancer."

There it was again, that affection in her voice. Maybe Loni was right and Arta really did care for him beyond simple gratitude. As he took her in, he did find her attractive.

Fear rose in him.

"You going to show me the rest of the ship?" Arta asked.

"Yeah, sure," Doug replied as he led her away.

———

Hours later, the four of them sat in the lounge, the image of the super weapon floating above the table.

Arta's mouth hung open.

"I can't…I can't believe anyone could do this."

"I know," Doug said. "It's pretty serious."

"No, I mean, I can't understand how it would be possible," Arta said. "Isn't the Federation ruled by a council of Admirals? For something like this, I'd think they would need unanimous consent or something. The Federation's always been peaceful. Sure, they were a military organization, but their entire purpose was to keep peace in the galaxy. How could *all* of the admirals suddenly agree to this? And what about the lower ranked people? Someone should have dissented and leaked the information. Can you imagine the manpower it would take to construct this? There's no way they could keep it quiet from the galaxy."

Loni, Doug, and Arch glanced at each other.

"She makes a good point," Arch said. "For something like this, there'd have to be mutual consent. And the cost of supplies and labor alone would make it hard to keep this thing under wraps."

"And yet, here it is," Doug said.

"Someone did leak out the information," Loni said, "and the Empire has been bent on eradicating *anyone* who seems to know about it."

Doug cast a worried glance at Arta.

"It should have been more widespread than just a few people on a derelict asteroid colony," Arch said. "Imperial organizational structure, mutual consent of all the admirals, almost no leaks.

People don't get along this well, especially as many people that are in the Federation."

"What does that mean?" Loni asked.

"That someone or some*thing* is controlling them," Doug said. "Whether from the outside or the inside."

"What, like mind control?" Loni laughed. "Doug, that's ridiculous."

"No, it's not," Arta said. "Hassa have very precise control over our minds compared to most other species. Our otouta act like near perfect memory banks, allowing us to recall anything we've experienced or systematically and intentionally forget anything we decide, from precise, to broad. It's conceivable there's a species we haven't encountered that can use their thoughts to manipulate others. The galaxy isn't fully explored. There's a lot of strange things out there, especially in the Interference in the Mid Dark, from what I hear."

"You're not wrong," Doug said. "But to manipulate that many people would be quite a task, even for one with those abilities." He rubbed his chin. "I know someone, a bounty hunter sanctioned by the Federation, so she has contacts inside it. She's seen some pretty strange stuff that I've only heard hints of. Maybe she knows something about this."

"Can you trust her?" Arch asked.

"With this, absolutely. She'll do the right thing. But I'm not planning on telling her about the weapon. She's a capable warrior, but I don't want to put anyone else in danger by knowing about this if I don't have to. But maybe she knows something about what could be influencing the Empire."

Arch's ears twitched and he shut down the holo projector. A few seconds later, Redneb loped into the room, alternating between walking on his four fists and his feet.

"Uba dunna," he said, holding out a data pad. Doug accepted it and skimmed over the ledger.

"This is ten-thousand more than you quoted, Red. What's the deal?"

"Uba job. Shupa doo palaoob."

Doug leered at the Ticksar who growled in response and motioned with his fingers for Doug to hand him back the datapad. Redneb made several taps, and handed it back. Doug nodded appreciatively and inserted the data chip from his pocket, then another Loni handed to him. The data pad chirped, Doug removed the one partially full chip and handed the pad back to Redneb.

"Hub jub," Redneb said, turning to leave.

"Hold on there a tick, Red," Doug said. "I left a little bit extra in my payment. I'll need you to take Arta back home."

"Wait," Arta said, getting clumsily to her feet. She glanced at Loni, then back at Doug. "I've decided something. I…I'd like to go with you."

Doug let out a hard breath.

"Go get the speeder warmed up, Red. Arch, Loni, will you excuse us for a moment?"

"Yeah, sure," Arch mumbled, hopping down and padding off with Redneb. Loni stayed where she was.

"Loni," Doug said, indicating for her to leave.

"I'm not going anywhere, Cowboy. You want to say something to Arta, you can say it in front of me." She spoke with an edge in her voice and crossed her arms.

"Fine," Doug said. "Come on, Arta, let's talk outside."

Doug led her down the hall and down the ramp. Loni followed at a distance, remaining at the top of the ramp as they reached the bottom and walked away a bit. The air had already grown chill, though the twin suns weren't fully set. Doug faced Arta who looked up at him expectantly.

"Listen, Arta," Doug began.

"Doug, I love you," she blurted and covered her mouth, her skin glowing slightly. Her eyes darted past him toward the ship and she removed her hand, speaking more boldly. "I love you, Douglas Lancer. I want to come with you."

"You don't love me, Arta. You're grateful because I saved you. But you can't confuse those feelings with love. Don't put your affections on me. There's someone more suited for you out there."

Arta lowered her head, soft sobs punctuating the cold evening air and whispered, "Someone who doesn't mind trash."

"Now, Arta, you're not—"

He put his hands on her arms, but she jerked out of his touch, her sobs coming more freely, though she was clearly fighting them.

"I'm not confused. I love you and I can't help it."

"Arta—"

"Just go, Douglas Lancer." She turned away and hugged herself. "Just go back to the stars."

Doug hesitated, not knowing what to do. Finally, he turned and walked back up the ramp. Loni met him, her arms crossed and a scowl on her face.

"What?" Doug snapped.

"You scum-sucking low-life. How could you say those things to her?"

Doug scowled back.

"I don't appreciate you listening in."

He attempted to move past her but she blocked his path.

"She's not confused, *Cowboy*. She's in love with you."

Doug turned away. "She'll get over it."

He tried to move down the hall, but Loni slammed her hand to the opposite wall, blocking him again.

"She thinks she's trash, Doug! A throw away. And what you said just validated that lie."

"She's smart enough not to believe that. Now get out of my way."

Loni stepped further into his way. "What is wrong with you? All she wants to do is come with you and you're abandoning her to loneliness."

"It's better than getting her killed!"

"So that's it. That same stupidity you tried to play on me. I can be patient with you while you work that out with me, but I'll be spaced if I'm going to let you hurt that poor girl out there."

"That ain't your decision to make."

"Oh?" Loni said, crossing her arms. "Who's going to fly your ship off this rock? Cause I'm not."

"Now don't be stubborn."

"Just following the example set before me."

"Loni—"

"You want me to fly this ship? You march back out there and you apologize to that girl and then you tell her the *real* reason you're leaving her behind. Or the only thing I'm flying is *my* ship *off* of *yours*!"

Doug stood there a moment, his jaw working.

"Fine!" he said with a dismissive wave. "I'll figure out how to do it myself."

He stomped down the hall, leaving Loni to stew. The cockpit door closed behind him and he plopped into the pilot's chair. His hands didn't move to flick any instruments. Anger and frustration circled the conversation over and over in his mind. Overtaking those thoughts, like a rising tide, were thoughts of Arta. Her declaration and staunchness that her feelings were genuine pulled at him.

Doug could see her from the cockpit window. She was still standing near the ramp, her shoulders convulsing in sobs. Redneb stood near her, speaking to her, his face sympathetic.

You know that was a lie, a voice spoke inside him. *You know she meant what she said. And you can't just walk away.*

He tried to push the thoughts out of the way and focus on the controls, but no amount of effort made any difference. His anger was melting into guilt, Loni's words ringing true. After several minutes of stewing, he took off his hat and threw it down in frustration, rose and marched back down the hall.

———

Arta tried to stop herself, tried to stop the convulsing of her body, tried to stop the thoughts from cycling again and again. No matter how hard she tried, her mind and body would not obey.

Stupid! You're so stupid, Arta! What were you thinking? Of course he doesn't want you. Who would want trash like you?

She wiped her eyes, but the thoughts only made the tears come more earnestly. She'd trusted Loni's words, taken a risk and put her heart out there. And like every other time, it got stomped into the dirt. No one wanted a defective Hassa with a sordid past, least of all a Ranger.

"Arta."

She barely heard the voice over the sound of her own weeping. She didn't answer. He'd already thrown her heart in the incinerator. What could he possibly have to say further?

"I'm sorry," Doug said, his voice quiet.

She tried again to compose herself, wiping her eyes. She didn't want to be weak in front of him.

"For what?" she managed.

"For lying to you."

His words were laced with something. Sincerity? Humility?

"You're not trash," Doug continued. "I hate that you would even begin to think of yourself that way. And your feelings aren't misplaced. If you say you love me, well, I believe you."

She shook her head. He was just trying to comfort her. Arta tried in vain to hold back the resurgence of tears.

"Doug, please don't do this to me. I can't take you just trying to comfort me. I'd rather deal with the truth, as much as it hurts."

"This *is* the truth," he said.

Her tears slowed, that tone of genuine humility still present in his voice. She knew him to be an honest man. Had she any reason to doubt his words?

She looked over her shoulder at him, her eyes feeling ragged. She probably looked a mess, but in that moment, she didn't care. His dark eyes searched her face.

"I, uh…well," Doug said, "I'm concerned for your safety. I don't want you to get hurt." He paused, his mouth hanging open, then turned his head downward. "The truth is…well, the truth is I have issues. Dust, that sounds so stupid."

She turned to fully face him and waited expectantly. He fidgeted with his hands, ultimately deciding to shove them into his pockets.

"I have a problem letting people get close to me. Frankly, I've always had that problem. It's just gotten worse over the years."

"What happened?" She found herself asking, surprising herself. She didn't want to get hurt again, but with him, she found she couldn't stop herself.

"It's not so much what happened as what always seems to happen," Doug continued. "Every time I get close to someone, something happens and poof, they're gone out of my life. They usually end up dying or going crazy. Once I was stabbed in the back. Now I know that ain't you, I truly feel I could trust you with my life. I really do believe your feelings for me are genuine."

Arta's defenses crumbled in the face of his honesty. She stepped up to him, hope blossoming in her heart. His dark eyes found hers and she thought she could see a longing in them.

"And…your feelings for me?" she asked softly.

"I can't say."

"Then stay. Why not see where this goes?"

Doug shook his head, looking at the ground. "I can't. My responsibility as a Ranger, with whatever is going on in the galaxy right now, I have to do what I can to stop it."

Arta lowered her head.

"I understand. And you don't want to put me in danger, which is why I can't go with you."

"No, that's not it. There's, something else. Something I can't talk about that's preventing us from…uh…being together. Even as an informal kind of thing, even for me to bring you on board. I'm sorry, Arta. I don't want to hurt you. Might be best if you just forgot about me."

I could never forget you!

That's what she wanted to shout. She wanted to throw her arms around him and kiss him long and deep. But she held back. She loved him, yes, but that also meant respecting his wishes.

"This thing that's preventing us. Is it something permanent?"

Doug floundered.

"I don't know."

His words were sincere. She could hear the conflict in his voice. He *did* want to be with her! She moved without thinking, her hand sliding up, feeling the rough stubble on his cheek, moving his head to look her in the eyes. Then her lips were pressing against his, the kiss soft and full of her love for him. After several moments, she withdrew, holding his dark eyes with hers.

"I'll wait for you, Douglas Lancer," she said. "You go. Stop the Empire from building its weapon. Then, if you can, come back to me."

Doug nodded.

"I'll come back to you. I mean, if I can."

Arta closed her eyes a moment, her mind diving into her memory stems inside her otouta tendrils. She found the memories and wiped them from her mind. She opened her eyes to see Doug staring at her, that same longing in his eyes.

"I've erased everything you showed me in the conference room except the enormity of the danger," she said. "I don't remember what we talked about so you needn't worry. But I still understand the danger. So, I'll stay and wait for you."

Doug didn't seem to know what to do with himself. Despite everything, or perhaps because of it, Arta felt peace cover her like a blanket, the only other thing remaining being a sliver of worry for him.

"Thank you, for sharing your heart with me," she said.

Doug nodded, awkwardly stalling as if he wanted to say more, but didn't know the words.

"You should get going," she said.

Doug nodded and turned away. He paused, and turned back to her, floundering a moment longer. She smiled at him and somehow, that seemed to be all he needed. He smiled back and walked up the ramp.

Arta stood in the frigid twilight, watching the ship rise into the air and rocket into the sky. She watched the deepening night until the cold forced her to move.

"Come back to me, Douglas Lancer," she spoke into the starry sky.

CHAPTER TWENTY-ONE_

"Where to?" Loni asked.

"Aren't you still mad at me?" Doug said, slumped in his chair, his mood still dark. He hadn't moved since take-off, eyes permanently glued to the endless star field beyond the viewport.

She shrugged. "You're still a jerk who needs to get over himself. I mean honestly, who turns away a girl like that? She's beautiful, absolutely adores you, is brave and not a dimwit. I don't know about you, Cowboy, but you manned up and confessed your faults to her, even if it did take someone kicking you in your rear to do it."

Doug's lack of a response brought with it a sting of regret. Didn't she have her own faults? Who was she to rail on him?

This was different, she told herself. *I couldn't let that girl suffer.*

He did the right thing, so drop it.

She cleared her throat.

"Where do you want to go?" she asked in a more subdued tone.

Doug's eyes remained on the stars.

"After this is over, if we survive, that is, I'd like to take you to New Texas. There's something there I need to show you that will help explain my…problem."

Wasn't expecting that, Loni thought.

"Anyway, that aside," Doug said, straitening, "I've been thinking. On an impulse, I deleted the file from the database. That only leaves one copy left besides the one on this ship."

"Grandus?"

Doug nodded.

"We don't know where they're building this thing. Maybe it's in the file, maybe it's not. But we can't hack it. The only slicers we know that would do it for free are either missing or unwilling, and we don't have the credits to hire someone or even rent a decrypt bot.

"The way I see it, our best option is to delete the other file. That way the Empire doesn't have the information to draw upon to build their weapon."

"Wouldn't they keep copies in other locations?"

"The facilities on Ifdil and Grandus are some of the highest secured information hubs in the Empire. It's a miracle we actually made it into the facility, much less out. Any other place is subject to leaks. And Lent didn't tell you it was located anywhere else. No, my guess is, those are the only two locations this file exists. We delete that file, we stop the Empire."

"I don't know, Doug. This sounds like a suicide mission."

"I know. But I can't think of any other option. And I can't just let this go for the galaxy to work out on its own." He activated the com. "Arch, can you come to the cockpit?"

A few seconds later, Arch padded into the room and hopped up onto the navigator's chair. "What's up?"

"Here's the deal," Doug said, swiveling to face him. "The only way to ensure the Empire doesn't build their weapon is to destroy their plans. I already deleted the file on Ifdil when we were there. That only leaves Grandus. Loni's slicer friend only identified those two locations as being where the file existed. I'm going to Grandus to delete that file as well."

"And what, you expect me to just go along with this?" Arch asked, crossing his arms over his chest. "Doug, that's suicide. Grandus is a core world. The Empire and the Rangers will be on the lookout for us, especially after that fiasco on Ifdil. You're walking right into death."

"That's what I told him," Loni said.

"Which is what I wanted to talk to you two about," Doug said. "My oath as a Ranger compels me to do something about this. I can't just sit by and let this happen. Yeah, this may be too big for me, but I have to do what I can. I have a responsibility to the galaxy. And I couldn't live with myself if this weapon comes to fruition and I don't at least try to stop it.

"Which brings me to you two. You're not Rangers."

Loni opened her mouth to object, but Doug held up a hand.

"Let me finish," he said. "Now I'm not going to object if you two want to come along. I know you both have your reasons and I'm not downplaying those. But I wanted to give you an opportunity for an out. This is it. If you're with me, you're all in, but I can't guarantee your safety, or even your lives. Dust, we'll probably all end up being executed by the Empire. At best we'll have prices on our heads so high every bounty hunter in the galaxy will be after us. I just wanted to give you both the opportunity to drop out."

Loni swiveled in her chair, exchanging a glance with Arch and said, "Doug, sometimes you are absolutely infuriating. I'm your partner and a fighter pilot besides. I don't back down from a fight. I'm in."

Arch kept his arms crossed and shrugged his black-furred shoulders.

"Yeah, sure. I'm in."

Doug raised an eyebrow.

"That's it? No explanation?"

"I got reasons. You don't need to know 'em all."

"Alright then," Doug said. "Let's head for Grandus. We can plan on the way."

Loni smiled.

"Calculations are already set."

She shoved the hyperspace lever forward, launching them into hyperspace.

Arch studied a data-pad, reviewing the inventory he sold and the profits he'd made. Not a bad day's sales. He generated more money while they were on Lavtak Three than he did in an entire week on Tapolas. Maybe selling off the ship would work out better than he initially thought. He just needed to order more inventory and—

The chime for his room sounded.

Arch growled, "Yeah, what is it?"

Doug poked his head in.

"You got a minute?"

"Not really," Arch replied, still poring over the data.

"Alright. Just thought I'd check out your shop. See if there's anything I could use."

Arch snapped his head up. "Oh, why didn't you say so in the first place?"

He tossed the datapad onto his bed and padded out the door, Doug following behind.

"You know you should learn to get straight to the point," Arch said as they walked. "Stop pussy-footing around."

Doug smirked, wondering if Arch even realized the pun he'd

made. They entered the cargo bay and Arch hopped up onto a crate, his salesy-air already about him.

"So, what interests you? You already got your blasters. I noticed you eyeing the Glok earlier back on Tapolas." He reached into a crate. "I got some nice old Earthean slug-launchers."

"I'm not really—"

Arch pulled out a long-barreled hand-cannon, silencing Doug. It was old, though well maintained with a rotating chamber and steel barrel glinting in the bright light of the cargo bay. Arch tossed it aside and pulled out something similar to the Glok.

"Here we go," Arch said, handing the weapon over, grip-first. "M1911. Single-action, semi-automatic, magazine-fed, recoil-operated pistol chambered, forty-five caliber slug-launcher. Grip the top there and pull back. Pull the trigger to close the breach. There ya go.

"If memory serves me, that's a piece of history there. Used by your species in a lot of the wars of your homeworld. Y'know, that lost one some of you Terrans are always yammering about."

"I'm New Texan, not Terran," Doug said.

Arch waved off his comment.

"Whatever. From what I understand, it was widely used by law enforcement of that planet as well."

"Earth was pretty fragmented before we left it. Hard to say one gun was used by every culture."

"You would know better than me, I guess. But it's a reliable weapon from what I'm told. Never fired one enough to find out."

"Drawbacks?"

"Only holds seven rounds. They're housed in a vertically stacked chamber in the handle. Hit that button to pull it out. Also, it's a pain to load the slugs in that thing. You'd want to keep a couple chambers on hand to switch out in quick order."

Doug turned it over, fiddling with it.

"Pretty sure they're not called chambers."

"Oh, listen to you, mister weapons expert."

"Kind of heavy for a hand gun," Doug said.

"Eh, that's what you get when you make weapons out of regular steel. Those things pack a punch though."

"What about this one?" Doug set aside the 1911 and picked up the hand cannon Arch tossed aside.

"That one? Forget it. Dealer gave it to me as a freebie. I think he just wanted to get rid of it. Thing's more ancient than the M1911. Slower too. Only holds six rounds. Might be the same caliber, I don't know."

Doug palmed the weapon. The grip felt natural in his hand. He held it out in front of him and took aim through the ancient iron sights. Just as heavy as the M1911.Somehow this one felt natural. He pulled the trigger. The hammer came back and clicked forward, rotating the chamber. Doug popped open the cylinder. The gun had been used, but was clean.

Then he saw it.

Stamped clearly into the metal of the barrel:

TEXAS RANGER.

Those words brought old memories back to him.

"Y'know, my granddaddy had one of these. Never saw him use it, but he'd often swear by it. Did say he used it back in the Alien Wars."

Arch stood silently by. The way Doug handled the gun, it was almost like it was meant for him. Doug glanced at the other gun and handed it back to Arch, holding up the Texas Ranger.

"How much does something like this run?"

"Eh, take it. I ain't making any money off that thing."

"Ammo?"

"Now that'll cost ya."

"Consider it rent."

"Rent?"

"Look, I got no problem with you setting up shop in here, especially since it was partially my fault yours got toasted."

"Partially?"

"But if you're gonna be making credits out of a hold on my ship, I'd appreciate some compensation. How much were you paying for rent on Tapolas?"

"None of your business, that's how much. Don't think I don't know what's going on here. The Rangers aren't paying your salary, so you have to make money any way you can."

"You think it's unfair to pay to use someone else's space, especially when that someone is also providing room and board?"

Arch growled, his ears flattening as he turned his head away. He crossed his arms and grumbled out how much he'd been paying in rent.

"Alright," Doug said. "Provide me a few more tools this time, and the occasional item or ammo, and I'll only charge you half that. Plus, if you want to make back some of those credits, you can help out with the bounties we catch."

Arch's ears perked back up.

"Yeah, alright. I guess you've got the right to charge. And if you're only charging half for a mobile shop, I guess I can't complain. Besides, it's not like you'll be depleting my inventory, unless of course you keep losing your blasters. That slug launcher will probably never leave its holster."

"What makes you say that?"

"Oh, please. You think I haven't noticed your blasters are always on stun? You don't like using lethal force. That's obvious. And guess what? That ancient relic you're holding doesn't have a stun setting."

"It does if you don't shoot something vital."

"That's debatable," Arch said. "But whatever. What else are you looking for?"

"What type of other things you got?"

"Well, I got grenades, remote blaster triggers, I don't know. I got lots of stuff. You gotta give me particulars or we'll be here all day."

"Maybe some items to use if I find myself in a pinch."

Arch licked his paw and rubbed his ear.

"Something for a pinch. Yeah, I got some stuff in a crate over there. Let's go have a look see."

CHAPTER TWENTY-TWO_

Commodore Ferris walked briskly through the halls of the *Dominator*, her mood darkening with every step. Two bounty hunters failed, technically three if you counted the Glipts as two. The renegades successfully escaped both Marines and Rangers at Ifdil, even managing to run a blockade of interceptors and the *Dominator* itself. Aoo was still out there, but she couldn't count on that incompetent blob. And Lo Jinal, even after his embarrassing failure on Terra, along with every other bounty hunter, were reporting no leads. The hunt was dead.

Incompetents, the lot of them. Based on their actions so far, the renegades' next move was quite clear. It was time to take more drastic measures.

The commodore arrived at the hanger bay and a deck officer walked up to her.

"Your shuttle is ready, Commodore."

"Thank you, Lieutenant," she said without breaking stride, walking up the ramp and into the cockpit.

"All systems are green, Commodore," said the pilot, a young man fresh out of the academy.

"Thank you, pilot. You are relieved."

"Ma'am?"

"I will be piloting the shuttle myself. You are on leave until I return."

She gave him an uncompromising stare. The pilot hurriedly unstrapped and disembarked. Ferris slid into the pilot's seat, strapping in and firing up the engines. She couldn't blame the pilot. This was highly unusual. But she didn't want to implicate anyone she didn't have to in what she was about to do. It was bad enough she was forced to resort to such measures in the first place.

The craft shot out of the hanger bay and down to the planet below.

The dead world loomed before her. She checked her coordinates and piloted down. Checking to make sure her side-arm was secure, she left the shuttle fort he harsh landscape.

Once a thriving planet, it was now ravaged and charred beyond repair. Despite the slim atmosphere, it was completely unlivable. Nothing would grow here ever again. Not even terraforming would be able to restore it.

There were a small number of worlds like this in the galaxy. More than there used to be. Such devastation would continue. Pirates and warring factions each taking their toll, reducing entire worlds to useless hunks of rock. Just like this one. Nothing short of complete unification would stop it. That's why they had to succeed. Then there would be peace. And scum like the one she was meeting would be wiped out once and for all.

Something in her peripheral caught her eye. A large, winged creature flying toward herat an incredible speed. She faced it, straight-backed with her hands clasped behind her. Ferris held her ground as it slammed into the dirt several meters in front of her, blowing up ash and dust. Out of the cloud stalked an enormous skeletal figure. Its boney wings collapsed into two writhing tendrils coming out of its back. Its yellow eyes glowed with menace at the Imperial officer.

"Commodore," Drexx said over her ear com.

The Commodore glanced around the ruined, rocky landscape.

"Interesting choice of location." She turned back to him. "Feeling nostalgic?"

Those glowing eyes narrowed. The beak opened, revealing rows of razor-sharp spines. "What do you want, human?"

"I have an opportunity for you," Ferris said, activating a holo-projector. An image of a blue, crescent-shaped ship rotated between them. Ferris tapped the device again to display a holo of a young woman with curly hair in a pilot's uniform overlaid with a leather jacket. "This is Loni Taraska. She's a fugitive from the Empire. She was last seen escaping on the ship I just showed you. I want you to track her down, and kill her and anyone else involved with her. Intel suggests her next destination will likely be the information hub on the planet of Grandus."

"I know this one," Drexx said. "She was with a Ranger, a very dangerous one."

"Is this too hard a job for you?"

Drexx snapped his head back to the commodore. He growled and took a crashing step toward her.

"Maybe it is. Maybe it would be easier just to feast on your bones and enjoy their crunch between my jaws."

The commodore held her chin high. A red dot flashed over Drexx's eye. It grabbed his attention. He looked down at his body where more dots were appearing, twenty or so covering its boney surface. He looked around, but she could tell he failed to see his assailants.

"You didn't really expect me to come here alone, did you?" the commodore asked.

Drexx growled again, taking a step back. The marks vanished.

"And what do I get if I kill this one for you? I'm no bounty hunter."

"How about the Kolos system?"

Drexx paused before saying, "This human must mean a great deal to you. What does she know?"

"That's not your concern. Take the job or don't. I don't have time for pointless questions."

Drexx crashed slowly to her. The same red dots appeared, but he ignored them, looming over her. She stared into that horrid beak, wrinkling her nose at the smell of rotten flesh.

His low growl sounded over her com.

"Pointless questions. Like, what are you building beyond the asteroid cluster in the far point?"

Ferris flushed.

Drexx continued, "Or what was really on that mining station in the Belt that you and your lackeys obliterated? Or perhaps what was in a certain cylinder someone raided from one of your transport vessels en route to Grandus?"

Despite herself, Ferris shook, unsure if it was from rage or fear.

"I am no simple Pirate, human," Drexx said. "I know far more than you realize. Your little toy guns do *not* impress me. And when it suits me, I *will* feast on your flesh and tear your precious Empire to shreds until there is nothing left but a handful of mind-warped sentients, cowering in their own urine, floating aboard a destroyed carrier abandoned at the edge of space."

He lingered there a moment, his sharp beak inches from her face. Drexx took the holo-projector from her, his touch sending electrified shivers down her spine. He backed away and launched into the sky with a soul-scraping screech. Ferris stood there for several long moments, calming herself.

We'll see about that, Pirate.

"Captain," she said into her com, "recall your men and return to the *Dominator*."

She got confirmation but remained, transfixed on the spot where Drexx had disappeared into the horizon, wondering on the genuineness of his threat. Was she afraid he might be telling the truth? Drexx had a reputation for ruthlessness. The rumors said he always got what he wanted eventually. She shuddered, then straightened. She would not be cowed by some alien scum who thinks he can intimidate her.

Let him think he can.

It will be all the sweeter to see his face when they obliterate his fleet once the job is done. She turned briskly on her heels and headed back to the shuttle.

———

"Commodore."

Ferris had barely stepped off the shuttle's ramp when the deck officer addressed her.

"What is it, Lieutenant?"

"Admiral Traik is requesting you contact him, Ma'am."

She hesitated, wondering why the Admiral would be contacting her.

Probably just a status update.

She didn't like the idea. Their status was unchanged with the criminals still out there. She smoothed her uniform and marched ahead, hands clasped behind her back.

"Thank you, Lieutenant."

The door to the commodore's office slid shut and she moved to her desk, activating the com. "Get me Admiral Traik."

She got an acknowledgement and attempted to steady her nerves.

"I have Admiral Traik," a voice said.

Ferris cleared her throat and folded her hands on the desk.

"Put him through."

A full-sized holo appeared on the other side of the table. The man facing her was older than she with gaunt features. But there was a hardness and cold cruelty in his eyes.

"Commodore, what is your status?"

"Sir, the fugitives are still at large. I believe they will head for the information hub at Grandus. We are currently en route."

"And what is your plan for capturing them?"

Ferris hesitated. So far everything she'd tried had failed. She couldn't tell him about Drexx, at least not directly, lest he be implicated as well.

"Sir, I have pursued five avenues of capture besides my own troops."

"I want specifics, Commodore, not vague promises. I needn't tell you the consequences of this information getting to the other branches."

"I'm well aware, Sir. At this moment, I have two bounty hunters after the fugitives. I have alerted the Marines on station at Grandus to be on the watch for Lieutenant Taraska. I have alerted the Rangers their rogue is heading to the planet as well. On top of that, I have an Armored Corps Trooper squad hunting them down. Their last report was that they were headed to the same location."

"That's only four, Commodore."

"Yes, Sir. The fifth is questionable, but effective."

"I see... The Armored Trooper squad, what is their designation?"

Ferris tapped some keys on a data display.

"Titan Squad, Sir."

"I'm familiar with them. I will contact them personally to ensure capture of the fugitives. Be sure you don't let these traitors slip through this time, Commodore."

"I won't, Sir."

The image disappeared and Ferris immediately hit the com. "Get me Marshall Deft of the Galactic Rangers and the Marine commander at the Grandus information hub. And get me intel on Titan Squad's destination."

"Right away, Commodore."

Ferris tapped her desk with a gloved hand. Her mind instinctively going to the implied consequences if she failed. A cold chill swept through her and she shuddered.

"Ma'am," squawked the com, "I have Armored Corps Commander Tain on long-range coms. He insists on speaking with you."

"Put him through," Ferris said.

A burley man in a crisp, richly decorated uniform appeared on the other side of the desk. His face was hard and serious.

"I understand you are looking for intel on one of my trooper squads."

How in space did he get word so fast? She didn't waiver, remaining as straight-backed as he.

"I don't see how that's any of your concern, Commander. They left from my ship and I want to know where they are headed. They *are* under my command, are they not?"

"Limited command, Commodore." The man's voice was authoritative. The kind of person who follows a single path and never deviates, come hell or high water. "This particular squad is operating under Corps Special Ops protocol. Their mission is the concern of the Corps and the admirals. You're not to investigate. Understood?"

The Commodore smiled. This fool didn't know the half of what was going on.

"Of course, Commander. We are all working toward a common goal, are we not? Peace among the branches and all that."

"Somehow," Commander Tain said slowly, "I doubt your sincerity."

"A shame. The peace of the galaxy requires all of us to work together. The Navy and Marines are as dedicated to it as the Armored Corps, as am I. Are you, Commander?"

"Don't try to play games with me, Commodore. Rumors that don't go away, often have a kernel of truth. Maintaining peace comes secondary to keeping each other in check. War and conflict are sometimes necessary to maintaining that balance. But things better be pretty edged unbalanced for that to happen, because the Armored Corps don't play nice. And neither do I."

The image disappeared, leaving the commodore alone. The message was clear. *Watch your step.*

The admiralty likely already knew about Commander Tain's suspicions. But she didn't like his implication. The branches *were* in fact designed to do exactly as he said, just as the Rangers did for the whole of the Federation and vice versa. No one ever believed things would get bad enough for actual conflict to break out. The Federation was dedicated to maintaining peace throughout the galaxy and had done so since the Alien Wars. What reason would the Armored Corps have to initiate a conflict?

But things were growing dangerous. If the Commander's statements were any indication, the Empire folding in the Rangers and becoming a united force didn't sit well with many. And this new weapon would change the face of that balance.

"Ma'am," said the com officer, "I have Marshall Deft."

Ferris cleared her throat. At least the Rangers were in their control and their loyalty was unquestioned. What the admiralty told Marshall Deft was unknown to her, neither was it her concern. He was with them. That was all that mattered.

"Put him through."

CHAPTER TWENTY-THREE_

Pen Olster dodged a stray animal darting across the ramp of his small shuttle. He sighed, hating the poor state of the space station. Pen wished he could have stopped at a nicer, more reputable place.

He took a bite of the bread-covered meat stick he held in one hand. The thing tasted terrible, but it was all he could afford after resupplying. He didn't have many credits left now that the Rangers weren't paying his salary. What could he do? He wouldn't go back on his decision. More so now that he knew there was another Ranger on his side.

Another Ranger.

He smiled with pride at the thought of his promotion.

Pen opened a storage compartment in the floor of the craft. He deposited the weeks' worth of food in the compartment, eyeing the tools and stun rod inside.

Wasn't much. At this rate, he'd either have to turn to bounty hunting, or find another side profession. Maybe security. No, that would leave him tied down to one location. He couldn't perform his duty as a Ranger if that were the case.

He replaced the panel, forcing it into its beat-up housing.

Maybe he could track down that other Ranger. What was his name?

"Hey there, handsome."

Pen whirled. Standing in the entryway at the top of the ramp was a female Sin-Sin, a race of near-humans with wiry-frames, large, colorful eyes, and an outer-coating of hardened, but shiftable skin that acted as clothing. She was mostly covered, but not enough.

Pen blushed and lowered his eyes.

"Ma'am. What can I do for you?"

"I'm looking for a Ranger. Thought you could help me find him."

"Someone specific, then?"

She approached him, her moves sultry. Her hand rested on his cheek and for a moment, all he saw was her gorgeous, color-shifting eyes.

"I certainly am. His name is Douglas Lancer. He helped me out of a rather tough scrape a few years back and I was hoping he could help me again. Do you think you could find him for me?"

Doug's name immediately threw up a red flag in Pen's mind. With an effort, he wrapped his head around the rest of what she was saying. Sin-Sins were notorious for their powers of persuasion. No one knew if it was pheromones or something else, but whatever the reason, this one wasn't working on him. He pulled her hand away, her thin wrist held firm in his meaty grip.

"What do you want with Doug Lancer?" he asked, eyes narrowed.

Her seductive look faltered, but she recovered quickly.

"Why, I told you. I need his help."

Pen drew his blaster and pressed the barrel to her midsection.

"I'd be more careful if I was you, girly. Messing with a Ranger always comes due."

"What do you mean, handsome?"

This broad was proving too shady for Pen's liking. He tapped a button on his blaster, causing it to whine as it powered up for an intensified shot.

"Get off my boat."

"Come now, big and burly, why don't we—"

Pen shoved her away and fired at her feet. She jumped back, slamming into the wall. Her form rippled and faded for just an instant.

Shape-shifter.

Pen switched to stun and fired center mass. The Sin-Sin dissolved into an amorphous blob that quivered before launching out into the hanger bay. Pen followed it to the top of the ramp just in time to see it slither into a vent on the bay's wall.

A form darted past him into his ship. He turned and fired. The brown and yellow feltil, something akin to a cat, jumped and yowled, darting back out of the craft.

Pen shook his head and slapped the close button.

Pests.

He holstered his weapon. The ramp slowly raised to form the rear wall of the shuttle. Out of the corner of his eye, he thought he saw another critter scurry by, but when he looked again, his ship was empty.

Sighing, he plopped into the pilot's chair and fired up the engines. He needed to figure out what to do next. That *thing* was after Doug for some reason. He needed to warn him. But how to reach him?

As his ship flew out of the hanger bay into empty space, he connected to the dock master at Eisen Ro. A few questions and a few minutes more of research and he had a likely idea of where he would find the Ranger. Entering the coordinates for Grandus in his nav computer, he sat back, waiting for the calc computer to navigate a course.

His mind went back to the shape shifter, wondering what the creature was after. Bounty, maybe? He'd have to ask Doug when he saw him. Swiveling around he noticed his meet stick lying on the floor next to the still open compartment. Thinking he needed to work on being more observant, he put the panel back in place.

CHAPTER TWENTY-FOUR_

"Overwatch, status update."

Ati scanned the information hub through his field mags. Like much of the rest of the nearly planet-wide city, the structure lit up with sharp lines of iridescent light that cut through the darkness and gloom of the nighttime rain.

"Wet, boss," Waters replied, clearly not affected by the weather.

"Aside from that." Ati suppressed a smile, knowing Waters was just making fun banter. That's what he did. The rain couldn't penetrate their armor, or the nerve-connecting body suit underneath.

"I'm all set up and have eyes on the entrance," Waters said.

"Good. Team two?"

"Ready and standing by," Bot said.

"Team three?"

"In position and standing by," Drawl replied.

"Good. Everyone remember, don't move when the target appears, feed me intel. We want to take this Ranger alive and as quietly as possible. Let's not stun if we don't have to."

"May not give us a choice, Sergeant," Bot said.

"Then he'll have made his. We know his tactics now, so we should be able to take him down."

Ati went over the scenario in his head. He had his squad spread out to cover all angles. They were far enough apart to prevent the Ranger from getting the drop on all of them at once, but close enough to lend support to any team that encountered him.

"I've got a taxi coming in from the west," Drawl said.

Ati swiveled his field mags. The taxi pulled up to the steps leading to the building. A hooded and robed figure stepped out and the taxi pulled away.

"Team two, grab that taxi and hold it there. We may need to use it," Ati said.

"Copy."

"Anyone have a visual on the passenger?"

The figure climbed the incredibly long stairwell. All teams reported negatives.

Probably just another patron.

The figure glanced to the side and Drawl's voice came back over com.

"Got a visual. Boss, you're not going to believe this."

———

Josh scanned the rainy night before him. Water dripped in thick drops from the edge of the overhang, soaking the marble steps not three meters away from where he stood guard.

Why haven't they perfected weather control? He groaned within himself.

His partner, Scott, stood guard alongside him at the front entrance of the Federation data repository. Scott's icon disappeared from his HUD. Josh turned expectantly to find Scott with his helmet off, flicking the visor in an attempt to reboot it.

"That thing giving you trouble again?" Josh asked.

"I hate all this tech," Scott grumbled. "Just give me a blaster and tell me who to kill."

"What were you doing?" Josh turned back to the night, not wanting to be distracted from his duty. Not that it mattered. Their shift was almost up.

"Nothing. I was just checking the guard feed and it fritzed out on me," Scott said with an edge to his voice. He was ready to blast a hole in his helmet.

"Alright, let's just see what happens at the reboot," Josh said. "If it doesn't work, just go without the electronics. You only have to bear with it a few more minutes anyway."

"Yeah, I guess," Scott grumbled.

Movement beyond the sheet of rain snapped Josh into readiness.

"Heads-up."

Scott hastily replaced his helmet and stood ready. A minute later, a figure in the hooded jacket of high-level trades-person made their way up the steps to the doorway.

"Halt," Josh said, and the figure pulled back its hood. A woman of tan skin, blue eyes, and loose, curly hair smiled, grateful to be under the overhang.

"Hi," she said.

"State your name and purpose," Josh ordered.

"Oh, uh, Loni Taraska. Here to do some research on behalf of the Taraska Royal family."

Josh glanced at Scott who was equally surprised.

"*Princess* Loni Taraska?"

"Yes, that's right," she said. "Do you want to see my I.D.?"

"That's not necessary, ma'am. We both know who you are. We just thought you were a fighter pilot for the Empire."

"Empire? Or Federation?" she asked, winking.

Out of the corner of his eye, Josh saw Scott smirk. Every

soldier had been informed of the change-over. As far as Josh knew, every branch had received changes in structure and responsibilities, and there were many who disagreed with it. It was no surprise this feather-head felt the same.

"Do you have a pass, your highness?" Josh asked, restraining his own smirk.

"Oh," she said, her smile dropping. "My friend was supposed to meet me to let us both in. I guess I beat him here. Is it okay if I wait for him?"

"I don't see why that would be a problem."

"Thanks," she said, her smile returning. "In answer to your question, I'm kind of on permanent leave. Didn't like the turnover to Empire, so I resigned my commission. I hear a lot of military aren't too happy with it."

"Ain't that the truth," Scott said, his eyes focused on the rain.

The door slid open and someone walked out. The princess stepped aside to make way, still chatting with the guards. A black cat appeared out of the rain and shook itself.

"Oh," Loni said, "It's so cute!"

A garbled transmission came over Josh's com.

"All sta—central—be on—over."

"Central, this is station one. Repeat your last transmission. Over."

The cat purred and rubbed against Josh's leg. He tried to maneuver away from it as he repeated his request. All he got was static and another leg rub from the cat.

"Get out of here!" Josh kicked at the cat. It jumped aside and darted inside the facility, causing the closing door to re-open. Both guards turned toward the door.

"Nice move," Scott said.

"Shut up and go in after it," Josh shot back.

"You're the one who kicked it."

"I hate pets," Josh grumbled, leaning into the doorway. "Why does this stuff always happen right before the shift—"

"What's that?" the princess said from behind him. Josh heard the sound of something powering up. His rifle came up as he turned. A quiet *POP!* and a tingly feeling washed over him, and everything went black.

———

Arch peaked out from the doorway. Loni and the two guards were unconscious on the marble floor. Worry crept through him for Loni. He dug in the dark pouch strapped to his belly, mostly hidden by the way it blended with his fur. Pulling a small device, he stuck it to the doorframe. The device would hold the door open until removed. Arch rushed over to check Loni's heartbeat as Doug crested the steps.

"She alright?" Doug asked.

"Yeah, she's fine," Arch replied, retrieving his stun grenade. "I'd like to state again that I don't like this plan of yours. Attacking royalty is not something we Ikati do, even if she knew it was coming."

"She wanted to participate. Felt our chances were better if she lulled the guards into idle chatter."

"Yeah, well, revealing her name wasn't too smart either. She runs into danger way too often for my liking."

"Can't say I disagree," Doug said. "And I understand about you not wanting to attack royalty. I won't ask you to do it again."

"Be sure that you don't."

"You got her handled?" Doug asked as Arch maneuvered Loni onto his shoulders.

"Don't make me stun blast you," Arch said. "Speaking of which, that stun grenade was only half-power. You have maybe twenty minutes before these guards come to, and less before backup shows up. I scrambled their coms, but one of these hull-busters was getting a transmission. Others may know you're here. Good luck, Cowboy. We'll wait for your signal."

Arch made his way down the steps. His footing was sure even in the rain, but he wasn't comfortable with it. One misstep and they'd both be in serious trouble.

This would be so much easier if I was bigger, Arch thought.

Once at the bottom, he hailed a taxi. A speeder slowed and Arch hauled Loni inside, carefully positioningher to lean against the opposite window.

"Whoa. An Ikati!" The driver said. "Haven't seen many of your kind around."

"Yeah, well now you have. West Central Space port."

"She okay?"

"Heh. A little too much to drink. Lightweight, you know?"

The driver nodded with a furrowed brow, taking in Arch's comparatively small size.

"Hey, step on it, will ya?" Arch said.

The driver hastily turned to face front and the speeder took off. Arch pulled a small vile out of his pouch. He waved it beneath Loni's nose and she roused slightly. Arch replaced the vile and gently slapped her.

"Hey, wake up," he said.

Her head lolled and she mumbled something incoherent. Arch's apprehension grew, wondering not for the first time if even the minimal charge of the stun grenade had done some damage. He gripped her face in his paws. *Should I? No, I shouldn't. But she might be...but I can't just...*His will finally caved and he began licking her cheek, working toward her eye and down the side of her nose. He stopped himself with some effort before he reached her lips, moving to her other cheek.

After a moment of this, she woke up and brushed him away.

"You okay?" Arch asked.

Loni shifted, getting her bearings. Her eyes landed on the driver and she hit the privacy button. A forcefield went up between them, blocking out sound and visuals.

Loni sat back and put her hand to her head.

"Other than a splitting headache, yeah." She eyed Arch. "Were you kissing me?"

Arch pawed at the seat.

"I was worried about you. You weren't coming 'round as fast as I thought you would. I-I didn't mean anything by it. Just…"

"It's fine, Arch," Loni said. "But next time let me wake up on my own."

Arch nodded. Then he snapped his head up. "Next time?"

Loni smirked.

"I'm glad you're here to look out for me."

"It's my pleasure, your highness."

"Loni."

Arch forced down a purr. "Okay," he said in a subdued voice, still pawing the seat, "…Loni."

"We headed for the spaceport?"

"Yeah," Arch said, wrestling his feelings under control. "We should be there…"

He trailed off, looking out the rain-streaked window. He stood on his hind legs and put his paws on the cool glass.

"Hey, this doesn't look familiar." Arch hit the com for the front. "Hey, driver. What gives?"

The driver didn't answer.

"Hey, I'm talking to you!" Arch said.

Still no answer. Arch hit the privacy button but the forcefield remained in place. He hit it several times, panic building in him. He pulled out his square from his pack.

"We gotta get out of here."

Arch's gun unfolded into its shoulder-mounted version. He fired into the forcefield. The green field flickered as the bolts struck, absorbing right into it. Arch's heart jumped into his throat. *That* was not standard on taxis. He tried the floor with the same effect.

"They beat us here," Arch said, eyes wide. "They set a trap for us. How'd they know we were coming?"

Loni reached into her robes, drawing her singularity gun.

"I don't know. But I don't plan on sticking around to find out."

She dug in her pocket and pulled out a selection of shells. She picked a yellow one and shoved the rest back into her pocket. She grabbed Arch and held him to her bosom, aiming at the far door. Arch's heart beat madly, his purr igniting despite the situation. She eyed him, her brow knitted. He gave a shrug. She rolled her eyes and fired.

Blinding yellow light and searing heat filled the compartment. Momentum pulled at them, then turned sideways. A loud *THUMP* sounded and Arch felt weightless. Loni held him tight, trying to curl around him as they were tossed around amidst the crashing and scraping metal.

Just as quickly, the chaos stopped.

Arch wiggled out of her hold, landing on the ceiling, the seats above their heads. He shook her and said, "Hey, you okay?"

"Remind me never to do that again," Loni slurred, pushing herself up.

"What was that?"

"Solar energy. Even military-grade shields can't withstand it in those levels."

Arch's blood ran cold.

"You shot solar energy in a confined space?"

Loni groaned, holding her head.

"I was betting the shield was of the make that would absorb any ambient energy. Now will you blast us out of here while we still have time?"

"You are some kind of crazy, your highness." Arch blasted away at the door with a full volley, and it fell away from its frame. He grabbed Loni under the arm, dragging her out into the beating rain. "C'mon. We need to get clear."

Loni clumsily got to her feet.

"Can you run?" Arch asked.

"Watch me," she said, though her heart wasn't in the words.

"All right. Come on." Arch bounded away, having to stop when he realized Loni was stumbling to keep up.

"Listen," Arch said, "I ain't too comfortable with you running like this. You might have a concussion."

"We don't have much of a choice," Loni said, continuing forward on shaky legs.

Arch darted into her path.

"Just hang on a sec. I can carry you and we can get to the spaceport twice as fast. Just give me a second to focu—"

"Freeze!"

Ten Armored Corps troopers surrounded them, weapons raised. Arch cursed. Their approach had been dampened by the downpour. Loni's hair was soaked, hanging half in her face. The slight glaze in her eyes and her heavy breathing tore at his heart. He couldn't let her get captured.

She must have seen his determination, because she shook her head. He ignored her protest. In a swift motion, Arch turned his gun on the nearest trooper. His claw didn't even reach the trigger before he was hit and his world went dark.

Ati ordered the teams to hold position while the scene at the entryway played out. When the Ranger showed up and the Ikati ran off with the princess, Ati called an audible to secure them instead, leaving Waters on overwatch to keep an eye out for the

Ranger. There was only one entrance which would work to their advantage.

Then it had all gone south.

The taxi Q rigged with a remote-activated forcefield swerved and rolled thirteen meters before stopping on its roof. The Ikati decided to play hero and get himself stunned, and Ati was betting that wasn't going to win them any points with the princess.

Tolso and Drawl had her secured. Q gently slung the Ikati over his shoulder, examining the cat's gun as he did so, while Vid checked on the driver.

"Your highness," Ati began. "I'm Sergeant Dole Ati of the Armored Corps. We need to ask you some questions about what happened on the *Dominator*."

The princess stared glassy-eyed at him. Ati signaled his men and they retreated into a nearby abandoned building they previously selected and secured for interrogating the Ranger. The princess remained lethargic.

"Do you need medical attention?"

She didn't answer.

Ati signaled Bot who stepped up and did a scan.

"Slight concussion. It's healing and should clear up in a few hours."

They didn't have a few hours.

"Your highness," Ati said, snapping his fingers in front of her face to grab her attention. "It's imperative that you cooperate."

Her eyes strayed to Q still holding the Ikati, then back to Ati. She nodded and lazily waved him closer. He did so, knowing there wasn't much she could do if she was trying to trick him.

"Go to the edge," she whispered, and grabbed his K-12 blaster rifle and sent a kick straight into his abdomen, which did absolutely nothing. Ati held his grip on his weapon as Tolso stunned the princess. She collapsed into Drawl's arms.

"That went well," Specs said.

"See if you can get her roused," Ati ordered. "We need to—"

"Sergeant Ati, come in."

The voice was in his helmet's com. And he didn't like it.

"Getting a com. Stand by." He switched frequencies to reply to the incoming communication. "Go for Ati."

"Sergeant, this is Admiral Traik. I understand you are in pursuit of the Ranger. What is your current location and status?"

Ati silently cursed. "Grandus, sir. About a click from the data repository in Jan City. We are watching the repository for the Ranger, have apprehended two suspects we believe to be working with the Ranger, and are preparing to question them."

"Very good, Sergeant. However, I'm calling off your investigation. The *Dominator* has just arrived over Grandus and will be taking over operations concerning the Ranger."

That explained how the Admiral got a transmission through.

"Bring the suspects to the *Dominator*, then resume your post on Tellus Four. Admiral Traik out."

Ati stewed inside his armor, his hands gripping his rifle so hard he might crack the thing in two.

"Boss?" Q asked.

Ati took a moment to compose himself. "Overwatch, stand down and rendezvous."

"Now? But I was actually starting to enjoy the rain. I even thought up a dance number that—"

"Now, trooper."

"Okay. Be there in a tick."

Ati addressed his squad. "Admiral Traik is recalling us back to Tellus Four. We're to turn over the princess and the Ikati to the *Dominator* and leave operations in their hands."

There was silence over the com.

"Sergeant, this is clud dung," Bot's voice had an uncharacteristic edge to it. "They're covering something up."

"I know. But right now we don't have any evidence, only

speculation. If we had more we could cite Corps protocol, but that's not the case. We follow orders."

"We can't hand them over," Bot insisted.

"We can and we will, soldier. I don't want to hear any more about this."

Ati felt some sense of satisfaction knowing the Ranger was still out there. If their encounter with him was any indication, he was a tough capture. Maybe the Empire was covering something up. Or maybe they had this all sideways and the Ranger and the Princess really were guilty of treason and sedition.

Maybe the galaxy would implode.

One could only hope.

CHAPTER TWENTY-FIVE_

Doug's boots squeaked on the polished stone floor of the information center. The place was empty, as was to be expected. Someone had likely spotted the commotion on holo-feed and ordered an evacuation. He should still have time before they locked the system down.

The hum of the data towers surrounded him as he approached the reference desk.

Not surprising, it was empty. Doug noted the still-fading wet marks on the floor heading off in different directions, the information desk at the epicenter. The pattern was consistent with Ranger standard issue, a specialized hybrid of combat and space boot. He sighed and slid his hands into the pockets of his duster.

"May as well come on out," he called into the vast building. "I know you're here waiting for me."

Footsteps sounded all around him. Figures crept out from behind data towers like a group of thieves. Their dusters were still damp from the rain, badges on full display on their shirts.

Rangers.

They were acting like snakes sneaking up on prey. It was no

way for a Ranger to behave and it made him sick. He hoped Loni and Arch got away safely.

Four in front, and by the sound of it, five in back. The Rangers kept their distance, blaster pistols leveled at Doug who remained relaxed, hands in his pockets. Most of them he knew. Stenson was among them, a vengeful expression in his eyes. The crowd shifted and the Marshall stepped up to the reference desk on the opposite side from Doug.

"Good to see you, Douglas," the Marshall said, his own blaster leveled.

"Wish I could say the same."

"Time to come home, Doug. You've been running long enough."

"I ain't the one who left," Doug replied. "Tell me, Marshall, what are the Rangers all about? Cause I don't recall there being anything in the code about going against your conscience."

The Marshall didn't respond, but Doug could see a pang of guilt in his weathered frown.

What was it that turned you? He wondered. He needed to get him alone and un-armed so he could talk to him, man to man. But that wouldn't happen as long as he was surrounded by his entourage.

"That's enough talk, son," the Marshall said. "It's time to hand over your badge and your weapons. Now let's see those hands."

Doug slowly withdrew his hands, one empty, one holding a gleaming badge.

"Recognize this?" he asked. "Stenson's badge accessed a highly classified Imperial file. The same file I was willing to send you. Ranger or not, we shouldn't have that kind of access without a warrant pass."

A few of the Rangers exchanged looks, some turning their eyes on Stenson and the Marshall.

"Maybe you should take a second look at your right-hand man, Marshall," Doug said.

"No one is looking at anything, Doug," the Marshall replied. "We trust our brothers."

"Sure you do."

"Now that's enough! You've disgraced yourself by taking another Ranger's badge. And I'll not have you slandering your brothers." The Marshall indicated with his finger. "Return his badge to him."

Doug turned to Stenson.

"Catch." He tossed the badge, and closed his eyes.

Stenson fumbled it in his hands, catching it in time for the device attached to its back to explode in a blinding flash of light.

Shouts of pain filled the room and blasters fired wildly. Doug whirled, drawing both blasters, eyes still shut, and fired off five quick stun blasts. Seeing from behind his eyelids the intense light fading, he opened them and stunned three more. Stenson, he charged, throwing an elbow into his face. The scum deserved worse.

Stenson fired, but being blinded, his aim was off. Doug ducked the still well-aimed blast and came up with an uppercut to Stenson's jaw. The man crumpled to the floor. Doug grabbed the badge off the floor and switched it with the one pinned to Stenson's shirt.

"Much obliged," he whispered.

He stood to see the Marshall standing before him, squinting while he leveled the blaster.

"Don't think I can't shoot you like this, Doug."

Doug straightened.

"You know about it, don't you? The weapon, Stenson; you know about all of it, because…"

Because you're part of it.

He couldn't bring himself to say it. This man he admired and looked up to. He'd been like a father to him. And all of it was crashing down around him. It was all he could do to hold himself together.

"Everyone leaves," Doug muttered.

"What?" the Marshall said.

"Nothing," Doug said, steeling his will.

He couldn't afford to let his emotions out. Not right now. There was too much at stake. He had to get out of there and hook back up with Loni and Arch. He stepped up to the Marshall until the barrel pressed against his chest.

"You know that I've never betrayed my badge. You know that I'll do the right thing to honor the Rangers no matter what. And you know that you're on the wrong side of this thing. Whatever this is you're involved in, you need to walk away."

"It's too late for that, Doug."

"It's never too late to do right. You taught me that. Walk away, Marshall. Be the man I know you are inside."

Doug willed him to make the right choice. His elder adjusted his grip on his weapon, his eyes glancing around, his mouth opening to speak, then closing again.

Finally, he shook his head and said, "I can't. You don't know, Doug. You just don't know. And I can't tell you. You're just going to have to trust me."

Doug sighed, his heart sinking.

"Guess neither of us is budging. Cause I can't trust a man who goes against everything he taught me. And I can't back down from this. If you pull that trigger, it better be set to kill and that bolt will have to be in my back."

Doug turned away and holstered his weapons. He waited a moment, bracing himself for the impact. He didn't know how far his mentor had fallen, but he was gambling, hoping that he hadn't fallen that far.

After a few moments of silence, unconscious Rangers all

around them, Doug stepped up to the console on the reference desk and used Stenson's badge to access the file.

"Don't do it, Doug," the Marshall said.

Doug ignored him. Locating the file, he deleted it and moved to walk away.

"Douglas," the Marshall called.

Doug stopped and turned halfway to face him. The Marshall's blaster was lowered to his side.

"Think maybe you better stun me too."

Doug shook his head, his respect for the man dropping even further.

"You taught me to always face the consequences of my wrong choices, no matter how harsh." He tossed Stenson's badge at him. It clattered to the floor, stopping at the Marshall's feet. "See you around, Marshall."

———

The exit door was locked. Doug growled, but he didn't have time for self-pity. He located a map and brought up the exits. Everything was locked down. He kicked himself for not hanging on to Stenson's badge. He tried his own on the front door, but it didn't work. No doubt that was the Rangers' work.

Maybe they hadn't thought of the roof. He found a service ladder and climbed up to a service hatch. He scanned his badge and the lock unsealed. Doug smiled and climbed through the open hatchway.

Rain poured down in a torrent upon him. He walked to the edge. It was a sheer twenty story drop. No chance of getting down that way. He'd have to have Loni and Arch pick him up. He commed the ship but got no response. He commed Loni and Arch individually, with the same result. A sinking feeling crawled into the pit of his stomach.

Movement in the corner of his eye caught his attention. He spun, drawing his weapon. He only needed a glance and he knew to pull the trigger.

The bolt bounced harmlessly off the personal shield of the bounty hunter.

Must have been up here in order to snipe me.

Doug drew his other blaster and fired off a volley while running for cover behind a transformer node. Bolts sparked on the roof at his heels. He ducked behind the node, bolts slicing the corner, and tried his com again.

"Loni, Arch! Somebody, come in!"

Doug peeked around the corner. The hunter was gone. He crept toward the opposite end of the huge node, glancing back and forth between the two corners. Then he bolted for another. The nodes covered the rooftop in a grid, creating a maze of pillars brimming with energy.

Energy.

Doug found an access panel and opened it. Chips and wires lay inside.

Hope this works.

———

Lo Jinal stalked across the rooftop. His shield deflected energy, but did nothing for the rain. Fortunately, he had his armor for that. Still, some of it was seeping through the softer parts. He needed to get upgraded to a vac suit.

Focus, he told himself as he rounded a corner.

No one.

This Ranger was a slippery one.

A blaster bolt sounded somewhere around him. He spun, seeking a target.

Nothing.

He cursed. This blasted rain was really fragging the bone conductors in his helmet.

Don't let your guard down.

This wasn't his first job, nor even his first Ranger. Every Ranger he ever faced had been a challenge. Of course, that's why he did it. The money helped too. He rounded another corner to find an open access panel. Electrical wires sparked in the rain.

I smell a trap.

Lo avoided the panel, walking wide of the EMP field his sensors warned of.

Ranger thinks he's clever.

He had to squeeze against the opposite wall to stay out of the field. Warning flags went up in his mind. He didn't like being in that position. He drew his other pistol, aiming both in opposite directions as he shimmied along. It was only half a meter, but he'd be spaced if he was going to be ambushed.

An enormous red bolt shot out of the ground ahead of him. It slammed into his shield, draining its reserve down to nothing. It would reboot in a moment, but he was more vulnerable until it did. He barely had time to process this before another bolt struck his jet pack.

Even as the overload alarm blared in his helmet, Lo spun, seeking his target. With the rooftop empty, the Ranger could be only one place. He scanned the top of the nearest pillar and found him. He fired off several rounds from both blasters, driving the Ranger back.

The overload alarm for his jetpack screamed in his ear. Lo slapped a button on his chest ejecting the jet pack. It flew a meter from him and exploded, sending him hurtling across the rooftop. He rolled into another pillar, slumping to the wet roof.

Get up! That Ranger isn't going to wait for you to recover!

He shook off the disorientation, forcing himself to his feet, blaster raised. With visuals rebooting, first thing he saw was his jetpack in a ruined heap ten meters away. Another object lay just a bit closer. Zooming in, he saw it was the destroyed remnants of a blaster.

Overloaded and triggered remotely. Clever, Cowboy. Very Clever.

His shields were gone, the small generator having been fried when the Ranger hit his jet pack. They were almost even now.

Almost.

He broke into a run back toward the pillar.

———

Doug stumbled backward as the bolts seared the edges of the pillar and flew past his face, missing him by millimeters. His foot slipped off the small ledge and he landed hard on the slightly angled side of the pillar. He slid uncontrolled, slamming to the roof below, sending pain ripping through his ribcage.

He'd kept his blaster in hand, thankfully.

He tried to push himself up, but his ribs protested.

Probably bruised them good.

A figure shifted in the pouring rain. Doug gritted his teeth against the pain and pushed hard, spinning over onto his back. In the midst of his spin, his keen eyes picked out the hunter raising both pistols. He fired off a bolt before landing on his back with a grunt of pain. The bolt struck the hunter's pistol just as Doug fired off another round, blasting the other to slag as well.

It all happened in the blink of an eye, but the exertion was too much. The hunter was on him in a second, kicking his blaster away and grabbing him by his coat. Doug twisted, slipping out of his duster and tackled the hunter to the ground.

A blade popped from the hunter's gauntlet. Doug caught the arm, holding it back, just barely. His ribs screamed at him, but he ignored it.

He had to end this quickly.

Doug blocked another punch and threw a knee into the hunter's exposed side. He rolled off him, going for his soaked duster. He threw it toward the hunter just as a quiet *ka-chunk* sounded and the blade shot through the coat, sticking into the steel surface of the pillar. The maneuver was only meant to buy him a second. It was all he needed to grab his gun and duck around the corner as another blade sparked and ricocheted off the corner.

He sprinted into the maze of pillars. He needed to get clear of this hunter. Going back down inside wasn't an option, it was crawling with Rangers.

He needed a way off the roof.

———

Didn't this Ranger know when he was beaten?

Of course, there was still the woman, Loni, to find. But once he dispatched this Ranger, she would be no problem to track down and eliminate, that is if that fool Aoo hadn't managed to muck things up.

Lo was getting angry. That wouldn't help things. He needed to focus. Except this Ranger was infuriating, he refused to die. On top of that he ruined four pieces of equipment.

Yes, he'd enjoy killing this one.

He stalked forward, no longer cautious. He wasn't worried about the blaster. He doubted the Ranger would be willing to sacrifice his remaining weapon, or that he'd try the same trick twice. His armor would deflect any regular bolts that came his way. Unless the Ranger was an extremely good shot.

That gave him pause. The Ranger shot both guns out of his hands in split-second timing.

"Gunslinger," he muttered to himself.

Some Rangers were known to be masters at the craft. This Ranger must be one of them. That complicated matters. If the Ranger had a good bead on him, he could easily get him between the armor. So why didn't he?

Probably some moral code to only kill as a last resort. Well, that would get him nowhere with Lo.

Lo pulled components from his belt. In less than a minute he assembled a back-up blaster. It had a recharging core that took twenty seconds between each shot. Not ideal going up against an opponent of this caliber, but it was all he had now. He hadn't anticipated this Douglas Lancer having such skill, and a gunslinger besides. He made a mental note to add extra ordinances to his inventory as he proceeded into the maze.

"Attention, Bounty Hunter," a voice said in his helmet. It was a Ranger frequency.

The Ranger must know he'd be listening in. Lo had seen the other Rangers enter earlier. Was he using that frequency to talk to him, alert the other Rangers, or both? Lo didn't like giving up his bounty, but he wasn't about to go up against a whole group of them. They likely wouldn't take kindly to a bounty hunter going after one of their own. He needed to finish the job and get out of there.

Good thing the bounty didn't require the Ranger to be apprehended alive.

"Let's have this out man-to-man," the Ranger continued. "North side of the roof. I'm here waiting for you."

Lo ground his teeth. The Ranger told his brothers where they were and the situation he was in. He was forcing his hand.

"Fine," Lo ground out, knowing his own com was muted, "let's see how good you are."

He stalked towards the indicated spot. Rounding a pillar, the Ranger was a distance away, standing at the edge of the roof, hands near his blasters. Lo didn't wait. He charged, holding his fire. He wanted to get as close as he could for a killing shot. The Ranger drew his blasters and got off two rounds before Lo closed the distance. He felt no impacts. The shots missed! Lo raised his blaster.

A body slammed into his left side, tackling him to the rooftop. They tumbled, falling *through* the Ranger and sliding on the slick roof.

Hologram!

Lo wanted to curse, but he was instead focused on the rain and the Ranger grappling him. The Ranger was going for his blaster hand. Lo punched him in his ribs when the floor beneath them gave way to open air.

Instinctively Lo tried to activate his jet pack when he remembered it was blown to bits. Before he could think further, the Ranger hit a button on Lo's arm console, activating his grappling hook. The projectile shot back towards the roof, but fell short.

The hook scraped and clinked along the exterior of the building. The Ranger bear-hugged him while Lo focused on keeping his hook arm steady.

The hook caught. The rest of the feed ran out, jerking Lo's arm out of his socket. Lo screamed. The Ranger lost his grip, slipping down before catching Lo's boot.

Lo fumed. Why wouldn't this Ranger die? Fighting through his pain, he aimed with his other arm. He just needed to hit the Ranger's shoulder with a blade.

The Ranger was already pointing his blaster up at him.

His aim not yet steady, Lo fired the blade in the same moment the Ranger fired his blaster. The blade missed. The bolt sailed past Lo, striking the grappling line and sending them both into freefall once more. In the split second after the line severed, the Ranger pulled and twisted, reversing their positions. Two seconds later and Lo slammed into the ground, the Ranger on top of him.

Pain ripped through him from above and below. The armor

was designed to deflect blaster bolts and some physical impacts. But it could only absorb so much.

Sleep threatened to take hold of him. Lo fought through it, he had to take out this Ranger before he got away. He struggled to raise his arm. The Ranger, coughing, pushed himself up and rolled off. Lo was barely able to turn his head and fire off a blade. The Ranger jerked and stumbled away into the rain.

Lo's world faded, his trailing thoughts on how much he hated Rangers.

CHAPTER TWENTY-SIX_

Arch groaned.

Everything hurt.

"Nala," he said, finding his mouth slow to respond. "Remind me never to go rock sledding again."

A hand caressed his side and he purred.

"Wake up, Arch."

The voice was gentle, but it wasn't Nala's. His lethargic eyes opened. He'd been lost in a memory that was quickly ripped away.

Loni. He'd been with Loni, trying to protect her. He stumbled up on all fours, his forepaw pressing against his throbbing head.

"What happened?" he asked.

"You got hit with five stun blasts at once."

Loni's voice banged in his head. He cringed, squeezing his eyes shut.

"Criminy. Don't those troopers understand weight to stun-blast ratios?"

"I don't think they were concerned with it at the time."

Arch forced his eyes open. They were in a small cell. Plain, gray bars on one side, plain, gray walls on the other three, and blinding light making his skull feel like it was being drilled.

"Where are we?"

"The *Dominator*. Imperial Starcraft Carrier. Sovereign Class. We're in detention level Alpha, cell thirty-two."

Arch turned his head toward her. Not counting her defeated expression, she appeared unharmed.

"You seem to know an awful lot. You okay?" Arch asked.

"Other than dreading our execution? Fine. And I know so much because I used to serve on this ship. I know it inside and out."

"Inside and out, huh?" Arch said, licking his paw and rubbing his head. It still hurt like all criminy, but at least it was fading. "You know how to get around if we get out of here?"

"Forget it, Arch," Loni said. "They took our weapons and the bars are electrified."

Arch trotted up to the bars, gingerly reaching out a claw.

"How much voltage?"

The shock caused him to cry out and jerk his paw back.

"One-thousand."

Arch examined the spacing. Maybe he could just barely fit. He sucked-in his mid-section, estimating his size.

"One-thousand," he repeated, backing up. "Yeah. I can take that. Which way to the control station?"

"Arch."

Arch turned his head. Her mouth hung open slightly, her eyes full of fear. Arch's own mouth opened in his Ikati smile.

"Relax, Princess. I'm tougher than I look."

He turned back to face the bars and bared his teeth, his muscles growing tense in anticipation. A low growl came up and he charged. The front of his body darted between the bars and he jerked to a stop.

Excruciating pain ripped through him and his throat let out a feline yowl.

"Arch!" Loni yelled.

He forced himself forward, wriggling through the bars as the voltage burned away his fur, charring his flesh, and ravaging his mind.

Keep going! Don't stop! Keep going!

His muscles spasmed. Fear gripped some distant part of his scrambled brain. Was he going backwards? Was he moving at all? He had no control over his own body. His own screams confused him.

And then it all stopped. His recovering mind told him he was through, the overall pain fading along with his strength. He wobbled, his legs shaking beneath him, until he collapsed onto the deck with a groan.

———

"Arch!"

Loni stood so close to the bars she could feel the electricity coursing through them. The smell of burnt flesh and hair and the sight of him lying there made Loni want to retch. Arch let out a brief groan.

Two guards appeared. One stopped to look down at Arch while the other pointed her rifle at Loni. Loni recognized her as Xandrie Kovak, a human with a head of blue hair and a blatant disregard for non-human life. The other guard was Po D. Everyone called him Pod and he was a hard case.

"Get back against the wall!" Xandrie ordered her.

Loni reluctantly backed up.

"Stupid cat," Pod said.

"Is it dead?"

"What do you think?" He stooped to pick up Arch's body and

the Ikati hung limp in his grasp.

Pod threw Arch over his shoulder and turned to Xandrie. Faster than Loni could blink, the Ikati raked a claw across the man's jugular then leapt off. Pod cried out. Xandrie whipped around in time to see Arch leaping at her, claws and fangs bared. She shouted, reflexively fired her gun and missed. Arch sank his fangs into her neck. Xandrie grabbed Arch by the scruff and pulled. She screamed as her skin stretched.

The woman too late brought her blaster up. Arch planted his feet and yanked his head back, ripping a chunk out of Xandrie's neck. The release sent Arch slamming to the opposite wall.

Xandrie clutched her neck. She staggered, reached for a panel, and collapsed, bleeding out next to her companion.

Arch righted himself and spat out the chuck of flesh.

"Disgusting," he said, face smattered in blood. "I prefer my human well-done."

Limping and wincing, he moved over Pod, avoiding the pools of blood, and stood on Xandrie's body.

"Which one of these lets you out?" he asked, staring up at the panel just out of his reach.

"Th-the red button," Loni stammered, tasting bile in her throat. "Uh, you have to enter the code first. Should be on the guard's wrist unit."

Arch flipped the dead woman's arm and activated the bracer. A holo of a six-digit code appeared in the air.

"Had to be more than one," Arch grumbled.

He leapt up, his jump cresting at the panel, and punched three buttons. He landed, causing the body to jerk and spurt blood. Loni turned away and covered her mouth to keep from retching. Images of dead colleagues threatened to overtake her mind. With an effort, she pushed them away, focusing on Arch and their need for escape. Arch repeated his action until all buttons had been pressed and the bars of Loni's cell de-powered and slid into the ceiling.

Gathering herself and focusing her mind on Arch, Loni rushed out and plucked the Ikati up into her arms.

He winced at her touch.

"Ah, easy, easy."

"Oh, I'm sorry," Loni said, cradling him and nuzzling his head. "Oh, my brave little Ikati. That was stupid. That was so stupid, Arch! Why'd you have to go and do that?"

"I had to do something to get you out of there," Arch replied through a purr. "Besides, I didn't particularly want to die today. Alright, alright. Enough of the mushy stuff. Let's get out of here before more guards come."

Loni kissed his head and set him down. She picked up the blaster rifles, offering one to Arch. He shook his head.

"Too heavy. No way I can carry it like this, much less wield it. I'll be better off without one until I get my own back. Which way?"

"Follow me," Loni said, slinging the other weapon over her shoulder and leading him down the hall.

Loni opened the thick impervasteel door and marched boldly into the guard station, a lone monitor officer standing at the console. He turned at the sound of her footfalls. Upon seeing her, he froze, hand on his blaster.

"Don't," she said. "Think, Del. You know me. You know what'll happen if it comes down to you or me."

The officer took in the both of them. He pulled, and Loni fired. The officer slumped against the console, a cauterized hole in his chest, his eyes wide. For a moment, his clothing changed from a monitor officer to an interceptor pilot. Loni closed her eyes, forcing the image away.

It's all in your head, she told herself.

She forced herself to breathe deep, calling upon her pilot

training. The panic receded and Loni opened her eyes. Del lay on the floor, slumped against the console, his gray officer's uniform restored. Loni lowered the rifle, the rest of her panic fleeing.

Why couldn't he just listen?

"Nice shot," Arch congratulated, limping to the console and hopping up with a grunt. "Now let's see which one of these lockers has our weapons in it."

Loni glanced at the lockers. "Number 45172."

Arch glanced at the lockers, then at her.

"How do you know that?"

"I know."

Arch slowly turned back to the console.

"Oookaaay."

He keyed in the number.

A locker clicked and Loni held out a hand. The door slapped open and Loni's singularity gun flew across the room and into her waiting palm.

Arch's feline eyes were impossibly wide. He slowly raised a paw toward her, then shifted it toward the locker, then back to her. He seemed to be trying to say something, but nothing would come out. Loni waited patiently for him to get over his shock.

"That…that was…how did you…"

"I thought you said you knew how this gun worked," Loni said.

"Nothing I ever heard said anything about space magic. What else is there that I don't know about?"

"Sorry. Family secrets."

Arch drooped. "Yeah, all right," he moped as Loni walked over to the locker.

"Galaxy's edge. They took my shells."

She sighed and tossed Arch his square and pouch. The Ikati dumbly watched the two items fall short and land on the floor with a *KLACK!* He glanced at his paws then held one out toward the square.

Nothing happened.

Loni rolled her eyes.

"Come on, cat wizard."

Arch grabbed his pouch and square and slapped it. It transformed into a blaster pistol and he limped after Loni.

———

Loni peeked around a corner, waiting for the patrol of Armored Corps Troopers to march away. She sprinted down the pristine hall.

"Hey," Arch whispered. "Slow down."

Loni went back for him and put him on her shoulder. Arch winced with a pained cry at her touch.

"Ugh! Why are you so heavy?" she asked.

"Why does everyone have to comment on my weight lately? You got a plan to get off this ship?"

"Get to the hanger and highjack a fighter," she replied, glancing down another corridor.

"You think the *Blue Moon* is here? If they caught us, they must have known where the ship was."

"That's a good point. Imperial procedure would have impounded any vehicle owned or operated by a fugitive."

She darted to an access panel and told Arch to keep eyes and ears open while she worked.

"Got it," she said after a moment. "Hanger bay twelve. That's three levels from here."

"Is that far?"

"Relax, kitty cat. You have a free ride."

"I'm just wondering about being exposed. The further it is, the more chance we have of getting caught. Someone's going to discover the mess we left in the detention block eventually."

As if on cue, the lighting flashed from white to red and an alarm blared.

"Detention breach," a voice announced. "Detention breach. Lockdown commencing."

"Galaxy's edge," Loni swore, and headed for a lift, moving around to the side.

She pulled away the paneling to reveal a hidden compartment and a ladder running its length. She stepped onto the ladder and pulled the hidden panel closed. They were trapped on the very ship she used to call home. Literally every person she encountered was out to either arrest or kill her. How would she ever make it back to the *Moon* alive?

Stop it, she told herself. *Don't be a scardak. You can make it. Just stay focused.*

Three levels and Loni reached for the panel, but paused.

"What's wrong?" Arch asked.

She eyed his large ears in the dim lighting.

"Do you hear anyone out there?"

Arch pressed his ear to the panel.

"Nah, it's clear. Wait, no. Heavy boots coming this way."

Loni closed her eyes, running through her fighter pilot calming exercises.

"Alright," Arch said after several moments. "They've passed us."

Loni exited the shaft and re-closed the panel. Hefting the blaster rifle she'd taken from the guards, she headed for the hanger bay.

———

Loni peered out into the hanger bay from behind a set of storage crates. The *Blue Moon* patiently waited for them, its deep blue hull reflecting the light of the bay. Two Marines stood guard at the base of the ramp. A few other figures walked about, but it was mostly empty. From her vantage point, she could see the command center overlooking the bay.

"Those Marines are gonna give us trouble," Arch said from his place at her feet. "How's your aim?"

"Better in my interceptor."

"Well, make it better here. Aim for center mass, you're more likely to hit something that way."

"Copy that."

Propping her blaster rifle on a crate, she took careful aim at one of the soldiers. She controlled her breathing, allowing her finger to move on its own.

Breathe.

The cold steel beneath her finger.

A gentle pull.

A red blaster bolt streaked toward the first Marine and absorbed into a forcefield.

"Edge!" she shouted.

The Marines returned fire with a full volley. She ducked behind the crate, blaster bolts sizzling by. The Marines had been standing inside the shield array of the *Moon*. Someone had turned on the shields, which meant—

"We have to go!" she shouted and grabbed Arch by the scruff.

"Whoa! Hey!" he shouted.

Loni pulled him to her chest and he bounced along.

"It's a trap. We have to—"

She cut off as she rounded a corner to find a squad of Armored Troopers. She dove back behind the corner, firing blindly to keep them at bay. Arch squirmed and she let the Ikati drop to the floor. His blaster fire joined hers.

"We're not going to last long like this! We need to get to the ship," Arch said.

Loni knew the area would be swarming with troopers. But what choice did they have?

"Go!" she shouted.

Arch pulled out a stun grenade from his pack and rolled it toward the troopers. They bolted back down the hall as a loud *POP* sounded behind them. The Marines were surprised to see them charging back toward them. That hesitation was all they needed to close half the distance to the ship. Loni brought up her rifle and fired. The bolts absorbed into the shields of the *Blue Moon*, but it also kept the Marines from firing back.

She charged the closest Marine, intent on spearing him. The Marine flipped her over his shoulder and onto the deck. The butt of his rifle came down. She dodged, and it to slammed against the deck. She managed to get in a right cross, but it barely affected the Marine who back-fisted her.

Loni's head spun, pain ripping through her.

Somewhere around her, she heard Arch's feline wail.

She grabbed the man's arm, pulling and twisting her body, attempting to reverse their positions. He was bulkier and heavier, and she was losing ground fast. She tried to reach for her rifle, but he pinned her hand to the deck, his other hand around her throat. She went for his side-arm with her free hand. No sooner had she pulled it from its holster, the end of a barrel raised into her vision.

"Drop the weapon!" came the synthesized voice of an Armored Trooper.

Loni hesitated. It wasn't in her to give up. She would fight to the end if she had any choice. Just beyond the trooper, she could see another Marine, his face scratched and bleeding, aiming his rifle at his feet. She twisted her head. Arch was pinned under the Marine's boot, the barrel of the rifle pressed against his feline skull.

"Drop the weapon, now!"

Loni released her grip, allowing the pistol to fall from her hand. The Marine released her throat. She coughed and was violently flipped to her stomach. A pair of cuffs slapped onto her wrists. Loni's heart sank.

They failed.

Now they would die.

CHAPTER TWENTY-SEVEN_

Doug stared at the empty lot where his ship had been docked, the cold, after-storm wind rustling his clothes. His back ached. His shoulder burned where the bounty hunter's blade embedded itself. It took some work and a lot of pain before he got it out.

Loni and Arch still weren't answering. He doubted either would take off without him. Something else must have happened.

If the Rangers knew he was here, it was possible they alerted the Empire. That wasn't likely, as Rangers always dealt with their own problems internally. But with the change, he didn't put it past them. At any rate, his ship was gone, and Loni and Arch were missing. Only the Empire would have the capability and authority to haul away an entire star ship.

"Lose something?"

Doug turned. Pen stood a meter away.

"Playing it kind of dangerous being here, aren't you?" Doug asked.

Pen shrugged.

"A Ranger doesn't turn his back on someone in need. I heard a call on the Ranger net for Rangers near the system to gather and keep a lookout for one Douglas Lancer, Outlaw. Figured you could use a hand."

"Much obliged. How'd you find me?"

"I did a search when we left Eison Ro on what type of ship was docked at the bay you headed for. Figured I'd need it if I ever wanted to find you. You never gave me your com notifier. Cross-checked that info with local docking reports. Weren't too hard to find. What happened to your ship?"

Doug eyed Pen. Something about him seemed off. But maybe he was just imagining it. He hardly knew the man, so how could he tell anyway? It was probably just the exhaustion from fighting the bounty hunter.

"Not sure. Think someone got a hold of my friends."

"Empire has a capital ship in orbit. Only ones around here I can think of that would have the means and reasons to take your ship and your crew. I'd be happy to give you a lift."

"You got a plan for getting in there?"

"Sure do. Come on. I'm one dock over."

———

Pen's ship was an old, beat-up shuttle, retro-fitted with a hyperdrive. The inside hadn't fared much better than the outside, the wall paneling made of old, partly tarnished chrome plates.

"Nice ship," Doug said, sliding into a passenger seat behind him.

"Thanks," Pen dead-panned.

"What's your plan?" Doug asked as the ship took off and headed into the atmosphere.

"We head in there, you as my prisoner."

Doug's hand drifted to his side.

"And what? You get me into the detention cells so I can spring my crew?"

"That's about the sum of it. I'll fake a coolant leak so I'll have an excuse to stick around. I figure you'll have twenty minutes to get your friends out before they get wise to my actions."

"Sounds as good a plan as any."

Something still nagged the back of his mind about Pen.

I must be going nuts with worry.

Doug caught Pen's reflection in one of the panels. The image was warped and fuzzy. He studied it, racking his brain. Why was this wrong? The birthmark above his eye.

It was the wrong eye.

Doug drew his blaster.

"Why don't you hold the ship right here."

Pen turned his head to the side.

"Pardon?"

"You heard me."

Pen swiveled his chair around, starting to say something, then stopped when he saw Doug's blaster leveled at him. Beyond the viewport in the distance, Doug could make out the carrier.

Pen held up his hands.

"Look, Ranger. I'm not sure what has you all riled up. I'm just trying to help a fellow out."

"Interesting, you calling me Ranger."

"Well, yeah. What else would I call you?"

"What do you think I should be called?"

Pen didn't lick his lips, wasn't sweating, didn't fidget. There were no signs of nervousness about him. He was either extremely confident, or not human.

"You're a Ranger. I'm just a deputy. What else would I call you?"

Doug unstrapped himself and stood, his head nearly bumping the ceiling.

"I promoted the real Pen to full Ranger status back on Eison Ro before we left."

"Calm down, Ranger, uh, Doug. I must have forgotten the promotion. Things got pretty hairy down there, if you remember."

"Where's the badge I gave you?"

"I stowed it. Was trying to be inconspicuous. You know how that goes."

"I never gave you a badge."

Pen was silent, his face unreadable. Then a twitch of movement. Doug fired his blaster. The thing masquerading as Pen split into a field of gray tendrils, his bolt hitting an empty seat. They shot straight for him. He tried to dodge, but it was hard in the confined quarters. Some of the tendrils smacked into his side, wrapping around his arm and leg. The blob moved with lightning speed, enveloping him.

Doug's vision went dark.T he gray mass blocked his air and coated his body, trapping him in a flexible cocoon.

He pulled the trigger on his blaster. The thing rippled. Doug tried to break free but it solidified again. His finger twitched on the trigger but his blaster was ripped from his hand. This thing was strong.

He had to find a way to escape. Except his mind was growing fuzzy, spots appearing before his eyes as his lungs commanded him to breathe.

He flexed his muscles with all his strength, but every flex was counteracted by pressure from the goo monster. He started seeing things and he knew he was losing consciousness, but there was nothing he could do.

A horrible vibration of electricity ripped through him. He fell to the metal floor of the transport, coughing in huge gulps of air.

"I warned you, blobby," said a familiar voice. Doug raised clearing eyes to see Pen, disheveled and red-faced, a high-powered stun rod in his hands. "Messing with a Ranger always comes due."

Pen jammed the rod into the gray blob on the floor. It convulsed, shooting out a tendril to the control board. The ship pitched, throwing the two humans into the wall. Alarms blared. Doug got his hands under him, only to be thrown toward the back of the craft where a storage hatch lay open in the floor. His body slammed into the wall next to Pen.

He heard a beep and immediately reached for the handhold on the side of the wall as the ramp opened to the torrid winds of the upper atmosphere. The ship rocked and jerked, the blob attempting to dislodge him and Pen. Doug slammed against the wall and felt his feet hit open air, only to slam back into the side again.

His hand was wrenched, his shoulder screamed in pain. He didn't know how much longer he could maintain his grip.

At last he managed to get his foot planted against the floor, bracing himself against the constant motions. Pen was holding on but fairing poorer. He was a big man and Doug couldn't help him stabilize or he'd get pulled out too. Their only chance was neutralizing the blob creature. The stun rod was clattering around the interior of the ship. Doug watched it, waiting for the optimal moment. The air was thinning. They were almost out of the atmosphere. He couldn't wait any longer.

Doug dove for the stun rod.

His sweaty hands slipped on its smooth surface before he got a firm grasp. Doug fought against the rushing wind and the pitch of the craft.

A tendril shot toward him. He dodged, and struck.

The blob convulsed.

It was the moment of stability Doug needed.

He leapt at the main body of the blob and rammed the rod into it. It convulsed, tendrils slapping wildly at him. The thing started to smoke, still writhing. Doug held it there until the creature burst into flames. It shot past him, falling out into the open air. Doug nosed the craft downward, diving back into the atmosphere several hundred meters before leveling out. He set the autopilot and turned to the ramp.

Pen was nowhere to be seen.

CHAPTER TWENTY-EIGHT_

Loni kneeled on the deck, her hair frazzled and her breathing labored. Her hands shifted, feeling minute vibrations coming off the stun cuffs around her wrists. Arch sat next to her, head hung and eyes closed. They'd hog tied him with wire someone managed to scrounge up. They must not have a pair of stun cuffs small enough for him. Troopers and Marines surrounded them, their rifles at the ready.

The crowd parted and Commodore Ferris appeared, her head held high, with hands clasped behind her back.

"Loni Taraska," she announced. "You are hereby charged with treason against the Empire, sedition, and conspiring with—"

"Stow it," Loni muttered, meeting the Commodore's eye.

The Commodore started, obviously not expecting such brazen defiance.

"You're building a super-weapon to wipe out the core worlds," Loni continued. The commodore signaled a Marine. "You had my entire squad wiped—"

The butt of his weapon slammed into her chin. Her head spun and everything went dark for a second. Then she felt a massive pain rip through her jaw.

"That will be enough Rebel lies from you, trai—"

"Is that protocol?" Loni shouted, blood pooling in her mouth, splattering from her lips. "Strike a prisoner when she's cuffed and immobile? You'd best kill me now, because your secret is about to be blown wide open and I am *not* shutting up about it, no matter how severely you beat me!"

She spat at the Commodore's feet.

"You ordered us to wipe out a peaceful mining colony because someone got a hold of your plans and you wanted to make sure no one knew about them. Then you executed my squad, using White Scars as a cover. You're a disgrace to that uniform, coward!"

The commodore rung her hands, her face tight.

"Troopers!"

They stood at attention.

This was it. They were going to execute her. She'd done everything right and all she got for it was unlawful execution. How? How could this have happened? Her throat tightened and her heart slammed against her chest. She didn't want to die. Not now. Not as a traitor.

"You sure know how to work a crowd," came Arch's tired voice from beside her.

For some reason, just the sound of the Ikati comforted her. Knowing he was there with her, even to her death, she wasn't quite so afraid. She turned her head toward him. His eyes were closed and his breathing was deep. Small bits of foam leaked out the side of his mouth.

"Ready!" The commodore said.

The troopers readied their rifles.

"Listen, Princess," Arch said, his voice low, muscles flexing.

"Charge!"

The rifles powered up with a whine.

"Whatever happens…"

"Aim!"

"…stay low."

"Fi—"

A roar, as if from some great, inter-dimensional beast bellowed out of Arch. His eye shot open, beaming golden light and his body exploded into a cat ten times his size. His fur, no longer patchy, was streaked with silver, wavy lines, and a main of black fur encompassed his neck. His tail, disproportionately long, ended in a gleaming, diamond-shaped blade. He landed on all fours, belting out a roar even louder than the first.

The troopers in front of him stumbled backwards. Those on the sides opened fire. Loni flattened herself against the deck.

The starship-sized cat turned its snarling maw on the troopers. He bit one in half, scattering the others. He raked half-meter claws across another group. His tail whipped around, slicing through others, their armor flimsy as paper against his razor-sharp talons.

The blaster fire intensified, but it only seemed to enrage the Ikati further as it wreaked havoc on the Imperial forces.

People shouted, screamed, and died. Bodies and blood were everywhere.

Loni snaked over to a dead trooper and twisted herself, maneuvering until her stun-cuffs lined up with his auto-key. Her locks fell away. She picked up the fallen trooper's weapon and blasted away.

She spotted troopers setting up a plasma burner at the far end of the hanger. Loni had seen first-hand what the anti-armor weapons could do. Arch might be shrugging off normal blaster fire as if it was nothing, but she doubted whatever was protecting him could withstand a blast from that thing.

She fired at the troopers. Their return fire forced Loni to duck behind the wing of a starfighter. She wasn't very proficient with a blaster rifle, while the troopers were expert marksmen. She had no hope of hitting them.

At least not with this weapon.

She closed her eyes, blocking out the blaster fire, the roar of Arch's rage, and the screams of dying men. She focused her mind on a single object, sensing its presence. It wasn't far. Eyes still closed, she reached out and a moment later felt the satisfying smack of her singularity gun impacting her palm.

She dug out an emergency shell she kept in a hidden, inside pocket.

White.

A few of the troopers were keeping Arch distracted by shooting from multiple sides and ducking under cover. They were paying for it with their lives. Arch was too fast, too strong, and had too long a reach for them to escape.

Loni loaded the shell and closed the breach. She prepared herself and leapt out into the open, the barrel of her gun aimed in the general direction of the plasma burner spooling up for a shot. Multiple rifle shots slammed into her chest plate and Loni crashed to the deck.

She forced herself to hold her aim with weakened fingers.

A yellow beam shot from the plasma burner.

She pulled the trigger, unleashing a tunnel of white-hot energy a meter in diameter, swallowing the beam from the plasma burner. Her arc of heat tore through the plasma burner and the team operating it, continuing past them through several bulkheads and out into space. The beam dissipated in an instant, leaving the hanger and several portions of the ship exposed to the void.

Everything and everyone not fused to the deck were sucked toward the opening. Loni grabbed onto a gouge in the impervisteel caused by Arch's claws. She held her breath, knowing she only had seconds to live.

At least I took a few of these scum with me.

Something like a large, wet hand enveloped her sides. She

craned her neck to see Arch lifting her up by his maw. He dug his claws into the deck, fighting against the vacuum of space.

Incredibly, he was winning.

He made it to the *Blue Moon* and collapsed, dropping Loni painfully onto the impervisteel ramp and reverting to his former state. His now smaller body slid away. She grabbed his paw with one hand and the ramp hydraulic with the other, allowing her gun to fly off into the void.

She hit the emergency close button on the strut and the ramp raised. Loni collapsed onto the deck, Arch cradled in her arms.

Air rushed into her lungs and she took large, coughing breaths. Arch stared back at her with his golden eyes, the glow now gone.

"That's quite a trick you've got there," she said.

"Me? You're the one that just defied the vacuum of space with one hand. I'm an Ikati. We can manipulate our own gravitational field. But you're a human. No human I've ever met can do what you just did."

"I guess we both have our secrets. But I don't think any of mine can top what I just saw."

"I'm flattered. Now can we burn outta here?"

"Glad to."

She got to her feet and rushed the both of them toward the cockpit.

CHAPTER TWENTY-NINE_

Commodore Ferris glared at the crescent-shaped ship soaring away from the *Dominator*, her vision as red as the emergency lighting of the bridge. All around her, people were scrambling, yelling out status reports and relaying orders.

Her ship was disabled, dead in space. Those Pirate scum hadn't shown, which she should have expected. Now the fugitives were escaping.

Not on my watch, she thought, tapping the com.

"Gunnery Sergeant, target all turrets on that ship and fire at will!"

"Yes, Ma'am," the voice called back. "Rerouting power now. We will have a firing solution in thirty seconds."

"Ma'am," called a sensor officer, "I have multiple contacts emerging from hyperspace!"

Several ships appeared above Grandus, moving to intercept the fugitives' ship. They were a hodgepodge of fighters from different species mixed in with black-market military-grade fighters, which meant only one thing:

Pirates.

She tapped the com again.

"New orders, Sergeant. Defend the *Dominator.* Any ship comes near us, I want it vaporized. And I want tracking on those ships. When I give the order, I want all guns, full salvo on the lead vessel."

"Understood, Ma'am."

"Should we call in ship support, Ma'am?" the captain asked from her side.

"Not yet, Captain. We'll call them in if we need them, but I doubt we will."

"Ma'am?"

Ferris turned to the captain.

"Did I stutter, Captain?"

The man quivered beneath her glare.

"N-no, Ma'am."

Spineless jellyfish.

Ferris lingered a moment longer, then turned to the viewport. These traitors would get their just due, as would Drexx for his threats. Let any who would defy the Empire and threaten the safety of the galaxy know the penalty for rebellion.

———

"Uh, Loni, we've got company," Arch said. "And I think they're gunning for us."

Loni craned her neck to view Arch's sensor display, and the many ships headed in their direction.

"Think you can still man the turrets?" she asked.

"If I'm conscious, I can still pull a trigger."

Arch leapt down from the co-pilot's seat and loped back to the tac room. The com beeped and Loni tapped the button. Doug's voice filled the cockpit.

"Loni, Arch. Come in."

"I'm here, Doug. Arch is manning the turrets."

"The turrets?"

"We have Pirates after us. Your pickup might be a little delayed."

"Alright, well, you're obviously in a hot mess. I'm down below you. I can see you from my vantage point. I'll see what I can do about getting some help."

"I don't think the planetary defenses will help much, not with that carrier doing nothing."

"I had something else in mind. Do what you can to keep the Pirates off you. Don't worry about me for now."

"Wasn't planning on it. Loni out."

———

Sergeant Ati tried to make his mind relax and become mesmerized by the brilliant colors of hyperspace. Normally he enjoyed the beauty of hyperspace travel. Right now, he hated it. He also hated his destination.

Black void of space would be nice.

He'd spent most of the trip back to Tellus Four attempting to get over his frustration. He was almost there, but was lapsing. He needed to focus on his duty for his troopers' sakes.

The shuttle was mostly quiet. Vid and Tolso spoke in low tones about the benefits of first-person simulation games, but that was it. No one was happy about their situation and their silence spoke volumes. Bot sat next to him in the pilot's seat, equally quiet and likely equally miffed.

He knew the trooper wanted to further object, but there was nothing more to say. Best to focus on what's ahead. Likely private missions to hunt down dissidents. His frown turned down even more.

"You're scowling, Sergeant."

Bot's voice lacked any of the menace he expected from the trooper, remaining even and calm.

"You're awful cheery," Ati said. For Bot, that was true.

"Can't do anything about it. Orders are clear."

Ati looked over at the suit of armor in the pilot's seat. "What are you planning, soldier?"

"What do you mean, Sergeant?"

"I know you, Rustner. I know how you got into the Armored Corps. I doubt your penchant for going rogue has changed in the last three months. You're staying on Tellus."

The leather of the yoke creaked as Bot's grip tightened. The trooper would probably be in the exercise room until the next morning. The console beeped and Bot curled a fist, punching the dump controls before almost yanking the hyperspace lever right out of the console.

The brilliant colors faded to normal space and the console beeped with a com message. Ati tapped the button.

"Go for Ati," he said.

"Sergeant," said a voice with a New Texan accent. "This is Douglas Lancer, Galactic Ranger."

Ati threw Bot a questioning glance.

"Yes, I know who you are, Ranger. What are you doing on this frequency?"

"Contacting you, obviously."

Ati pursed his lips. This Ranger was a sarcastic one.

"*How* are you contacting me? This is an Imperial channel. And how did you—"

"Look, not to cut you off, but I don't have much time and I have some information you need to know."

"You're a wanted criminal, Ranger. Why would I listen to anything you have to say?"

"Cause you don't blindly follow the Empire. You're a good

soldier, near as I can tell by our brief encounter. Between that and the fact that you're an Armored Corpsman, you may be one of the few individuals I can trust. I know I'm taking a risk here, but it's one I'm willing to take for the sake of my crew. I have an opportunity your squad and the Empire may be interested in, if you're willing to listen."

Ati chewed his lip. He had his duty to the Empire. He should be tracking the signal, but he'd been ordered off the assignment. He wasn't ready to believe a criminal in a situation he couldn't control. However, he'd seen the evidence against this Ranger and was convinced the charges were questionable at best. And if his "crew" was the princess and the Ikati, it might mean the Empire was trying to finish what they started. He wasn't going to defy orders, but he wasn't going to pass up an opportunity to learn more either.

"Alright, you have my attention," Ati said.

———

Loni jerked the yoke. The pirates closed in and opened up on them.

They didn't even hail us. And why are they after us instead of going after the carrier?

The planet loomed in the distance. They needed to get away from its gravity well in order to jump. She wasn't worried about Doug. He could take care of himself. So why wasn't she leaving? All it would take was a simple reversal to run the Pirates chasing them.

Arch's voice crackled over the com.

"Did I forget to mention this was a nice choice of weaponry on this bird? What are these, AL-twelves?"

"Twenty-fours," Loni replied, sweat beading on her forehead as she adjusted their heading. She hoped this ship could take the trick she was about to try.

"Twenty-fours? Those are heavy emplacements rated for war cruisers! You don't mess around, do you, Princess? I'm liking you more all the time."

Loni smirked even as the planet drew closer.

"Uh, Loni, why are we headed into the atmosphere?"

"Trying something," Loni replied, her hand ready on switches as the ship began to vibrate. Outside the viewport, fiery streaks formed and multiplied, her focus locked on the altimeter spinning down.

Just a little further.

Her muscles tensed.

Almost there.

"Arch, hold on back there."

She killed the engines and hit aft thrusters. The ship free-fell into a slow spin. Loni waited until she could see the pursuing craft out of the cockpit viewport and fired up the engines, full burn.

She slammed into her seat, the ship groaning under the strain. Four Pirate ships shot past her, continuing on their momentum toward the planet surface where they impacted in a series of explosions and wreckage. Loni tried not to think of the loss of life she'd contributed to. The Pirates could have stopped chasing her after all. The *Blue Moon* hovered in place, fighting against momentum and the planet's gravity. Its inertia faded out and the ship shot back up toward the upper atmosphere.

"Uh, Loni," Arch said, his voice sounding sick, "does this ship have a cleaning bot?"

"Maybe a basic unit."

"Well, you may want to send it to the tac room. No particular reason. Just, y'know, a little dirty in here."

"Sorry, Arch. But that got four birds off our tail."

"Great. Only twenty more to go. These Pirates don't do anything light, do they?"

"Just take out as many as you can. Doug's getting some help. We just need to buy him some time."

The ship emerged from the atmosphere into a blockade of Pirate ships. They opened up on the *Blue Moon*, forcing Loni to alter course and weave. Even still, the ship took plenty of hits.

"How are the shields doing?" Arch asked as a few more ships vaporized.

Loni glanced at the readout.

"Holding. But won't be for long at this rate."

The ship bucked and a message flashed across the viewport.

IMPACT.

Now what?

"Arch, did something just hit us?"

"You mean besides seventeen blaster bolts?"

"Scan the hull and see if you see anything."

A terrible screech echoed from down the hall.

"What in the nine hells?" Arch said. "There's some kind of creature on the hull of the ship. It's tearing away the plating. I can't get a low enough angle to blast it."

Loni got a sinking feeling in her stomach. "What does it look like?"

"Hard to see. Looks like it has a long beak. Really thin, like maybe a skeleton. It's in shadow. I can't see much of it. But it's tearing up the hull like it's paper."

Drexx.

Loni's hand went to her side and she felt the empty holster.

Edge!

She closed her eyes, willing herself to block out the horrible screeches of metal, the blaster fire impacting the shields, and Arch's panicked voice.

She could sense it, far out, near the limit of her reach. Eyes still closed, she pulled on the yoke, whiplashing the ship in the reverse direction toward her singularity gun floating forgotten out in space.

A blaring alarm broke her out of her revere. Red words flashed across the viewport.

HULL BREACH.

A crash thundered down the corridor.

"Swore I'd never use one of these things," she muttered, locking the coordinates and transferred controls to the A.I.

She hit the final button just as the cockpit door screeched open. Drexx's frightening form took up the whole of the doorway. He shuffled into the room and brought a massive claw down. Loni leapt from her seat, rolling between his legs onto her haunches and sprinted down the corridor. Drexx roared, the horrible sound playing across the ship-wide com like some inescapable hell spawn as he crashed after her.

She could sense it, even without concentrating. They were close. She reached out a hand, summoning the gun to her as she dashed onto the hanger bay lift. She slammed a fist on the door close button. Two impervisteel doors slammed closed behind her, causing Drexx to impact them with a loud *BANG!*

"Activate voice controls!" Loni said, clinging to the railing as the lift slowly descended.

Above her, the doors dented inward. Drexx's roar shook her to her core. A horrible screeching sounded and the doors were forced open. Loni jumped the rest of the way to the floor. She landed in a controlled tumble, scrambled to her feet, and ran for her ship. Drexx slammed to the floor behind her.

She always kept a couple shells for her singularity gun in her cockpit for emergencies. This was definitely an emergency. She was almost there when something grabbed her ankle. She went down, the floor rising up to meet her.

A sickening *CRUNCH* and everything went black for a split

second. She felt herself being lifted as her sinus cavity filled with liquid.

Drexx held her off the ground, his glowing eyes hungry for her flesh.

Loni choked, coughing out, "Open hanger bay doors."

The hanger door obediently slid open, creating a vortex. Drexx dug his clawed feet and the claw of his free hand into the impervisteel, holding himself firm. Loni dangled from his other claw, holding her breath.

Drexx's razor teeth glinted in the light of the hanger bay.

"Where are the plans for the weapon?" his rumbling voice sounded in her com.

Loni felt her gun's presence close. She could summon it in an instant. But without a shell, it was useless. And she couldn't get to her ship. Fighting down her fear, she glared back at the monster as if to say, *I'll be spaced if I tell you anything.*

She made a rude gesture and Drexx moved his other claw toward her.

A black form leapt onto Drexx's shoulder and spat a small object at her. She caught it on instinct. Arch activated his blaster and simultaneously rammed the barrel into Drexx's eye socket and fired. Drexx roared, dropping Loni and losing his grip on the deck. He jerked back in an uncontrolled tumble, but managed to get his claws back into the floor.

Loni was flying toward the open door. She scrambled and her hand grabbed hold of the *Barracuda*'s landing strut, painfully jerking her shoulder. She could feel the object Arch spat at her in her hand.

A shell.

Arch was leaping around Drexx, firing at him with a rapid spray of blaster bolts that did little to harm to the monster. Drexx swiped the air, missing the nimble Ikati as it danced around him in its own gravity field.

Loni maneuvered herself so that she straddled the strut, and reached out a hand. Drexx's claw swiped, catching Arch in one of his leaps. Phosphorous, yellow blood splattered before getting sucked out into space. Arch smacked against the deck like a rag doll.

Loni nearly cried out, but kept her breath held. Spots formed before her eyes. An object flew past Drexx and into her outstretched hand. She loaded the shell as quickly as she dared and aimed.

Get off my ship!

She pulled the trigger and a red beam slammed into Drexx, sending him hurtling through the open hangar door. The shell ejected and Loni aimed the gun at the control panel. The gun went flying toward it, smacking the emergency close button. Loni let out her breath, coughing and gasping.

Standing on shaking limbs, she stumbled over to Arch. Blood pooled around him, gushing from a large gash on his side, his tactical vest sliced wide open. His lips were moving ever so slightly. Loni leaned her ear to his mouth.

"Med—bay."

She picked him up and rushed to the med bay, tears already stinging her eyes.

Please don't die, Arch. Please don't die.

Gently, she laid him on an operating table. Arch groaned, then whispered something. Loni leaned down to hear him.

"Go."

"Just tell me what to do," Loni pleaded, stroking his head.

"Go," Arch whispered. "Pirates…still out there."

"I don't care," Loni practically shouted. "I'm not leaving you."

"Have to…can't help."

Loni's heart rent in two. She'd left her squad when she fled the *Dominator*. How could she do it again, leaving Arch to die? How could she do what he asked?

"Leave me. Go."

Loni blubbered, unable to find the words.

"Go," Arch said.

He was right. There was nothing she could do for him. She had to get them away from the Pirates. Which meant she had to leave him to die.

She kissed his forehead and ran for the cockpit. She slid into the pilot's seat, disengaging the A.I., doing her best to pull herself together. She wiped her nose on her sleeve as the com chirped to life.

"Loni Taraska," said a familiar voice, "Traitor to the Empire. You seem to be in a bit of a predicament. Announce your surrender and turn over your ship and we will be glad to render assistance."

Loni could see the carrier out the viewport.

Her anger burned white hot. She adjusted her heading, angling her ship toward the carrier, then pushed the throttle all the way forward. The *Blue Moon* shot toward the *Dominator*. Pirate ships trailed behind her. Their blaster fire reduced the shields to nothing and an alarm blared. It didn't matter. She wasn't going to be alive much longer anyway. But neither was Ferris.

"Taraska," called a voice over com, "lower your speed. You are on a collision course."

"That's the point, clud dung," she said, knowing her com was muted.

She didn't mute their side though. She wanted to hear their panic as they continually warned her away. They'd probably open fire on her as soon as she got too close. Then she would die. She and Arch would die together, making a suicide run on an Imperial carrier.

A smirk formed on her lips. Neither of them would have it any other way. She was almost at the point of no return. Any moment and they would open up, and that would be it.

A stray thought entered her mind that she was about to leave Doug without a ship or crew.

Sorry, Cowboy.

Another carrier shot into the empty space next to the *Dominator.* Then another on the other side. Then a third. The space around the carrier filled with Imperial warships. They immediately opened fire. The high yield blaster bolts flew past the *Moon,* obliterating the Pirate forces behind her and scattering the rest. Loni veered off, bringing her ship out of range of the *Dominator.* Her com came to life with a new voice.

"*Blue Moon,* this is the Imperial warship *Excelsior.* Do you require assistance?"

Loni gaped, but quickly gathered herself and unmuted her com.

"That depends. Are you requiring my surrender?"

There was silence a moment.

"Is this Lieutenant Colonel Taraska I'm speaking with?"

Loni hesitated, unsure if she should trust this person.

"Yes," she finally said.

"Lieutenant, this is Admiral Kezzik. I have received word from the Admiralty that you are no longer an Imperial officer and that you have resigned your commission. I have as yet to know the circumstances of said resignation, but I will be speaking shortly with Commodore Ferris and the crew of the *Dominator.* Your cooperation in this matter would be appreciated. But you are a member of the royal house. If you resigned your commission, you have nothing to fear from us."

Loni breathed out a sigh of relief.

"You have my cooperation, Admiral. Though I would appreciate if I could conduct any interviews via holo."

"I don't see that being a problem. Now back to my original question; do you need assistance?"

"Appreciated, Admiral. But we're still flying. Just need some credits to repair my ship and I'll be fine."

"Will thirty-thousand do?"

Loni blinked.

"Sir?"

"We were tipped off by a member of your crew that there was a gathering of Pirates at these coordinates. We've captured a good number of them."

Loni glanced at her scope and saw more ships behind her, stalling the Pirate ships in tractor webs.

"As I understand it, you are working for a Ranger that has turned bounty hunter," Kezzik continued. "I'd say the Pirates we've captured is a bounty worth at least that much. Will that suffice for repairs?"

"More than suffice. Thank you, Admiral."

"I'll have the payments transferred immediately. We'll be in touch. Kezzik out."

Loni sighed, leaning back in her seat, energy draining out of her. Every limb felt like it was made of permacrete. Her eyelids sagged. She quickly rubbed her face, fighting through the fatigue and inadvertently smeared blood from her nose. She grabbed a gauze from an emergency kit and held it to her nose as she leaned her head back. She immediately faced forward again.

She couldn't rest. Not yet. Not until she buried Arch. She glanced back at the hallway, and balled her free hand into a fist. Forcing herself to stand, she loped down the hall toward the med-bay.

CHAPTER THIRTY_

Doug searched for a while, even combed the local holo news for word of a body having fallen from the sky. But there was no sign of Pen. In a core world city like Grandus, he'd probably never find him. He decided to do a search for his family when he got back.

His com squawked.

"Douglas Lancer, come in."

It was a general broadcast, a frequency used for announcements and searches for lost individuals, and used only by the Rangers and local law enforcement. Doug knew the voice. And it gave him an idea.

"I read you, Marshall," he said.

"When are you going to quit running, Son? You need to come in."

"Only things I need to do are stay human and die. But I'll be dusted if I'm turning my back on the code like the rest of you."

"Douglas," the Marshall said, hesitation clear in his voice, "there are things happening that…well, quite frankly, they'll spell the end of the Rangers."

Doug felt his blood run cold.

"I know your love for the Rangers," the Marshall continued. "You were the best deputy I ever had. Honest to goodness. And yeah, I know we're on public com right now, but I don't care. It's the truth and needed to be said. You're a fine Ranger, Douglas. Always have been."

Doug's hands gripped the yoke, his knuckles turning white as he struggled to hold himself together. The Marshall wasn't just flattering him or buttering him up. He was being sincere. He was the most honest man he knew.

"That's why I want you to come in," the Marshall continued. "I'm doing what I can to preserve the Rangers from what's coming. But I'm old and I'll need someone to take my place. You're the right man for that job, Douglas."

Deputy Marshall. He'd be the deputy Marshall of the entire Ranger corps. He could steer them back on the right course and fix the problems that lingered. As Marshall, he could weed out those unfaithful among them and finally find out what this whole mess was all about. But it would mean becoming slaves to the Empire and doing exactly what his mentor had done. Douglas swallowed and closed his eyes, steadying himself.

"I can't do that, Marshall," he said, quietly.

The coming silence seemed to penetrate his very soul.

"I figured as much," the Marshall said. "I think it's pretty useless to keep chasing you. You slip away each time. Even if we did catch you, you're not budging and I'm not having you jailed or executed. That's not the Ranger way."

Doug cleared his throat, diverting his mind from the situation.

"Yeah, about that. You mind cancelling the bounty on my head?"

"Bounty?"

The Marshall sounded shocked.

"You can probably thank Stenson. He never did like me."

A dark tone laced the Marshall's voice when he said, "I'll take care of that. At any rate, I can't sanction your status as a Ranger. You do what you know to be right, but if you ever have a run-in with any Rangers—"

"I know. One last thing, though. I'm currently flying the ship of a deputy named Pen. I don't know his last name. Olster, I think. But he gave his life to save me from what I suspect was a bounty hunter. I'd appreciate a last name and address of his next of kin."

"Hold on a tick."

Doug could hear the Marshall working some holo controls.

"Yeah, I've got it here. And I've got his ship's regular frequency. I'll send over the coordinates."

"Much obliged."

"Take care of yourself, Douglas."

"You too, Marshall."

Doug killed the com and hovered in the atmosphere. He closed his eyes, leaning back in his seat. The Marshall's words rang in his head. Tears formed at the edge of his eyes.

There are things happening that will spell the end of the Rangers. I'm doing what I can to preserve the Rangers from what's coming.

Doug opened his eyes, his brow knitted. This couldn't just be about the weapon. If the Marshall knew about the weapon, he and the rest of the Rangers could move in and arrest the Admiralty. There was something more to this the Marshall wasn't saying or *couldn't* say. Not unless he got the man alone.

First thing's first, he thought, reaching for the controls.

He tried hailing them, but got no response. A sinking feeling leaked into his gut. A few taps and he was flying Pen's ship up into outer space, headed for the *Blue Moon.*

———

Loni had gone back to the med-bay and covered Arch's body with a blanket. It was all she could will herself to do. Now, she sat in the pilot's seat, holding a cloth to her nose. Oddly enough, it was more comforting than her quarters. Here she felt in control, felt less like her world was falling apart.

"Loni, Arch. Come in."

Loni eyed the com. Apathy drowned her. She didn't see the point to anything right then, and certainly not talking to anyone. Nevertheless, she forced herself to hit the com button.

"This is Loni," she slurred out.

"You alright?" Doug asked.

"No. What do you need, Doug?"

"Well, I'd appreciate it if you'd open the hanger bay door so I can dock."

She tapped the controls, opening the door. A few minutes later, Doug appeared in the doorway. She turned haggard eyes to see him looking worriedly at the deep gouges in the doorway. His shoulder was bandaged with what looked like a portion of his shirt. When he saw her, his face grew even more concerned.

"What happened here?"

"Drexx," Loni said, turning back to the controls, replacing the cloth. She felt like crying again, but didn't want to in front of him. "Shot him out into space."

"Where's Arch?"

"Med bay."

"He all right?"

Loni shook her head, her will breaking down.

"No," she squeaked out. She put her head in her hands, attempting to use her military training to steady her emotions and the thoughts of her squad, the people at the colony that she helped kill, and Arch's severed body trying to save her. It was all too much.

"He died defending me, Doug," she blurted between sobs. "I couldn't save him."

Doug was silent. She turned on him.

"Say, something, will you?" she shouted.

Doug opened his mouth to speak, but another voice spoke first.

"How about 'Arch isn't dead'?"

They both turned to see Arch sitting in the doorway, staring up at them.

"Arch!" Loni rushed over and picked up the Ikati in a tremendous hug, sobbing once again, this time out of relief.

"Whoa!" Arch yelled. "Easy! I'm still healing."

"Healing?" Loni said, pulling him back to look him in the face. His legs dangled helplessly with his arms straight in front of him in a comical sight. "You're supposed to be dead."

"Oh, well, pardon me for disappointing you. Didn't anyone ever tell you? Us Ikati are immortal, well except for fire. That's about the only thing that can kill us. Why do you think Mao was firebombed? You bi-pedals don't know much, do you?"

Loni turned him this way and that.

His fur had grown back and Loni had trouble locating the wound. When she did, the flesh was whole with only the faintest hint of a scar, new hairs already sprouting around it.

"You told me there was nothing I could do to help you," Loni said accusingly. "You told me to leave you to die."

"No. I told you to leave me. Period. You needed to get us away from the Pirates and I needed to be left alone so I could go into my healing state. After transforming, getting wounded—"

"Hey," Loni interrupted. "Speaking of which, why didn't you just transform like you did on the *Dominator?* You'd have made short work of that nightmare."

Arch glanced at Doug.

"It's, uh, not something we can do anytime we want. There's

conditions. Look, I'd rather not get into it right now. Bottom line is, I've still got some more healing to do, but I wanted to find out what our status was. Hey, set me down, will ya? Thank you."

Loni wiped her nose with her cloth and gained back some of her composure.

"Well, our ship is scrap. But we're free of the Pirates, no thanks to me. You know I almost rammed the carrier because I thought you were dead."

Arch's ears flattened back against his head.

"You what? You really are crazy. How'd we get away?"

Loni turned to Doug, raising an eyebrow.

"I tracked down the Armored Corps Troopers that cornered us back on Tellus Four. Once they heard about a bunch of Pirates in one location, they jumped at the chance and called in the cavalry."

"Score one for the Armored Corps," Arch said. "At least somebody in the Empire has some brains. Does this mean they aren't hunting us anymore?"

"I suspect my parents found out about the bounty and inter-vened," Loni said. "Strong as the Empire is, they don't want to arouse the anger of the Tarsek System. We're free and clear, assuming the inquiry on the *Dominator* goes well. And we have the credits to get this ship repaired, thanks to Doug's work and a generous Admiral."

"Golden," Arch said. "Let's high-tail it out of this system and get the ship fixed up."

Loni raised an eyebrow.

"What?" Arch asked.

Loni shrugged.

"I just thought you'd be gone once we accomplished our mission."

"You bi-pedals. Don't you pay attention? I like you, Princess. And the Cowboy isn't half bad either. Stupid, maybe. Crazy, definitely. But I like you two. I can operate my shop out of the cargo bay, long as Captain Looses-his-blasters doesn't have a problem with it. I see you lost 'em again. I'm charging you this time."

Doug shrugged, then winced. "Fine with me. I mean on both the blasters and sticking around. Besides, we may not be done."

They both paused.

"There's a couple factors here that don't add up," Doug continued. "We all agreed that the admirals must have had mutual consent to approve and build the weapon. So why is it this admiral Loni communicated with was so eager to exonerate her? I don't buy that they would whiplash from hunting her like a dog in order to shut her up, to buying her off. My guess is this admiral doesn't know anything about the weapon."

"Or he's sticking to his integrity like a certain cowboy I know," Loni said.

Doug smirked.

"Good thought, but doubtful. If the whole Empire is like the *Dominator,* I suspect they'd have made him quietly disappear if he wasn't with them on this. Like I said, just doesn't add up. Also, there's the fact that they're not coming after me for deleting a high-level Imperial file. And besides all that, something the Marshall said makes me think there's more to this than just the weapon. I'm not sure what yet. It's just a hunch at this point. But we may need to do some investigating."

Loni smiled.

Doug threw her a questioning look.

"I just like that you said 'we.'"

"Well, don't get too excited. It ain't all glitz and glamour. Before we get to that though, we should get the ship repaired. And I have a couple things I need to take care of."

"Are we heading back to Lavtak Three then?" Loni asked, eagerness in her voice.

Doug grimaced.

"I ain't ready for that yet. Oh, keep your shirt on. I ain't abandoning her. I ain't heartless. I'll give her an answer soon one way or the other. No, there's another place that's closer and on the way to where we need to go. We'll stop and make repairs, then I need to drop off a shuttle to someone, then on to New Texas."

"New Texas?" Loni asked. "What's there?"

"Your explanation as to why I'm not going back to Lavtak Three. Set course for Glixsol and punch it as soon as you're ready. I need some medical attention and then some sleep, so I'll be in my bunk. You both may want to get some yourself."

"Heh," Arch said. "You don't have to tell me twice."

He padded out of the cockpit. Loni breathed out, the dried blood on her nostrils itching, her emotions finally steadying, but leaving her drained.

"You all right?" Doug asked.

"Now that I know Arch is okay, yeah. I'll be fine. Definitely need some sleep though, if I don't wind up having nightmares about Drexx stalking me through the ship."

She eyed Doug whose face held a smirk.

"What?"

He shrugged and winced again. Why did he keep forgetting that?

"Just seems to me you've grown some affection for Arch, same as he has for you."

Loni rolled her eyes and moved to the pilot's chair. "Good night, Cowboy."

Drexx stalked into his private chambers aboard the Pirate mothership and slammed an over-sized fist onto the close door panel. The large monster rubbed his skeletal chest where Loni's beam struck him. It hadn't hurt. But when it finally dissipated, he found himself severely weakened. It was fortunate he didn't register on most sensors as a life form, enabling him to float in space until the Empire left the system. Only then was he able to call in the mother ship.

He growled. If there was one thing he loathed, it was being weak. He'd spent his whole life doing everything he could to escape that pathetic being he once was. He had no memory of that creature who'd died so long ago so he could be born. But he knew it was weak, helpless. He had power now, both physically and otherwise. He was strong.

And yet that flimsy human made him feel weak. And that Ikati! His eye was just beginning to regenerate. How dare they challenge his strength.

He raged, slamming his fist into the floor, adding yet another dent to its already pocked surface, swearing to himself to hunt them down and tear them apart.

"Temper, temper, little dragon."

Drexx whirled on the figure standing in a shadowed corner of his room. He was in no mood to deal with her, but he wasn't stupid. He knew her capabilities and restrained himself, though not by much.

"My queen," his voice sounded over the room's speakers.

She wasn't really. She did very little with the Pirate Conglomerate. But she had sway over them he couldn't quite explain. Over them, and over him.

"Did you recover the plans?" she asked.

Drexx hesitated. What choice did he have but to tell the truth? What did he care anyway? Let her face some failure.

"No, my queen. The human female—"

"I do not want excuses, microbe." Her words were edged.

A tan hand reached out of the shadows and touched the hard surface of his beak. He shuddered at the touch. She caressed the smooth surface and he inwardly sneered at her mockery.

"Do you know how important those plans are?"

"Of course I do—"

The touch turned to a tight grip and his hardened skin burned, the smell of smoke entering his nostrils. He squirmed, the searing pain and pressure driving him to his knees.

"You know nothing. Your knowledge is insignificant compared to what lies ahead."

"Y-yes, m-my queen."

Drexx winced, feeling as though his beak might shatter. Her grip released and he gasped, the pain lingering.

"For now," she said, her voice softening, "stay and recover. I know you are feeling weak after your encounter."

Drexx raged within himself. She was prodding him, mocking him. His fear of her was the only thing that held him in check. A fear heightened when she stepped closer, her curly hair brushing the side of his face.

Her breath was like sweet flowers, hot upon his hard skin as she whispered in his ear cavity, "Do not fail me again."

She walked out of the room, leaving Drexx alone with his rage, fear, and weakness.

———

"I'm afraid I don't know what you're talking about," Admiral West said.

Etana raised an eyebrow at the admiral's holo-image.

"There is no sense in denying it. We have seen the plans ourselves. Why not be open about this?"

"One cannot be open about something of which one has no knowledge."

Her husband, Sen-ichi, spoke next. "Then you will investigate, of course."

"I hardly see that as necessary," the admiral said, lounging in his chair. "Just because someone presents you with a schematic, doesn't mean we're involved, or even that it's real."

"That someone is our daughter and heir to the Tarsek system," Etana said. "Your underlings tried to have her killed for this knowledge. Doesn't that warrant investigation?"

"That matter is exactly what is under investigation. I assure you, Princess Taraska has been temporarily cleared of all charges and her resignation is passed. She need not fear the Empire."

"And what about the rest of the galaxy?" Sen asked.

The Admiral leaned forward over his desk. "The galaxy is what we're here to protect. That's why the Federation was formed. That has not changed."

"Hasn't it?" Sen asked.

The admiral raised an eyebrow.

"We've been watching your movement over the past months," Etana said. "The 'Empire' has made some very aggressive moves,

moves the Federation of the past would never have made. Moves that belie the nature of your new title. Be aware, Admiral, no Empire either in name or force will rule this galaxy. We will oppose any forces who attempt to do so."

"I expect nothing less," the admiral said. "Know that that is not our intention."

"And know that we will hold you to that," Sen said. "Good day, Admiral. We'll be watching."

Sen killed the transmission. Etana looked to her husband, the king. Her look told him exactly what she was thinking.

What will we do if they try to take over?

They both knew the answer.

They would go to war.

———

Loni followed Doug down the pristine hall. This place was strange. The plainness of the building and the tight security, though none possessed guns, only stun rods, unnerved her. And all the workers wore the same white body-suits. Most were friendly to them, but there was an edge about them she didn't like.

They walked up to an elderly man staring through a window into a room. He rested his hands on a cane and his eyes, though spectacled, were sharp and observant. He turned and smiled warmly.

"Welcome back, Douglas."

"Doctor Falshian," Doug greeted. "This is my partner, Loni Taraska."

"A pleasure," the doctor said, taking her hand in a firm grip.

"How is she?" Doug asked.

The doctor turned back to the window. Loni moved around to get a better view. Inside was draped in the same drab off-white with only a bed and a side table. The only splash of color was a vase of flowers on the side table. Another vase was held in the hands of a young woman sitting on the bed. She was dressed in comfortable, loose clothing of the same drab off-white withthick bracelets around her wrists. Her auburn hair fell freely over her shoulders. Her beautiful face smiled, her mouth moving in words Loni couldn't hear as she arranged the second set of flowers.

"She has been lucid for three months," Doctor Falshian said. "She accepts her life here rather readily, expecting to one day be released, but not pressing for it. When confronted with the reason for her being here, she acts as if we did not speak. She takes her medicine without complaint and seems overall content."

"And when you mention me?" Doug asked.

The doctor sighed. "The same result, I'm afraid. It's as if she cannot hear. I would say the new medicine is working, but…"

"What's she saying?" Loni asked.

The doctor pressed a button on the wall, and the woman's voice sing-songed a gentle tune out of a speaker.

"I left my home
To travel far
To find that which I sought.
But what I found
Is darker far
That which from fate I bought.
Beware, beware,
Ye space faring folk.
I have no other words.
Once freedom is
Granted my soul
My fate you all will learn."

. . .

The woman started the song over as the doctor spoke.

"She sings it sometimes, hums it others, but always the same tune. It sounds like an old mariner song, perhaps something in her past?"

He directed the question at Doug who shook his head.

"I've never heard it, but the words make sense. I'd like to see her."

The doctor nodded as if he expected as much. He shuffled to the door and placed his palm on the reader next to it. It scanned his hand and the door slid quietly open. The woman ceased her humming and looked up, that pleasant smile still on her face. The doctor stood out of the door way and gestured Doug inside. Loni watched the woman's smile fade when Doug entered the room.

"Hello, Mera," he said.

Mera's hands shook, her face growing tight and turning down into a scowl. She threw the vase, scattering the flowers and ran at Doug, screaming, hands out like claws. Doug held his ground, not even flinching. Half a meter from him her wrists halted in mid-air while her body continued forward. She stopped only millimeters from him, screaming and snarling, her arms held behind her by some unseen force.

Grav bracers. That's why Doug didn't move.

Mera's face was a mask of hatred, the beauty from before vanished away like smoke in a vacuum. Loni realized Mera would kill Doug if she was set free.

Doug cupped her head firmly in his hands, though she tried to bite him, and placed a gentle kiss on her forehead. She screamed and struggled all the more, but Doug was stronger than her and the bracers would not give.

"I love you," Doug said. "I'll be praying for you."

He withdrew his hands quickly, not giving her opportunity to bite him and walked from the room, her incoherent screams following him. As soon as the door was shut, her screaming stopped. Her face relaxed, growing tired. She backed up to where her arms had more movement and collapsed to the floor. Her head bowed, her long, auburn hair covering her face. The doctor killed the audio.

"I'm sorry, son. We'll keep trying."

"Thank you for all you're doing for her."

The doctor nodded and moved away as Doug turned to view the seemingly comatose woman inside the room.

"She does this every time I come to see her," he said. "Doesn't matter what mental state she's in beforehand, my visit always evokes the same reaction."

"Who is she?" Loni asked, fearing the answer.

"My fiancé. Six weeks before the big day she started hearing voices. A week later and she tried to kill me. What you just saw is how she's been every time I visit for the past five cycles. Every time a new medicine comes out, they try it. Results are always the same."

Mera remained motionless on the floor. The only indication that she was alive was the slow undulation of her breathing.

"Look, Doug..." Loni hesitated to say more, but it had to be said. "I'm sorry, but...I mean if nothing changes, why haven't you given up?"

"Would you?" he said, looking her in the eye.

"No, I guess not. It just...I don't know. It seems so hopeless. I don't know if I could stand that."

"Did you see it?"

"What?"

"That look in her eyes, just before she ran at me and just after the door shut. It's the same every time, a desperation. She's pleading for me to help her. I know she's locked in there some-where. I can't give up on her. But I can't help her either. I just have to trust these doctors. They're good at what they do. If anyone can help her, it's them."

He turned away from the window and walked down the hall.

"Okay, I get that," Loni said, hurrying after him. "But why not tell Arta about this? She deserves to know. Space, you're not even married. You can still help her, but you can also move on with your life."

Doug stopped and sighed. His shoulders slumped as if the weight of the galaxy were pressing down on them.

"And what if she comes out of it one day? She wakes up and finds that I've moved on to another. Would break her heart."

"And what happens if she wakes up an old woman and you've passed on? Do you think she'd be happy to know you pined your life away waiting for her?"

"Well, that's where I'm stuck. I can't just give up on Mera, and I can't outright tell Arta no, either. I care for her. I think I always have. Dust, maybe I should just tell her and let her decide. I don't know.

"But there's one more factor to this. My mother died when I was eleven, beaten to death by her husband."

"Your father?" Loni asked.

"Yea. He went on the run. Rangers tracked him down and arrested him. He's currently serving a life-sentence on Terra. The man who took me in, the Marshall, raised me like his own son, taught me everything he knows about being a Ranger, and walking with integrity. Now he's gone and turned his back on everything he taught me.

"My mother, my father, my fiancé, and now the Marshall. Seems like every time I allow myself to get close to someone, they leave, one way or another. No matter what I do, I can't seem to protect them. I ain't saying it's fate or anything hooky spooky like that. But I took this badge to protect others from harm. Seeing so many people I care about suffer despite my best efforts, well, just makes it hard to allow myself to get close to anyone."

Loni wanted to tell him how she respected him for his

integrity, not wanting to endanger others, even if it meant a life of loneliness. But the words seemed hollow in light of his grief.

"You ready to go?" Doug asked.

Loni nodded and they walked out of the facility.

In Mera's room, the young woman sat unmoving on the floor, quietly humming.

———

Doug plopped onto his bed, feeling the fatigue of the encounter and the bruises from the days prior. He rubbed his face and reached for the light controls. His eyes spotted the com and he remembered something.

Instead of the lights, he typed up an encoded com frequency he'd only used once before. He typed out a quick message, pulled the fob from his shirt pocket and inserted it into the node. After attaching the file, he paused.

Did he really want to involve her? He considered all he'd witnessed; the Empire, Loni, the Marshall's veiled confession. This was way bigger than just him.

He hit the send button, then considered another action. Bringing up the file access menu, he hit the delete key.

Are you sure? The prompt asked.

Doug tapped the "Y" button.

FILE DELETED.

He sat there for a few minutes, contemplating the action.

"Well, guess we'll see."

He hit the lights, laid back, and closed his eyes.

It was hours later, when Doug was deep in a dream about Mera that his console winked to life. The words "FILE DELETED" once again appearing on the screen.

The "D" on the end disappeared. Then the "E."

One by one, the letters vanished until only "FILE" remained.

The background faded into a shower of ones and zeroes into which the word melted, becoming one with the stream.

In the constantly shifting binary waterfall, a *1* turned from blue to red and became static. In another place, a *0* did the same. In short order, several ones and zeroes isolated themselves. They gathered in a corner, shaping into a curve.

The process repeated, moving faster than before. These formed another curve, connecting with the first.

Bit by bit, the pieces fell into place until incalculable ones and zeroes coalesced into the shape of a long tube surrounded by concentric rings. The image shot out of the console in a holo-projection. It rotated silently in place, Doug snoring peacefully with his back to it. Another stream of ones and zeroes in the shape of a human hand eased into the projection field. It reached for the rotating image, wrapping digital fingers around it.

Doug stirred. The console and the holo-image winked out, plunging the room into darkness. After a time, Doug's soft snoring once again filled the cabin.

A circle appeared on the screen. Then another inside that one. It rotated and blinked, shaping into an eye before it disintegrated into a set of numbers that fell like debris across the bottom of the screen. The numbers tumbled together, arranging to form the letters of a single word. It stayed there until enough time passed for the image to be burned into the screen.

The console went dark, leaving the after-image of a name.

JACK.

The story continues in Book 2: Artificial Malevolence.

THANK YOU FOR READING
HYPERSPACE OUTLAWS_

We hope you enjoyed it as much as we enjoyed bringing it to you.
We just wanted to take a moment to encourage you to review the
book. Follow this link: Hyperspace Outlaws to be directed to the
book's Amazon product page to leave your review.

Every review helps further the author's reach and, ultimately,
helps them continue writing fantastic books for us all to enjoy.

———

You can also join our non-spam mailing list by visiting www.
subscribepage.com/AethonReadersGroup and never miss out on
future releases. You'll also receive three full books completely
Free as our thanks to you.

Facebook | Instagram | Twitter | Website

Want to discuss our books with other readers and even the

authors? Join our Discord server today and be a part of the Aethon community.

LOOKING FOR MORE GREAT SCIENCE FICTION?

The Complete Battle Ring Earth Series Bundle is here. 1000+ pages of military sci-fi action about the defense of Earth against aliens, fighter pilots, and the last hope for mankind. Technical Specialist Simon Brooks was no soldier. More suited for the academy than combat, his assignment to a rear echelon support squadron seemed a good fit. Everything changed when the Sleer attacked Earth's newly salvaged spacecraft, UEF Ascension. In a flash, Brooks goes from fleeing a burning transport plane to piloting a broken mech and learning the habits of a fighter pilot from Lt Sara Rosenski, the terror of Nightmare Squadron. But his rising star takes a hit when he learns to talk to the Sleer AI, Genukh...and suddenly the UEF doesn't know whose side he's on. Now Brooks and Rosenski are stuck aboard Earth's Sleer weapon—the Battle Ring--and they may be all that stands between Earth and its induction into the Sleer Empire... **Experience this complete Military Science Fiction Series perfect for fans of Rick Partlow, Jamie McFarlane, and Joshua Dalzelle. Books in the Set:** Book 1: Megastructure Book 2: Colony Book 3: Grand Reversal

Get Battle Ring Earth Now!

Grant Masterson is a man with nothing left to lose... A disgraced ex-cop, framed by a crooked politician, abandoned by his family, he's forced into the life of a bounty hunter just to survive. Tracking down a traitor who stole military grade weapons to sell on the black market, Masterson finds out things aren't as simple as the wanted poster made them seem. Because Delia Beckett isn't a traitor, simply a patsy, and the forces manipulating her may be the same ones responsible for Masterson's fall from grace.

GET ABSOLUTION NOW!

In the West, there are worse things to fear than bandits and outlaws. Demons. Monsters. Witches. James Crowley's sacred duty as a Black Badge is to hunt them down and send them packing, banish them from the mortal realm for good. He didn't choose this life. No. He didn't choose life at all. Shot dead in a gunfight many years ago, now he's stuck in purgatory, serving the whims of the White Throne to avoid falling to hell. Not quite undead, though not alive either, the best he can hope for is to work off his penance and fade away. This time, the White Throne has sent him investigate a strange bank robbery in Lonely Hill. An outlaw with the ability to conjure ice has frozen and shattered open the bank vault and is now on a spree, robbing the region for all it's worth. In his quest to track down the ice-wielder and suss out which demon is behind granting a mortal such power, Crowley finds himself face-to-face with hellish beasts, shapeshifters, and, worse … temptation. But the truth behind the attacks is worse than he ever imagined … **_The Witcher_ meets _The Dresden Files_ in this weird Western series by the Audible number-one bestselling duo behind _Dead Acre._**

GET COLD AS HELL NOW AND EXPERIENCE WHAT

PUBLISHER'S WEEKLY CALLED PERFECT FOR FANS OF
JIM BUTCHER AND MIKE CAREY.

Also available on audio, voiced by Red Dead Redemption 2's
Roger Clark (Arthur Morgan)

For all our Sci-Fi books, visit our website.

www.ingramcontent.com/pod-product-compliance
Lightning Source LLC
Chambersburg PA
CBHW051214130726
47988CB00001B/87